The Election

The Election

Landon Wallace

Trinity River Press

Copyright © 2017 by Landon Wallace
www.authorlandonwallace.com

Trinity River Press
Fort Worth, Texas 76102

Printed in the United States of America
Published 2017

Library of Congress Control Number: 2017957933
ISBN: 978-0-9861731-9-6 (paperback)

Cover design by Sheila Cowley

CHAPTER 1

September 6

Twenty years of his life melted away when he saw her. State Senator Blake Buchanan had several important guests to shake hands with before he navigated his way through the crowd to the podium, but her appearance had thrown him. He hadn't thought about Catherine Alexander—Cat, to him—in years, but her presence overwhelmed the need to court the political heavyweights hovering nearby. Before heading off, Blake peeked at his wife, Faith, who was busy working the room and visiting well-wishers several tables away.

"Senator Buchanan, we've got Pickens, Butts, and Perry in front of you," whispered the young, black-haired assistant who pawed at the senator's arm to guide him to his donors.

Blake resisted his aide's tug toward the moneymen. "Give me a minute, Kristen. There's someone I need to talk to first."

"Sir, these men have been waiting," Kristen protested.

Blake ignored the admonition and bobbed his way through the throng of supporters to the far end of the bustling reception. The woman standing in the distant corner under a *Buchanan for Governor* sign glanced in Blake's direction as he made his way toward her, their gazes locking through the sea of bodies. The candidate assessed his wife's proximity one final time before reaching the woman's side.

"I can't believe my eyes," Blake gushed, while offering a brief hug that he hoped would appear innocent to anyone watching. "Are you lost, Catherine?"

"It appears that way," she replied. Cat returned his embrace while pecking him on the cheek. "And, for better or worse, it's still Cat."

Blake backed away to a safer distance and immediately noticed a platinum wedding band and emerald-cut diamond on Cat's ring finger. His eyes then darted to her face—the slight dimple in her right cheek, the familiar tiny freckles dotting her nose—which carried him like a daydream to a happier place. Except for the tiny crow's-feet that appeared when she squinted, Cat hadn't changed. Blake marveled at how gracefully she'd slipped into middle age during the many years since he'd last seen her. Cat's youthful appearance made him wonder how she viewed the thick lines that now crisscrossed his fifty-year-old face. "I can't believe you came," he said.

"Neither can I." She shook her head. "I'm in town for a couple of days to see Mom, but I couldn't help myself when I saw the newspaper this morning."

"Yep, buried on page three of the Metro section." Blake laughed in spite of himself. "I'm not much of a news story, it seems. You must be a thorough reader."

Cat grinned and shuffled her feet. "I turned around three times in the lobby before I came in." She wrinkled her nose in just the way Blake remembered she used to when she had something important to say. "Hey now, shouldn't you be shaking hands instead of wasting time with me? I think that's your assistant over there waving her arms at you."

"I'm not wasting time, but I do have to get back and address these folks." Blake stopped himself. "Maybe not as many here to address as I'd hoped." He raised his eyebrows. "Can you stick around? Better yet, how about dinner? And bring your husband along if he's with you." Blake glanced to his left to confirm Faith hadn't drifted their way.

"It's time, Senator," Kristen announced from behind him.

"Go on," Cat encouraged, sidestepping his dinner invitation. "Get these people fired up."

Blake turned around and strode to the podium. As he bounded forward, he tried to reboot his brain and focus on his remarks, but his mind had careened off course. His thoughts were now on Cat Alexander and the life he'd known before Faith, before children, before politics had changed everything.

―――★―――

As soon as Blake headed off, Cat maneuvered herself so she could fix her attention on the stage. The room wasn't large, and the strategically located tables with their assortment of oversized red, white, and blue balloons made it seem even smaller. This familiar campaign trick was often used to ignite excitement in a crowd; Cat had seen it at rallies she'd attended back at home. She fidgeted as she surveyed the area, hoping she wasn't going to need to explain her presence to some acquaintance from her past.

"Friends," Blake started as he began to switch on the charm. "Thank you for being here. If I could hug each one of you, I'd do it right now." He smiled, revealing a curtain of wall-to-wall gleaming teeth that reminded Cat just how much had changed since the days of his endearing gap-toothed grin. The cosmetic work his dentist had performed, whether tied strategically to this political run or some exercise in male vanity, fit him well. He was more handsome than ever, and time had only enhanced his searing green eyes and sculpted cheekbones. "All of you know I'm an even bigger underdog than my Texas Longhorns these days," Blake continued, "but some of you still remember the glory days of Vince Young and—with your help—I'm counting on that same kind of magic."

Cat joined in the crowd's applause but worried the reaction to Blake's hometown launch sounded more polite than heartfelt, and she wondered if his campaign was faltering before it even got out of the blocks.

"My opponent, Grace Striker," Blake stated as his voice smoothly transformed from folksy to somber, "embodies everything wrong with politics in this state . . . and in our nation. She's wrong on women's reproductive rights, wrong on protecting our border, wrong in polarizing our minority and transgender communities, and she even thinks climate change was an idea cooked up in some laboratory by a Democrat from New York."

Cat nodded approvingly, but the looks on the faces of those in attendance indicated that many found Blake's unusual approach to Republican orthodoxy confusing. She'd come expecting Blake, as a Texas Republican, to be openly hostile to the policies she believed in, but Blake was spouting anything but Tea Party dogma. His eyes seemed to float toward the back of the room. *Did he wink at her?* When she'd impulsively decided to attend the event that afternoon after reading about it in the morning paper, Cat had held no expectations for seeing Blake. In fact, she'd doubted he'd even spot her in the sea of supporters, let alone have time to greet her. But the unanticipated spark when they'd said hello had exposed her. And now as his penetrating gaze reached through the fortress of heads between them, she sensed he was glad she'd came.

"As Republicans," Blake asserted while pounding his fist on the podium, "we have common purpose, to stand for what we know is best for our children, for what is right for our state, and not give in to the cynicism and hate that Striker's campaign breeds."

When Blake finished about ten minutes later, he drew some cheers and nodding heads but Cat still didn't feel any urgency in the room. She'd bristled when several attendees escaped before he'd even stepped away from the rostrum. Cat, however, swelled with pride for the politician, and perhaps the man, too, because she understood that a speech like the one he'd just delivered was truly courageous. Few Texas politicians would even challenge the brand, much less succeed doing it. She planned to tell Blake as much after accepting his dinner proposal . . . one he'd offered again after casually mentioning that his campaign manager and aide, but not his wife, would be joining them.

CHAPTER 2

Tony León sat in the conference room at Attorney General Grace Striker's campaign headquarters awaiting feedback from another associate who'd attended Blake Buchanan's fundraiser. Beside him were fellow staffers Debbie and Josh, both newcomers to the job as well. Tony already could see that his fresh-faced colleagues were in way over their heads. A ringing phone interrupted his thoughts, and Tony watched Debbie Adams, the perky twenty-two-year-old former sorority girl, punch the speakerphone.

"Michael?" she answered.

"Hi, everyone," replied the fourth member of Tony's team, Michael Huffines. "Buchanan's just finished, and the response was polite at best. He's a decent enough speaker, but most of the crowd was left scratching their heads wondering why a RINO thinks he's going to win the Republican nomination. He sounded like a freaking Democrat."

Crack. The table rattled as the door snapped against the wall. Tony turned just as campaign manager Marshall Phelps and Attorney General Striker marched into the room. They acknowledged the young staffers with salutes and plopped down in their seats. Phelps gave an impatient hand signal for the call to continue. Tony's fellow staffers quivered, as if overcome by the presence of the presumptive future governor of Texas.

"Hold on, Michael," Debbie said, "General Striker and Mr.

Phelps just arrived. Can you start over?"

"I was saying the event was poorly attended—no more than a hundred, max—and the senator did nothing to light a fire under the few donors who showed up. He poked the Tea Party in the eye and gave an unconvincing explanation about how he could defeat the attorney general. Not much new."

"What subjects did he cover?" Phelps asked with a frown.

"Abortion, the environment, even the transgenders, most of the positions he promoted in his announcement. You know, the stuff that won't sell in Texas." Huffines cackled.

"Won't sell to conservatives," Phelps corrected.

"Yes, sir," Huffines replied.

"Who was there?" Phelps pressed.

"The only Republicans of importance were Clarence Pickens and Stripling Butts. There were a handful of businessmen and an assortment of college types, but it was a weak crowd. Very few elected officials, other than Mayor Chalk."

Tony snickered under his breath. He knew that inviting a Democratic mayor to attend a Republican primary event, even a big-city mayor from Houston, wouldn't help drive up the primary vote. He glanced at Striker to make his point but she avoided his gaze.

"What about his wife and kids?" Phelps inquired.

"His wife was there," Huffines explained. "I saw the ice princess shake a few hands. In his speech, Buchanan mentioned his two daughters but I never saw them. About the only other thing I can tell you is that he spent the last few minutes before he went on stage chatting with a woman in the back of the room."

"What's your point?" Phelps snapped.

"I don't know but the body language between them just seemed odd. And the lady was attractive, blonde, about five foot six, probably in her mid-forties. Never seen her before."

Phelps scratched his chin but didn't respond. The balding black man looked at Striker and raised his eyebrows. "Thank you, Michael. That's enough. We'll see you at headquarters later tonight."

As Debbie flicked off the speakerphone, the attorney general rose from her chair unspooling her slender, five foot nine frame and whisking her shoulder cut brown hair to the side. "Senator Blake Buchanan," she announced, "can't be dismissed this easily." Striker paused as if to emphasize her point. "The man's well-known in Republican circles, unconventional, and hard working . . . plus his wife is a fountain of money so he'll be well financed. I want all of you to dig deep and fight to keep him from gaining any traction." Striker pounded her fist on the table while her eyes roamed the eager faces staring back at her. "That's why Marshall Phelps is running this campaign. He will be giving you daily instructions and duties. I'm glad you've come on board. Next stop . . ." She then confidently raised two fingers in a mock victory salute.

Tony didn't know how to respond to the impromptu pep talk but felt he should remind his co-workers of the significance of the attorney general's appearance at their meeting. Turning toward Striker, he stood up and applauded. His fellow aides joined him.

"That's enough," Phelps interrupted. "General Striker's leaving now. Sit back down. We have work to do."

CHAPTER 3

Cat now wished she'd declined Blake's dinner invitation. The connection that she felt ignited earlier at the reception had dimmed during their dinner table discussion about politics, politics, and more politics.

"Well, Cat," Blake said, finally focusing on her, "we've excluded you most of the night and that's my fault. You must not think much has changed in twenty years."

Cat was about to respond but the senator's aide Kristen jumped in first. "Sir, there are a number of other issues we should cover before we finish." The young brunette leaned in and brushed her shoulder against Blake's arm while showing him the iPad that seemed surgically attached to her hand.

Blake ignored Kristen and looked toward the fourth member of their dinner party, his longtime strategist, Raymond "Rags" Beckham, a man Cat had learned was the mastermind behind Blake's twenty-year political career.

"We're finished with politics," Rags announced. "But, Blake, don't forget you've got a heart-doc appointment tomorrow. He won't refill your script unless you show up."

Blake flipped his hand at Rags as if to say *sure, sure.* He whispered to Cat, "Arrhythmia, no big deal."

Cat sensed it was time for her to leave. "Nice to be with all of you," she said while pushing her chair away from the table. "But I have an early flight back to New York tomorrow. I'll be following the campaign with great interest from home. Good luck to you, Blake."

"Wait a minute," Blake interjected. "I know we've bored you to death, but we're done now. I mean it. Kristen and Rags are leaving. Please stay a little longer so we can catch up. No more politics, I promise."

Cat flinched slightly at the smooth certainty in Blake's voice. His tone conjured up images of some of her less favorable memories of the man. "Sorry, but I need to get back to the hotel," she explained. Cat felt Kristen's penetrating glare as she spoke.

"Just a minute," Blake responded as he turned to Rags. "Please get Kristen back safely. I'll see you both tomorrow. Thank you for your hard work. Great job tonight."

"Thanks, boss," Rags replied with a wink. Within a minute, Cat and Blake were alone and she'd eased back into her chair.

"I won't keep you long," Blake promised.

Despite her resolve to leave, Cat couldn't avoid the sense that she had some unpacking to do with her former boyfriend. So many years had passed and she had so many questions.

"What's on your mind?" she asked.

"I don't know . . . twenty years."

Cat tilted her head back.

"That's a long time," Blake continued. "I want to hear about your life."

"We've got a lot of ground to cover then," she suggested. "Where do you want to start?" Cat drew in a deep breath.

"How about Asheville?"

Cat brushed her fingers across her chin before answering. "Hmmm, I guess that's the last time we saw each other."

"Nineteen ninety-three, the River Arts District. You were cooking at a place called Cúrate."

"That's right. The politician has a good memory."

"The man has a good memory. The politician would have forgotten that long ago. Let's get a drink. It's only ten. The Cat I remember enjoyed an occasional nightcap."

Cat nodded but wondered if ordering a drink at this late hour was opening a door she wanted to remain closed.

"I messed up in Asheville," Blake acknowledged. "In a lot of ways. And it's time I properly apologized to you."

Cat raised her eyebrows, encouraging him to continue.

"I should have done this years ago." Blake leaned in closer to the table. "About the only good thing I can say for myself now is that I lived up to my promise after I left."

The waiter took their drink orders—Johnny Walker Black and a glass of Cabernet—and scurried away.

"So what do you want to apologize for?" Cat smiled, knowing the answer.

She had not forgotten Blake's sudden departure that night, the disaster of their short reunion. By that time, she and Blake hadn't been together in over five years, since their teary farewell in Puerto Vallarta, Mexico, when the still-in-love couple had decided to separate to jump-start their careers after a final holiday together. Cat to Miami to begin her cooking career as an assistant line chef at the famous Forge restaurant, where her culinary degree and fluency in Spanish had given her the necessary edge to win the coveted job. And Blake, under the guiding hand of his dominant father, to Houston to rev up his political resume with the kingmakers at the influential Vickers & Nelson law firm. Cat hadn't truly expected their kiss at the Puerto Vallarta airport to be the end—young and starry-eyed, she'd anticipated their love would pull them together again—but the trajectory of their careers never allowed that to happen. And just as she'd made peace with the fact that her future with Blake was truly dead and buried, he'd shown up in Asheville, forcing all those dangerous emotions to surface again.

"You're not going to go easy on me, are you?" Blake asked.

"Why should I?" Cat answered.

They nursed the drinks the waiter had quietly set on their

table and stared at each other. In that gaze, Cat's mind drifted back to Asheville and the last time she'd seen Blake Buchanan.

———— ★ ————

He arrived at her restaurant unannounced in a blue Ralph Lauren shirt, cowboy boots, and jeans and asked for her as if the past five years—including his marriage two years earlier—meant nothing. When the hostess summoned her from the kitchen, Cat couldn't believe it was Blake sitting alone at the bar. The minute she approached him he jumped up and pulled her into his arms with an inviting grin and a familiar hug.

"B-Blake," she stammered as he released her. "What are you doing here?"

"Hi, Cat. Surprised?"

"Stunned might be a better word."

"Someone told me about this great new restaurant in Asheville and I thought I'd give it a try."

Blake's cavalier attitude immediately turned her off. "What are you doing in Asheville?" she asked, her voice diving an octave. Her clenched jaw delivered the rest of her message.

"Let me start over," Blake responded in a more serious tone. "I have a deposition in Charlotte tomorrow afternoon, so I rented a car and drove over. I wanted to come by for some dinner and see how you're doing."

"I'm doing great," she said curtly. "I'm sorry to be short with you, but I'm the sous chef and I have to get back to the kitchen. Lots going on here tonight." Blake's disappointment spread across his face but she was indignant that he seemed to have expectations about seeing her. She didn't care that he'd made the two hour drive from Charlotte. "I'll try to stop by and visit with you when I get a break," she added. "If you're still here, I mean. Enjoy your meal. We have a fun little band that starts at nine. They play seventies tunes." With that, Cat pivoted and walked back to the kitchen with a frown on her face.

It was a long uncomfortable night for Cat, but as she tried to stay focused on the kitchen business in front of her, memories flooded through her head. By the time food service finally shut down, Blake had moved to a table near the stage and was nursing a beer while listening idly to the band. Cat was tired from a busy night, and that weariness had stripped away much of her annoyance over his presumptuous attitude of two hours before. She hadn't spoken to him while she'd been working, though she and the head chef had popped into the dining room a couple of times to say hello to a few of their patrons. She was grateful Blake had, at least, shown the good sense to leave her alone while she did her job. His patience had earned him a few minutes of her time.

"It was good seeing you again," Cat said once she arrived at his table. She purposely wore her jean-jacket and carried a bag over her shoulder to suggest she was heading out.

"Give me a minute," Blake requested. "I know it's been a long time but there are some things I want to say to you."

"There's really nothing for us to talk about. You know that."

"Cat, please sit down, or at least let me walk with you to your car. I've come a long way."

She sighed and signaled with her hand for him to stand up. "Come on. My car's down the street."

Cat led Blake to the dimly lit surface lot where she'd parked her gray Honda Civic. "This is me," she stated.

"Let me guess, probably the most fuel-efficient car on the road." Blake grinned.

"You remember some things accurately." Cat swung her keys around on her key ring as if to validate his comment. "Now tell me the truth," she continued. "Why are you here? It's not like I somehow missed the fact you got married."

Blake gave her a wry "you got me" smile, one of those boyish looks she remembered had once melted her heart. His expression confirmed he hadn't made the long drive on a lark. Blake walked to the front of her car and leaned against the hood. He tapped the spot next to him. "Sit down," he pleaded. "I need to say a few things."

Although again frustrated with his behavior, Cat had wondered most of the night what Blake was doing here. This was the man she'd once loved and planned to spend her life with before he'd unexpectedly found a better deal. So what in the world could he possibly want with her now? "I'm not sitting on that dirty hood," she protested. "There's a little park about a block away where we can visit. But I will have to leave in about fifteen minutes. That's it."

"Thanks," Blake said appreciatively.

"Well, how's married life?" Cat asked as they walked down the sidewalk shoulder to shoulder. She knew it was a snarky comment but he deserved it.

Blake recoiled but didn't hesitate. "Complicated is the best answer I can give you."

Cat shook her head as they approached a series of benches situated in the middle of a landscaped, tree-encircled park. The red brick pavers that framed the seating area captured the spotlights beaming down from a large cluster of maple and walnut trees.

They sat down several feet apart on one of the benches. "Thanks for not shooing me away," he said softly while swiveling toward her.

"Don't be so sure I still won't do that." Cat half-smiled, hoping to relieve the tension she could see building in Blake's face.

"I probably should have called first," Blake acknowledged, "but I wasn't sure you'd see me if I did. And now that I'm finally here sitting next to you, I still don't know what I came to say. I guess you can tell that my marriage isn't, well, the most stable of situations."

Cat bristled, sensing from his remark that Blake really might have objectives beyond just talking. "Blake," she pronounced brusquely while staring at him with narrowed eyes, "I don't know your wife and don't know what that comment's supposed to mean, but I bet she wouldn't like to know you're sitting on a bench with your ex-girlfriend thousands of miles away."

Cat could see the edge to her statement had caught Blake by surprise. "You're right," he replied, "and I'm feeling more unhappy about that every minute I sit here. The truth is my life will soon change forever and that's what pushed me to come see you. I'm about to run for office, just like we used to talk about, and . . . well, it felt lonely not being able to share that with you. You were always the one who believed in me, and you're the one who encouraged me to take the job at Vickers and Nelson, even when I thought it was a terrible idea. I wouldn't have this chance if it hadn't been for you."

Cat couldn't ignore the emotions stirring within her, emotions she had zero interest in rekindling or even trying to understand. Blake had no idea what the final collapse of their relationship had done to her, or what she'd gone through to start a new romantic life in Asheville. Cat had worked years to break down her wall of distrust before she'd allowed another man close, but she'd finally done it, and her life was actually better now. She was stronger and more confident than before. But now Blake was here . . . and none of that seemed to matter.

"You've always been a mess," she teased, sensitive to the intimacies he'd shared and those he couldn't. "But I'm glad to hear you're going where you've always wanted to be. I'm happy for you."

Blake reached over and placed his hand on Cat's just as a cool breeze rippled through the trees and across their backs. She didn't move and without speaking rolled her fingers around to interlock with his.

"Thanks for being here, Cat," he whispered.

"I think we should head back now," she replied softly. "It's been a long day. I'm very tired." She stood up, still holding Blake's hand, and encouraged him to follow.

Blake complied even while giving off the sense that he wanted to say more. She suspected he wanted to talk about his marriage, and what a political career would mean to the future of that relationship, but there was no reason to go there. And she wasn't about to give him that chance. He'd moved on and made his future, and that's what she was doing as well.

Blake continued to hold her hand as they walked quietly back to Cat's car. When they arrived, she took control.

"I'm still not sure why you're here, but one thing's very apparent." She slid her hand out of his. "You're married, and I've got a life here in Asheville. This, whatever this is, can't happen again. We both need to move on with our lives once and for all."

"I don't know what I expected," Blake responded, "but you're right. This was a moment I wanted to share with *you*—to celebrate with someone who really knows me—but I understand what you're saying. I'm sorry. I shouldn't have come here."

Cat opened her car door and hastily scooted inside, as Blake stood frozen in place staring at her. His look cracked a piece of her heart.

"Be safe driving back," Cat said through her open window.

Maybe he really did still love her, but she knew that she'd made the right decision not letting him in that night in Asheville. Nothing good could have followed, and she could not go back to the painful place she'd worked so hard to leave.

Twenty years later, now sitting alone in the Houstonian Steakhouse with Blake, Cat realized her former lover had stayed away just as she'd asked him to do all those years ago.

———————— ★ ————————

I really went to Asheville," Blake explained, "to talk to you about my race and . . . well, once I saw you I started believing we could turn back time, at least for one night. But please know my intentions were honorable when I drove up, despite how it played out."

Cat raised her eyebrows to feign surprise. "I think I figured that part out." She chuckled. "It's fair to say men are a bit more . . . compartmentalized . . . than women. Looking back, I'm sure I could have given in just as easily as you, but I'm glad I didn't, for both of us."

Blake sighed before turning serious. "I wanted to tell you that after I left Mexico I thought I was doing what I had to do to build my future. That included marrying Faith. Frankly, my ambition blinded me to what my actions would mean. But more than anything, I wanted to tell you that I was excited that I'd found a state-rep race I could win, and that I was petrified as well. So much of my past, my dad, my marriage, and my future was wrapped up in that decision. And I guess to be truthful, I was panicked because I still had such strong feelings for you."

"Well, it appears that all worked out just fine."

"That's a longer, and much more complicated, discussion."

"Sounds a little difficult to believe sitting here today, mister governor."

"Yeah, well, I do have a shot now, but you saw that crowd tonight, or what passed for a crowd." He winced. "My message may not be resonating yet, but what I'm trying to do is to tap into the better angels out there. But I'm not sure speaking to half-empty rooms and Tea Party glares is what Rags had in mind when he talked me into this race. It sure wasn't the strategy my father and I discussed before he died." Blake paused. "But it does mean I'm going to do it my way, even if I end up speaking to a lot of empty rooms."

"I was sad when I heard about your father," Cat offered. "I thought about getting in touch with you at the time . . . what was it, maybe a couple of years ago? I'm sorry I didn't reach out."

"Thank you, but I understand why you didn't. I still do miss him a lot. He had a sudden heart attack, the widow-maker. He was always so strong and vigorous. It caught us all by surprise." Blake's eyes moistened and he paused to catch his breath. "You know I always thought the old man was indestructible."

"Of course you did," Cat said in a hushed tone. She'd known Walter Buchanan very well at one time, and had observed the towering shadow the investment professional had cast over his son's life. She wanted to hear more about what Blake thought about him now, how his father's death may have freed Blake to become his own man, but she knew it wasn't the time to take on that delicate subject. "I'm not easily surprised," she continued after a moment, "but you're surprising me, Senator Buchanan. Your independence was front and center in your speech tonight, and I must say it plays to my personal brand of politics."

"Good then, but you're an easy target. I've known that liberal conscience of yours for a long time. Good thing it found the right home in New York." Once again, Blake's easy wit reminded Cat of the young man who'd captured her heart.

"I'll accept your comment as a compliment coming from a Republican candidate for governor, but Blake Buchanan deserves a swat." She raised her arm as if about to swing at him. "I guess it doesn't say much for your electoral chances that a New Yorker is drawn to your politics."

"Very true. That alone makes me a million-to-one long shot, but that doesn't mean I don't have a plan, or at least Rags does. But seriously, I really believe if people are spoken to honestly, as peers and adults, and not pandered to with easy fixes, they'll give me a chance." He shrugged his shoulders. "And then again, I might get beaten in a landslide."

Cat shook her head in disagreement. She liked this sincere, surprisingly humble Blake Buchanan. This was the man she'd always envisioned he'd grow up to be. "I'm not buying your long shot line," she countered. "You're the most competitive human being I've ever known, and I'm guessing you wouldn't be running unless you think you can win."

"I never could get much past you," he conceded, "but the answer's yes, I do think my opponent's vulnerable." He then looked into the air as if to signal that he wanted to avoid talking anymore about politics. "Cat," he said with his jaw set, "I still wonder what we thought we were doing back then. Back in Mexico. Why couldn't we figure out a way forward, where we could both have the careers we wanted and stay together? Florida or Texas, did it really matter? We could have made it work. We should have at least tried. What happened?"

"Blake, I can't say I haven't thought about the same thing over the years, but what did we know then? We were twenty-five-years old. We had no idea how each decision lead to another and that suddenly we'd be on different paths. Ones we never expected."

Blake nodded. "You're right. But please understand that I've always read about you and followed your career. And I know you've done incredibly well for yourself. Assistant line chef, line chef, sous chef, and ultimately head chef and owner of a fancy Spanish restaurant in the West Village. I want to hear more about all of that. From what I can tell, you've made a lot more progress on your goals in life than I have."

"Hardly."

"No, really. I saw that travel magazine story about the lovely proprietor of a charming Spanish restaurant called Abrazo, and how the ambience and food makes one feel like they've dropped themselves onto the Iberian coast. I was on a transatlantic flight when I saw that one." "Don't even try to deny it," he continued. "You're a star."

Cat blushed at the unexpected praise. "We're a tiny dot on the Manhattan landscape, but I must admit I'm very proud of our place. But it hasn't been easy. Not at all."

"I can only imagine."

Blake reached across the table and took Cat's hand for a moment before pulling away.

Cat scolded him with her wagging finger. "Careful, Senator," she said.

As they talked their way down toward the last bit of his Scotch and her Silver Oak, Cat grew more comfortable as the alcohol kicked in. She didn't even think about interrupting Blake when he signaled for a couple of fresh glasses of wine. At this point, the liquid courage pushed her to press on the one subject they hadn't crossed into—his family.

———— ★ ————

As the waiter poured the Cabernet, Blake was reminded again of the celebrity that came with running for governor of Texas. The fuzzy-faced server, or any amateur sleuth with a cell phone for that matter, could derail his campaign if he made another inappropriate gesture—like handholding—with Cat.

Blake took a deep breath. "Tell me about your family."

"Well, my kids are my lights," Cat answered, carefully evading any mention of her husband. "Mitch and Paige, they're everything to me."

"How old are they now?"

"Mitch just turned eight and my daughter's closing in on her teens. I'm not looking forward to those mother-daughter battles ahead. You may remember I was rather headstrong in high school. Like mother, like daughter, I'm afraid." She raised her glass and held it for a second. "I'm in the midst of the busy years right now," she finished with a laugh and then took a sip.

"Tell me about it," Blake replied. "These past years with Finley and Shana have been a roller-coaster ride with their . . . mother." Blake wanted to cover up his awkward hesitation but realized he'd signaled his discomfort about introducing his wife into the conversation. He had no desire to discuss the complexities of his marriage or why he'd stayed. "My girls are great," Blake continued. "Fin will be heading off to college next year."

"Hmm. College already. I've got a long way to go before I get to that point. And I'm sure Sam and I will be the oldest parents in the senior class by the time Mitch gets there. Where does Fin see herself?"

"I don't know yet—maybe, UT—but she's worked hard and while I'd like to keep her in Texas, I'll be happy no matter where she goes."

"That's a good attitude." Cat then looked up as if contemplating her next question. "And how are you doing?" she asked. "I mean you . . . not the candidate."

"Other than my cholesterol levels? That's not what you're asking about, is it?"

Cat grinned but her piercing look showed the familiarity of a woman who knew the real Blake Buchanan, even after twenty years.

"Let me answer you this way," Blake proposed, staring at Cat. "You may think this is a line but I've thought about you a lot over the years. It wasn't only curiosity about your professional life that kept me reading whatever I could find and Googling you. And it's sure not just because I like Spanish food. I've missed you, Cat. So now it's your turn. Why did you agree to come to dinner with me tonight?"

Cat's blank stare gave much away but she was saved when the waiter approached them.

"Senator," the young man interrupted. "I held back until the place cleared out, but do you mind taking a picture with me?"

Blake glanced at Cat and raised an eyebrow before standing up next to the bushy-haired server. "Sure," he replied.

As soon as the waiter left, Blake noticed Cat picking up her purse off the floor.

"You're right," he said. "It's time to get out of here." Blake looked away for a moment and took a deep breath. It didn't matter that he was tipsy and attracted to Cat, he knew what his next move had to be.

CHAPTER 4

By the time Phelps finally got around to the announcement Tony had been waiting for, Michael Huffines's earlier report on Senator Buchanan's fundraiser seemed like a distant memory. Tony watched as Phelps posted the list on the white board.

Striker Campaign
Marshall Phelps—campaign manager
Tony León—policy and opposition research
Michael Huffines—advance and fundraising
Debbie Adams—scheduling
Josh Carraway—volunteer coordination

"This will be a horizontal structure," Phelps declared. "And we'll have consultants by the carload, but this staff is the nucleus of our team. I want you to work together and make me look good. Understand?"

Tony nodded along with his co-workers, but he recognized immediately who'd wield the most clout among the young staff. The other newcomers didn't have his experience or educational background, and they'd defer to him on most day-to-day issues. And since he and Phelps were the only non-Anglos on the team, he realized the campaign manager would need him more than anyone, particularly for the critical outreach work into Hispanic communities. Never mind that Tony's mother was as white as the descendants of the *Mayflower*, he had three rare commodities in

23

the world of Republican politics: black hair, brown skin, and a fluency in Spanish. Plus, Tony knew that his appearance—"God, he looks like a young Antonio Banderas," he'd heard Debbie Adams whisper—would hold him in good stead for a media-driven campaign.

"Listen to me closely," Phelps continued. "You're on a twenty-four-hour schedule and you're never to be late for meetings. Are we on the same page?"

"Yes sir," the group replied in unison. Given it was already past 10:00 p.m., Tony found the twenty-four-hour warning redundant.

"That's all then," Phelps stated. "You're dismissed for the night. Tony, I need you to stay behind."

Tony waited to address Phelps until the others exited. "Mr. Phelps?" he asked, tilting his head.

"Tell me a little more about yourself. Your father was Mexican-born?"

"Yes sir, he met my mother while on a work visa and naturalized after they married."

"And your mother?"

"Born and raised in The Valley. I only moved to San Antonio after law school."

"How'd you meet General Striker?"

Tony fidgeted and looked at the floor before answering. He was glad Phelps didn't appear to be aware of the rumors that had swirled about him in San Antonio. "I was introduced by friends at a fundraiser at the Alamo," he answered. "She gave a great speech that day."

"And why are you here?"

Tony's heartbeat accelerated. "I want to be on the team that wins the governor's race," he replied. "I believe the days of the middle-aged white male in the Republican Party are over. Senator Hutchison set the table for the next generation of female and minority leaders in Texas, but there have been few since her to take over that mantle. General Striker is her logical heir."

"And you think you can help us recruit more Hispanics onto her team?"

"Yes sir. We need to make Hispanic outreach a priority in this race because even if General Striker wins—yet Republicans fail to build that coalition—Texas will likely end up blue within the next decade. I want to be part of the effort to reverse that trend."

Phelps rubbed his fingers against the stubble on his chin. "So how do you plan to do that?" he asked.

Tony realized the grizzled veteran already knew the answer to his question but he welcomed the test. "I have it mapped out in my head," he started. "The Latino population has exploded in The Valley and is now spreading within all of the major metropolitan areas of the state. Hispanics are populating at six times the rate of Anglos and not just because of illegals. I think if we go where Hispanics live, and speak to them about abortion, immigration reform, jobs, and all of their hot-button issues, they will respond to a conservative platform like General Striker's. Her values are their values. I can help deliver that message."

"And you also want to be ready for the day a Latino Republican runs for governor in Texas, don't you?"

Tony knew better than to answer that question. "I'm here to do a job," he replied. "The most important thing for me is to work hard. I'll do whatever it takes to win."

Phelps smirked. "You're a young man beyond your years. Sounds like you're planning a political future of your own. That'll be all, Tony."

Tony nodded and left the room thinking he'd connected with Phelps but worried he might have gone too far with his enthusiasm. He understood that most sharpshooters like Phelps didn't care for ambitious pols on their staffs; they wanted worker bees. What Tony hoped Phelps took away from their meeting was that he could make an impact if given the chance. For now, however, he had to put his head down and get to work. To that end, Tony was pleased that Michael Huffines was waiting for him in his small office when he arrived.

"What's up?" Michael asked as Tony walked in.

"Thanks for waiting, *mi amigo*," Tony said. "I know you're ready to get out of here. Just a quick question so I can get going with this project for Phelps. He's asked me to jump on oppo research right away."

"Shoot," Michael replied, rubbing his hands together.

"You mentioned a woman at the Buchanan event. Remember?"

"Sure I do. Phelps already asked me about her."

"I know," Tony lied. His curiosity intensified, knowing that Phelps had interrogated Huffines about the mystery woman. "She's part of the research I need to do."

"Really? He told me not to talk about her with anyone."

"No worries," Tony responded with a wave of his hand as he sat down behind his desk. "I was just looking for the name and address you got off the sign-in register. I can call Phelps for it. No big deal."

"No, no, don't do that," Michael said while biting his lip. "I'll give you the name, but I'm just a little confused. I thought Phelps wanted to keep this to himself. But okay. All of this is new to me."

"I understand," Tony sympathized. "We've all been there."

"Her name is Catherine Alexander," Michael said, "and she lives in New York City. That's all I could find out."

Tony scratched the name down on a piece of paper, nodded toward Michael, and swiveled toward his computer screen. "Thanks, Michael," he replied. *"Eres el hombre."*

CHAPTER 5

Cat understood Blake's reluctance to advance beyond briefly clasping her hand, but even as the restaurant emptied and it was just the waiter and the two of them, he remained a model of rectitude. She hadn't gone looking for an opportunity to turn him down, but she'd almost grown disappointed he'd never given her the chance.

"I'm not sure I've enjoyed talking to anyone like this in a long time," Blake said when they approached her rental car.

The moment came with a hug, strong and familiar, his arms sliding around the soft contours of her body in a gesture that was both intimate and innocent. She held back at first, but his warmth broke down her willpower and she lifted her arms around his shoulders, gently caressing his back, as their bodies swayed in the late-night air. "I enjoyed it too," she whispered in his ear.

For ten glorious seconds that filled two decades of her life, she hugged Blake. And just as she lost herself in that world, he pulled away.

"I'm sorry, Cat."

She didn't respond but found the strength to step back. She straightened her hair—why did she do that?—before removing her keys from her purse and unlocking her car door.

"Got a little carried away," Blake said with a wink.

"You've never made these reunions easy on a girl," Cat replied, shaking her head as she tossed her coat and purse onto

27

the passenger seat. "Here I am again, saying goodbye to you as I climb into my car and drive into the night. Haven't we been here before?"

For a silent moment, they both took in that sense of déjà vu.

"Well, Senator," Cat said, "good luck with your race. I'll be watching and keeping my fingers crossed."

Blake gave her a thumbs-up and backed off so she could motor away.

Cat was headed back to her family, back to the untidy routine of her life in New York City, and that reality transformed her as the distance grew between her and temptation. Ahead of her were the joys of packing school lunches, attending parent-teacher conferences, yoga with girlfriends, and managing her restaurant. Her brief, harmless dinner with Blake Buchanan would be a nice memory in time. As her mind moved to matters ahead, her hand reached over into her coat pocket and pulled out a keepsake. Blake had slipped her a business card with his private cell phone number and email address. She looked at it, smiled, and dropped it into her purse.

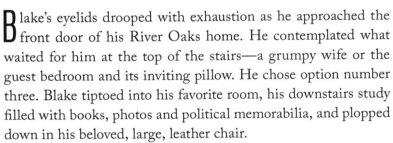

Blake's eyelids drooped with exhaustion as he approached the front door of his River Oaks home. He contemplated what waited for him at the top of the stairs—a grumpy wife or the guest bedroom and its inviting pillow. He chose option number three. Blake tiptoed into his favorite room, his downstairs study filled with books, photos and political memorabilia, and plopped down in his beloved, large, leather chair.

Blake reclined, thought about the campaign, and pondered his encounter with Cat Alexander. He looked down at his iPhone and considered sending her a text to say how wonderful it had been to see her, but he quickly realized that would be a mistake. Their turn-back-the-clock moment needed time to breathe, and any message he sent now might easily be misinterpreted. His mind then wandered to the computer staring at him from his desk. How dangerous it was . . .

"Dad?" a voice called out from the hall.

"Hey, Fin," Blake responded. "Sorry I woke you up."

"I wasn't sleeping. Can I come in?"

"Are you kidding? Get in here."

Blake's blonde-haired, seventeen-year-old daughter entered the study in a pair of furry slippers and a cotton knee-length nightgown that swallowed her slender-framed body. "What are you doing?" she asked while walking over and sitting on the arm of his oversized chair.

Blake scooched over and Fin's small body slid in next to him.

"I had a long night with the campaign folks and they got me thinking about social media. I was about to experiment on my laptop. It's time I learn what my staff does on this thing."

Fin giggled. "And who am I then?" she joked. "As I remember, I set up your first Facebook page. Until then you didn't know what a 'like' was from a 'tweet.' Probably still don't, do you?"

"Very funny," he replied. "I'll have you know I'm tweeting and Facebooking more and more every day. At least, someone on my team is." He chuckled.

Fin squirmed out of the chair and stood in front of her father. "Are you okay?"

The question jolted Blake. It was the kind his mature girl often surprised him with these days. "Yes, sure," he answered. "I really am. But you're sweet to ask."

Fin looked at her feet. "Mom's been drinking tonight, you know. Ever since she got home." The young girl then turned her head and took a deep breath.

Blake stood up, opened his arms, and hugged his daughter. "Your mom will be fine," he whispered. "This race is tough on both of us."

"I hope so. I'm worried."

"Please don't be."

"C'mon, Dad. I know Mom's tired of politics. She wants more of your time, I think, and less of Rags Beckham's. All she does now is hang out at the club and play tennis with her girlfriends."

Blake nodded. "I'm sorry you've had to deal with all of that."

"Maybe you can talk to her tomorrow. She's inviting those ladies from the club to the house almost every day, and all they do is gossip and drink wine. It's a different group, not even her old friends. She's unhappy. Anyone can see that."

"You're something." Blake squeezed his girl around the shoulders. "I didn't think it was that obvious to you guys."

"Dad," Fin said while curling into her father's shoulder, "Shana and I are with her every day. We're not blind."

Blake sighed. "I'll talk to her. I promise."

Fin kissed her father. "Love you."

Blake smiled and tousled his daughter's hair.

"I'm tired now," Fin said in a relieved tone, walking toward the hall. "Time for this sleepy girl to go to bed. You too."

Blake called to his daughter, "I love you. Don't worry about me. I'll be right up after you."

As Fin blew him a kiss, and he caught it, Blake fell back into his chair. He laid his head against the cushioned leather and surveyed his study, taking in the many pictures and keepsakes scattered around the room. The one that never failed to move him was the framed shot of his indomitable father hugging him after his first political victory, with Faith standing by his side beaming a megawatt smile. That night was among the happiest moments of his young marriage, a time when his wife genuinely shared his dream of a political future leading to the governor's mansion. As Blake compared that image to the reality of his life now, he remembered why he'd come into his study in the first place.

He picked up his phone, opened his Facebook app, and sent the woman from New York a "friend" request.

CHAPTER 6

Over-caffeinated, Rags Beckham bounced around his small office at Buchanan headquarters, unsure of what to make of his dinner with Blake and Cat Alexander. The five-foot-seven ball of energy paced in figure eights around the large stacks of campaign signs filling his room, each waiting for its chance to be deployed to the field. Every single one of them was needed for a candidate twenty points down in the polls. It hadn't taken Rags long to figure out that Cat Alexander was his boss's old flame—Blake's introduction had confirmed that—but despite the obvious chemistry between the two, Rags didn't think he had anything to worry about. His candidate was tough and smart and had waited far too long for his political moment to give it away on a fling. He would never be that foolish. Instead, Rags had to focus on a different, but imminent, problem brewing down the hallway.

"Kristen," Rags called out to the young scheduler.

"Yes, sir," she replied, motoring his way with a wide smile.

"Shut the door, please," he directed as she entered the room.

"Is something wrong?" Kristen asked. The energetic brunette wore a blue pantsuit that accentuated her toned figure, but it was her open white blouse revealing a hint of cleavage that captured Rags's attention.

"I want to talk to you for a minute," he said. "Please sit down."

Kristen eased into the chair across from Rags's desk and waited with an expectant look on her face.

"Do you know how Senator Buchanan and I met?"

"No, sir," she answered.

"I was a struggling campaign manager wannabe back in the nineties, bouncing from election to election, hoping for a break. I'd worked on the first Bush campaign, actually serving on the back bench for Lee Atwater. Boy, I thought I was ready. I wanted to be a lead consultant more than anything in the world but I couldn't catch a break with any of the big guns."

Kristen nodded.

"And then I met Blake Buchanan. He changed everything for me."

"Yes, sir." The confused-looking woman slightly adjusted her posture in her seat. "I know you two have had a successful partnership ever since his first state-rep race. That was almost twenty years ago, wasn't it?"

Rags nodded, the realization settling in that Kristen was about five at the time. "So you know I'd do anything for the man, don't you?"

"Yes sir, of course."

"I like you, Kristen. You're organized and disciplined, and I think you're going to be a great asset for this campaign. But you need to remember that Senator Buchanan's married. Do you understand?"

Kristen shuffled her feet, then frowned at the floor, before looking up, red-faced, toward Rags. "Do you think I acted inappropriately last night?"

"No, but I think you know what I'm talking about."

Kristen's skin color shot from red to deep crimson. She reached toward her blouse with her right hand and pulled her shirt together as she lowered her head. "I understand, Mr. Beckham," she replied. "I'll be more careful from here on out."

Kristen's instinctive move to cover up her cleavage reinforced Rags's observation that she'd accentuated it the night before. "Thank you for understanding," he said with a paternalistic smile. Rags liked the young girl, maybe too much, and trusted this would be the last time he'd have to slap her wrists. He gazed at Kristen, her fresh face and brown doe eyes now guilting him in response, and hoped she'd captured the gravity of his message. Even then, he sensed trouble ahead with his star-struck assistant.

"That'll be all," he said.

CHAPTER 7

The *humm.*

Cat had returned to the old paces of her life—from walking her kids to school in the morning to bouncing around her restaurant at night—but thoughts of Blake, and how they'd reconnected in Houston, now pushed their way into her consciousness, tilting at the windmill of the comfortable, safe life she'd built for her family in New York. The *humm* had reinvaded her world. The tantalizing feeling, romanticized by the passage of decades, created pleasurable and overwhelming daydreams, no matter how dangerous she knew they were.

With those distracting thoughts in her head, Cat placed bread, condiments, and a number of Tupperware containers on her marble kitchen island. She'd left the restaurant early tonight to work in her own home. The minute Cat popped off a couple of the plastic tops, her husband Sam entered the room. He was dressed in a pair of baggy cargo shorts that extended to the knees of his five-foot-ten frame, a New York Yankees T-shirt, and sandals. His sparse, once-blonde hair swirled around his head like a windblown bird's nest and his reading glasses dangled from a cord around his neck. This was the distinctive look Sam threw on most days when he worked from his study at the apartment. Cat rarely thought much about her husband's uniform as she went about her business but she now realized how attractive she'd found the crisp, tailored, navy suit Blake had worn that night in Texas.

"Why're you home early?" Sam asked.

"It was a slow night . . . and I wanted to make sure I had everything I needed to prepare these sandwiches for the fund-raiser tomorrow night."

"Why didn't you just order them from the deli?"

Cat looked at Sam and shook her head. "Because I told Mitch that I'd make them. I'm in the food business for God's sake, so I don't want anyone thinking that our son's mother's a slacker."

"You know that's what all the other mothers do?"

Cat dug her knife into the homemade pimiento spread and bit her lip. "Maybe so," she fired back, trying to keep her voice even. She didn't know if Sam meant to criticize her, but his arrow hit anyway. "Well, that's just not me. Did you kiss Mitch good-night?"

"After I read him a story," Sam explained while opening a bag of chips he'd grabbed off the table. "Paige is studying."

"Hope she's not just snapchatting friends."

"Don't know," Sam replied. "At least she had her books out." He crunched down on a mouthful of Lay's. "By the way," he mumbled while chewing, "we never talked about your trip to Texas. How'd it go?"

The question stomach-punched Cat. She looked at her husband, thought about her answer, and shrugged. "Same as always," she said. "Mom's getting pretty crusty these days." Cat couldn't help contrasting her memory of Blake's hug with the image of Sam chomping his potato chips. "There's going to come a time when it won't be good for her to live alone," Cat continued, steering the focus away from the only part of the trip she wanted to think about.

"What's the school fundraiser for tomorrow night?" Sam asked.

"We've talked about this several times," Cat answered with irritation. She took a deep breath and sighed. "It's New York Cares."

"Oh yeah," Sam sniped with a wave of his arm. "We've been giving them money for years."

"Yes, because they do remarkable things around the City. They revitalize green spaces and teach kids how to protect the environment. I think they may ask me to join their board."

"Good for you," Sam said. "But that's likely a prelude to some big-money ask."

"That's offensive," Cat responded tartly. Why did he always feel the need to take her down?

Sam balled up his chip bag and threw it into the trash. "I'm not itching for a fight. Just saying . . ."

Cat pierced her knife deeper into the pimiento spread as if stabbing the conversation in the heart. "I'll be back in a minute," she announced. "I want to go check on Mitch." Cat took a deep, audible breath and stomped out of the room, flipping her hand in the air as if whisking Sam away.

———————— ★ ————————

Blake sat down at his conference table with Rags, Kristen, and their new fundraising consultant, Susan Wilde, a petite firecracker from Austin with the staccato delivery of a woodpecker banging on a tree. A small brain trust for a gubernatorial campaign, but one that fit Blake's budget. This meeting was intended to help remedy that problem.

"We have four fundraisers on the schedule next week," Rags began. "These events are critical because we have to raise some real money or no one is going to take us seriously."

"I understand." Blake nodded his approval.

"So our goal is to raise ten million dollars over the next few months," Rags continued. "We have to shake every tree and call every one of our prospects, some of them three or four times."

"Let me cut in," Susan interjected. "Don't be overwhelmed by that number because we're going to raise that amount and more."

Blake shook his head. "I'm not intimidated at all," he stated.

"Rags and I have talked about this many times before I got in the race. We knew this campaign couldn't be managed without huge money. Striker already has fifteen million in the bank. I have five hundred thousand. That puts me at more than a slight disadvantage, but I'm ready."

Wilde then volleyed back with the question Blake knew was coming. "And is your wife's father still willing to loan the full five million?"

"Yes," Blake snapped. "But remember we're not counting any of that money until we've worked all of our targets. Faith knows that and so does her father. We all on the same page?"

"Of course," Susan replied, casting her eyes down. Blake could see his comments disappointed the almost-perpetually sunny Wilde. The fundraising juggernaut had been reluctant to hire onto the campaign given the popular attorney general's big lead, but Rags had convinced her based on the promise of the five-million-dollar loan as a kick start. Money rarely flowed to insurgent candidates like Blake, but the Cantrell pledge gave him a solid chance to raise his profile, which Susan knew would open doors for new dollars. His announcement to refrain from taking that money early on had undercut her strategy and likely had her questioning her decision to join the Buchanan team.

"So where are we going first?" Blake asked.

"We have events planned in Dallas, San Antonio, and Houston," Wilde explained, "but the first thing we need to do is mine Wall Street. That old friend of yours, Chance Mitchell, promises he can raise one or two million dollars in a single visit. They hate Striker and all of her Tea Party cronies up there. You're leaving Sunday. The event's Monday night."

Blake showed no reaction to the news of his New York trip—he'd planned it weeks before—but hearing it aloud made his heart skip a beat. Yet he was the only one in the room who knew why.

CHAPTER 8

An affair, if that's what Blake Buchanan had going on, was a tricky subject to exploit. Tony León realized his hunch about the woman from New York could be a big bunch of nothing, but the information he'd extracted from Michael Huffines was nonetheless too tantalizing to ignore. Tony also understood that while social conservatives considered morality a very significant issue, these kinds of disclosures could backfire on the candidate outing the story. Plus, the last thing he wanted to do was create an atmosphere that might bring out Grace Striker's own peccadillos. That's why the preferred method for embarrassing an opposition candidate over a secret romance was siccing the press on the trail of the presumptive lover and, like hogs to truffles, setting them loose to unearth the prize. Think Gary Hart in 1988, Bill Clinton in 1998, or even the infamous client number 9 episode with Eliot Spitzer. The stories were infinite, but not always disqualifying. Tony risked a lot by putting this plan into action without Marshall Phelps's approval; however, he believed that if he uncovered an affair he'd become a hero. And if his plan imploded, his fingerprints would never be found.

"Hey, Jackson," Tony greeted from his office phone when the reporter answered, "it's Tony León. How've you been?" Tony hadn't spoken to his former UT law school classmate in over a year but the fact that Jackson Goodrich had become the chief political writer of the *New York Enquirer* was a card he'd always kept close at hand.

"Hi, Tony. Have you taken over our state yet?" Jackson chuckled.

"Not quite, but I am working for the next governor of Texas. Attorney General Grace Striker."

"Gone to the dark side, huh?" Jackson replied.

"If you mean I'm working for a true conservative, I guess the answer's yes."

"I meant she's to the right of the Tea Party itself, don't you think? A wack job like Striker has a different name association in this newsroom."

"You're supposed to be objective," Tony replied, as he rolled his eyes.

"Keep your shirt on, buddy. I'm just messing with you. What's on your mind? I know you're not calling to shoot the shit."

"Did you know my candidate's opponent, Blake Buchanan, is hosting a fundraiser on Wall Street next week?"

"Can't say I did. But why should I care?"

"This is a big deal. A Texas candidate raising money in New York City before he even hits Houston or Dallas. Don't you find that odd? Might be worth covering just to see who shows up."

"What are you suggesting?"

"Nothing, but you might want to look at the list of attendees. That's all."

"Tony, I'm not interested in the Texas governor's race. The polls sure tell me I shouldn't be. Doesn't your candidate have a twenty-point lead? Seriously, why should I give a shit about an obscure fundraiser for some second-tier candidate?"

"You're right," Tony said. "Forget about it."

Jackson's pause gave Tony the assurance he needed.

"Message delivered, Tony," Jackson acknowledged. "I'll check it out. Hope you're not bullshitting me. Talk to you later."

Tony hung up the phone and smiled. Step one of his plan was under way.

——— ★ ———

Marshall Phelps gnawed on the last piece of lukewarm pizza and wiped his mouth with the sleeve of his shirt. His office clock said it was after midnight. He turned to his pollster, Stanley Braxton, aka the Source, with a look of disbelief.

"Our girl's unhinged," Phelps said.

"Yeah," replied the graying politico from across the table. "She's spinning some crazy shit here."

Phelps glanced at his longtime colleague and imagined that each crease in his friend's face represented one of the many political battles the two had fought together over the years. They came from different backgrounds—Phelps, the black projects in New Orleans; Braxton, white suburbia in Dallas—but both practiced politics the old-school way: vote-by-vote. They'd built a thirty-year relationship, often joking by helping to elect vain, self-indulgent pricks neither of them much cared for. Both were jaded by what they'd witnessed over the years and they agreed Grace Striker was among the worst of the bunch.

Phelps slammed his hand down on the work of "nonfiction" they'd spent the night reviewing. Striker had decided, like many other politicians with national ambitions, to publish a memoir filled with self-aggrandizing stories, in an effort to frame her life journey before others did. It was a deceptive attempt by the candidate to recast her comfortable middle-class upbringing into an earnest tale of struggle and perseverance. "Get this," Phelps observed. "She's decided that *laboring* at her father's construction company as a receptionist was heroic and fighting sexism there comparable to MLK's battle for civil rights. And that's just the start. The two chapters she devotes to that East Texas stunt at the Harrison County Hospital are something to behold."

"She's a trip," the Source agreed. "And check out the pictures. I must say she's a good looking woman, but the more she tries to look like Jennifer Lawrence, the more pathetic it seems."

"I wouldn't flatter her that much. I'm thinking more like our very own Abe Lincoln in heels and a push-up bra."

"That reminds me," the Source interrupted as he chuckled at Phelps's comment. "Is that *People* magazine spread still coming?"

"Fuck yeah. As if *People* was the *Washington Post*. I at least got her to dress down for the photo shoot, but she damn sure wasn't happy about it. She didn't want to hear that her photo spread might otherwise turn out like that of some desperate, middle-aged TV reality star's. The problem is our Lubbock everywoman likes hearing she's the most searched politician on the internet."

"Just hope no one starts doing before-and-afters," the Source joked. "They might think Dr. Frankenstein had come back to life."

Phelps laughed and flung the empty pizza box toward the garbage can. He took a deep breath and stared at his friend. "Can you do something about the damn book?" he asked.

"Yeah, I'll get Fricks to tone it down."

"She can't know." Phelps paused. "You understand that?"

"Of course. Fricks is a pro. As long as you're paying him, he doesn't care what the thing says. Whatever you don't like can be deleted. He'll tell her, if she asks, that his editor made some last-minute changes. My guess is she'll never take the time to read it anyway."

"Good . . . and thanks." Phelps stood up from his chair and stretched his arms. "So let's get the hell out of here. It's almost one in the morning and I've got a campaign to run."

The Source smiled and reached over and slapped his friend on the shoulder. "In the day, you'd just be pouring me another Scotch right about now."

"Times change," Phelps pointed out.

"And we're old," the Source replied.

CHAPTER 9

September 16

The guest room was Blake's de facto sleeping quarters at home. His wife had handed off his place in their king-sized bed to the family's wheaten terrier, Red. Although the change in sleeping arrangements had been gradual, Blake often wondered how he and Faith had lived as husband and wife without discussing their beloved dog's displacement of his master. It had started one night several years earlier, after one of their more blistering arguments, when Blake had left the room to avoid further confrontation. By the time he'd returned to bed, his wily hound had left his customary place on the floor for a more comfortable location: the mattress. Blake hadn't objected to retreating to the guest room that evening—it was a welcome exodus—but he'd never expected the arrangement to become permanent. After a certain amount of time had passed and tempers had cooled, Blake realized that loveable Red had become the couple's white flag of truce.

When Blake woke up the morning of his flight, he wondered whether he should talk to Faith before heading to the airport. He tiptoed past his sleeping wife to shower and pack his bag in the master bathroom, but when he emerged and saw her still slumbering, he made up his mind to sneak away. Her closed eyes fooled him.

"Where you headed today?" she asked sharply.

Blake stopped and veered over to Faith's bedside. Red was

unfazed, snoring through her question. "New York fundraiser," he answered. "An old friend, Chance Mitchell, is hosting."

"Did you even wonder if I wanted to go?"

"No, but I'd be glad to have you. We'll need to check on flights right away."

"I'm not going," she said without moving from her pillow. "But you should've asked."

"My fault," Blake conceded. "I'll make sure you have a copy of my advance itinerary from now on in case you want to participate. They have me moving around quite a bit and I honestly don't know where I'm going to be half the time."

Faith yawned. "Don't forget your daughter's game on Thursday. Do you have *that* on your sacred itinerary?"

Blake didn't respond at first because he had no desire to exacerbate the tension with his wife. "I'll be there," he agreed, knowing that it would be impossible for him to attend given his schedule.

"Have a nice trip," Faith said before rolling onto her side. "And," she added in a muffled voice, "please put the alarm on when you leave."

———— ★ ————

B lake had met Faith at a mutual friend's wedding in Dallas about eight months after Cat moved to Florida to pursue her job at the Forge restaurant. He hadn't even thought about bringing another woman into his life at the time. His work as a young law associate had made social events scarce and dating even scarcer. Faith Cantrell had changed all of that.

"Who's she?" Blake had asked his friend Peter while surveying the numerous bridesmaids at the reception.

"You're such a dumbshit," Peter had replied. "You don't know Faith Cantrell? Gorgeous, isn't she? And that's only half of it. Her daddy's one of the richest oilmen in Texas. She's way out of your league, pardner." Peter had nudged his arm and

Blake had understood the challenge. After several more min-utes of prodding, Blake had coaxed Peter into introducing him to the stunning five-foot-nine blonde, who was dressed in an emerald-blue, chiffon dress.

"So you're Jake's fraternity brother?" Faith had asked Blake after Peter had diplomatically stepped away to leave them alone.

Blake hadn't been close to the groom in college, but they were friends. "Yes, we had some good times together at UT," he'd replied.

"And what do you do, Blake Buchanan?" Faith had asked.

"I'm an associate at Vickers and Nelson in Houston. Finished law school last year. Peter told me you went to SMU."

"Sad but true," Faith had said. "Couldn't leave the bubble." She'd laughed. "You know my father's good friends with Craig Vickers. They're big political cronies."

Blake's temperature had risen with that revelation. "Are you here with anyone tonight?" he'd asked.

She'd shaken her head signaling "no," before casting her eyes down and then directly at his.

From that moment on, the evening had been theirs. They'd danced, joked about the perils of post-college life, and discov-ered the many common friends they shared between Dallas and Houston. And later on, as they toasted the newlyweds with champagne, Blake had reached for her open hand, and she'd accepted, confirming what he'd sensed from the moment they'd met. When the party had shut down, Faith had taken him back to her place and they'd consumed each other in a fiery fit of love-making that lasted till dawn.

After that first night, Blake had realized he'd started down an inexorable path with Faith Cantrell that had no escape routes. Within weeks, she'd invited him to meet her parents at a holiday party at the Cantrells' Turtle Creek estate, a gala that had included a guest list with both of Texas's senators, the lieutenant governor, and an assortment of Republican Party politicos and millionaire donors the likes of which Blake had never seen. Blake's eyes had been opened wide to a world and a circle of people he'd only read about. And as his fling with Faith had blossomed into a full-blooded romance, the seductive pull of the Cantrell wealth and power had grown more irresistible each day.

———★———

B lake pushed back his seat on the plane to the reclined position and read the grim news in the paper, a bemused look crossing his face. His announcement for governor had barely registered on the radar screen of Texas politics, one writer projecting his chances for defeating Attorney General Striker somewhere south of Walter Mondale's forty-nine-state massacre at the hands of Ronald Reagan. Another drew comparisons to the Alamo. Blake had expected to be an underdog, but not a dead dog.

Despite the negative news, Blake pushed himself to remain positive, believing that Texans had tired of opportunistic Republicans like Striker and feeling secure in his campaign manager's plan. Rags's advice still echoed in his brain: "Keep your head down through Christmas and don't look up till New Year's." Patience was Rags's mantra. "Texas Republicans haven't seen a candidate like you before," he reminded Blake at every turn. "They will need time to adjust."

"Not much to get excited about here," Blake whispered to Rags while patting the newspaper. Rags shook his head as he nestled himself into the middle seat of the row, fidgeting in his cramped quarters next to a flabby-armed woman who'd assumed control over their armrest.

"What did I tell you about reading that crap?" Rags replied. "And remember, we have a strategy." Rags winked. "As a matter of fact, I'll bet you a Coca-Cola that you'll pick up five points in the polls within two weeks. Maybe more."

Blake looked at his campaign manager and laughed. "I guess," Blake said, "that will move our chances from not-in-a-million-years to something just under impossible." Blake smiled but wondered if Rags truly believed any differently. Yet, he refused to question his quirky campaign manager. From their very first meeting, over eighteen years earlier, Rags had proven he had better instincts than his slicker, more polished competitors in the political world.

"Tell me about yourself," Blake had asked at their initial interview.

Before answering, Rags had fumbled for several seconds with the pen he'd clutched in his hand like a relay-baton. "I'm from West Texas," he'd begun. "Which means I was supposed to play football. But look at me. I'm scrawny, no more than a hundred-fifty pounds dripping wet. I wasn't going to be a football star. So while the other guys were at practice every day, I studied math equations. The math equations eventually turned into political algorithms."

Blake had cocked his head, encouraging Rags to go on.

"My father was a diehard West Texas Republican at the time," he'd continued. "The kind who thought Jimmy Carter was Satan and Ronald Reagan divine . . . and he had some influence over me as a young kid. Plus, I loved history, especially biographies of the presidents who changed America—Washington, Lincoln, FDR—and the two ideas collided in my head. Voila, the algorithm."

"What became of it?"

"The internet. While I thought I'd built something unique, the internet made personal data, voter profiles, and the various inputs I needed for my program so available that any political consultant with a laptop and half a brain could come up with his own version. My genius was commoditized."

Blake had found something about Rags's raw honesty and self-deprecation compelling. Two hours later, the men had finished their meeting and shaken hands.

"I'm hiring you as my consultant," Blake had said. "Think you can get me elected?"

Rags had shuffled his feet before looking at Blake with moist eyes. "To what office?" he'd finally responded. "You've got what none of the others I've met have—a real heart for making the world a better place. And that is a quality any good consultant can take a long way."

Blake had smiled at Rags that afternoon and known he'd made the right choice for his future. He reminded himself of that fact as they relaxed in their airplane seats and zoomed off to New York.

————— ★ —————

Cat shopped at the local market and picked up a prescription for Sam on her way to meet the kids that afternoon. As many days as possible, Cat greeted Mitch and Paige near the front of the Trinity School on the Upper West Side to escort them home. Soon-to-be-teenager Paige was newly resistant to having her mom near campus but Mitch still enjoyed the fifteen-minute walk with his parent. Cat waited patiently outside the school building, soaking in the warm sunshine that snuck out from behind the puffy afternoon clouds. Mitch bounded out first through the front doors and beelined to his mother.

"Hey, Mom," he yelled before tumbling into Cat with a short bump of a hug.

"Hi, Mitch," she replied. "How was your day?"

"Good," he answered.

Cat smiled and fluffed her son's hair.

A few minutes later, Paige emerged from the building and made eye contact with her mother and brother. The preteen then turned and chatted with a couple of friends for several minutes, waited until they dispersed, and only then moseyed over to her family for the walk home. Cat didn't worry about her daughter's disrespectful antics; she figured every day she got to spend with Paige was a blessing. They were about halfway down their Central Park West route to their apartment when Cat's phone beeped from her pocket. She wondered if—actually, hoped—it was a text from Blake.

Cat reached for her phone but Paige beat her to it.

"Want me to read your message?" Paige asked, holding Cat's phone in front of her.

"No, that's private," Cat said, but she was already too late. Her heart jumped as her perpetually nosy daughter swiped in her mother's birth year to unlock the screen. Cat had thought about changing her too-obvious password many times in the past but had never seen a real need . . . until now.

"It says," Paige announced, "'*Just got here, staying at the Lowell. Come by Chance Mitchell's house around 6 if you can. B.*' Who's 'B,' Mom?"

"Must be my friend Beth from Connecticut," Cat lied, hoping the fictional name would chase her amateur sleuth off the trail.

Paige appeared satisfied with the answer.

"Hey, Mom, can I play a game on your phone while we walk?" Mitch asked.

"Give me that thing," Cat demanded. "You guys need to pay attention to the road." Cat pulled her phone from her daughter's hand.

By the time the trio reached their destination, Cat had considered and reconsidered Blake's invitation, then reconsidered it several more times. While the new Blake appeared to be a different person than the cad she'd written off years before, Cat knew that showing up at his fundraiser was a bad idea. He was a married man, with the eyes of a state on him, and no matter what spark had passed between them in Texas, the risks were too great for even a mild flirtation. And while time had softened the ill will she'd harbored for Blake over his abrupt marriage to Faith, the fact was she still believed he'd chosen a wife for political access and power over his heartstrings, and that still smarted. Now that she'd spent years in Manhattan, becoming successful, respected, and fulfilled, re-opening the Blake chapter of her past was a risk she couldn't take.

Cat had changed a great deal after Blake had left Asheville, so much that she wondered what he'd really think if he got to know her as a fifty-year-old adult. She was a nester nowadays, having built a good life with Sam and her children in the City. She volunteered, donated to causes she cared about, and held deep animus for Republicans hostile to her political ideals. Maybe Blake wasn't that kind of Republican—his campaign speech had suggested as much—but what did it matter? She was a Democrat and a New Yorker now, a busy mother, and yes, a wife. For all those reasons, after she arrived home and the children scurried off to their rooms, she dialed The Lowell's front desk and left Blake a voice mail message.

"Thanks for the invitation," she said into the recorder, "but I have a full night ahead at the restaurant. It will be too late to get to your event and I'm sorry I'll miss you. Good luck with Chance."

CHAPTER 10

M arshall Phelps leaned back in his office chair and reflected on his candidate's transformation over the past few years. From an unknown West Texas legislator who'd ridden a Tea Party wave of support into the attorney general's office, Grace Striker had remade herself into a Bible-wagging, gun-toting, antiabortion advocate—the reincarnation of Sarah Palin, at least the popular, pre-Tina Fey variety. Now Phelps had to broaden his candidate's appeal beyond the activists who'd thrust her into statewide office because his woman had set her sights on bigger quarry.

Tony León burst into Phelps's office with his hair on fire. Since coming on, the young man with the movie-star looks and oily personality had grabbed every opportunity he could to gain his boss's attention.

"What is it?" Phelps asked, his patience with the staffer's congenital eagerness growing thin.

"I've got some big news," Tony whispered, as if someone outside might be listening.

"Speak up. I can't hear you."

Tony shut the door and walked closer to Phelps's desk. "I just got a call from a Dallas friend who gave me some very surprising news."

"Spit it out, Tony. I can handle it." Phelps yawned.

"Reverend Davis Dodds is getting in the primary."

Phelps looked at his young assistant and shook his head. "Reverend Dodds talks about getting in every race, but he never does. His game is to force the candidates to pay attention to him and generate a little more cash for his offering plate. Nothing more."

"Yes, sir," Tony replied, "I understand that. But I'm told he's actually running. He apparently is saying that God told him it's his time."

Phelps shrugged and looked at Tony with a wry grin. "God, huh? Well, I guess I can't argue with that."

Tony stood still as if he wanted a prize for his news, but Phelps merely asked him, "Is that all?"

The excited staffer nodded.

"You can go then."

Tony left the room with his tail between his legs as Phelps leaned back in his chair. Phelps knew that Dodds, the black, wheelchair-bound leader of the largest charismatic, evangelical church in the nation, was a nonfactor in the primary, but his small, dedicated base of voters would cannibalize some of Striker's support. Phelps scolded himself for allowing a political event to bubble up outside his control. He realized that he hadn't fully dedicated himself to the race and that working solely for money, even a lot of money, would lead to even more mistakes.

Tony popped his head back into Phelps's office as if he'd forgotten something.

"What is it?" Phelps growled.

"Dodds's speech is going to be carried live by the networks."

"Are we done now?" Phelps asked, clenching his jaw.

"Yes . . . yes, we are."

The news about Dodds made Phelps realize it was time to get back to the nut-cutting part of the business he knew best. He slammed his fist down on his desk. Whether he liked Striker or not, Phelps vowed that Dodds's candidacy would be the last turn in the race without his hand on the wheel.

CHAPTER 11

Upon landing at LaGuardia, Blake had traveled straight to Wall Street where he'd met with two native Texans who Rags had reached out to about supporting the campaign. The sessions had gone better—and longer—than Rags had expected, which prevented Blake from stopping by his hotel before heading to Chance Mitchell's home. During the taxi ride over, Blake straightened his tie, combed his hair, and thought about his remarks. The pony-tailed cabbie pulled in front of a dramatic five-story townhouse on East 66th Street just off Fifth Avenue, and Blake marveled that his wealthy old friend—a one-time tuba player in his Houston high school band—lived in one of the City's toniest neighborhoods, just next door to U. S. Grant's former home. Blake's adrenaline surged. He knew what a big night in New York could do for his campaign. But even as he focused his mind on prying money loose from potential donors, he couldn't help wondering if Cat would show up.

Rags had scheduled an interview for Blake before the fundraiser, with a political reporter from the *New York Enquirer*. The newsman, a young Texan named Jackson Goodrich, had told Rags that he'd heard rumors of an upset brewing in his home state and wanted to get ahead of the story. While Blake scoffed at that ludicrous explanation for the meeting, Rags had convinced him that free publicity, no matter what the motive for the coverage, would be senseless to pass up. The baby-faced writer with a prematurely receding hairline waited for Blake on the second floor of Chance's townhouse.

"Nice to meet you, Senator Buchanan," Jackson said as Blake entered the room.

"Appreciate you taking the time," Blake countered. "I guess I'm something of a novelty item . . . a Texas candidate in New York."

"Not necessarily," Jackson replied. "We see more than a few out-of-staters drag the hat in Manhattan. But, admittedly, very few Republicans. I guess that's a good segue into the interview. Why here? Why now?"

"Fair question," Blake answered while taking the chair across from his interviewer. "Chance Mitchell is an old friend. It's very gracious of him to host this event for me."

"Tell me about the guest list," Jackson requested.

"I can't tell you much. That's been up to Chance. I just hope I can convince a few of them to support me."

"There's not enough money in Texas for you?"

"I'm willing to go anywhere people will listen." Blake smiled.

"I understand that, but what's the attraction to New York? The polls I've seen say you're a huge underdog. Why would a New Yorker want to step into that?"

"You'll have to ask Chance, but I believe his guests will respond positively to my message."

"Which is what?"

"That it's time for a change in Texas politics and around the country. We need leaders who offer a hand up, not a turned shoulder. Fiscal responsibility can coexist with a humane approach to government."

"That's a little too abstract for my readers, Senator. What do you mean by that? Are we talking about social issues, immigration, the wall?"

"Those issues and many, many more. Republicans can't be afraid of what the base will say if they truly want to lead."

"How about your family," Jackson pivoted. "Do they engage in the political process?"

The quick departure from policy suggested to Blake what the reporter was really up to. "My wife and daughters are supportive but their privacy is important to me. That's about all I want to say about them."

"Do you think that's a reasonable position to take?"

"Reasonable or not, it's mine."

Rags had told Blake that at the very least he'd get a favorable puff piece from the reporter, something in the vein of the tall Texan taking on Manhattan, but instead Jackson's meandering Q and A dealt entirely with personal and New York issues. Blake thought he knew what that likely meant—a less than flattering story—and intentionally kept his answers concise, and bland. The two men chatted idly for a while longer, but the interview came to an abrupt end ten minutes early, with Blake shaking his head wondering why he'd even bothered.

Blake then bolted downstairs to the much larger entertainment area on the first floor, where the host was scurrying around preparing for his guests. Never was a man more perfectly named than Chance Mitchell. He sprang toward Blake when they spotted each other across the room.

"Welcome," Chance bellowed.

"Thanks for letting me do the interview upstairs," Blake responded with his hand extended. "I'm glad to find out a Republican can survive in this hostile territory. And, by the way . . . wow . . ." Blake spread his arms.

Chance smiled, the extra chin he'd acquired since Blake had last seen him sagging as his face expanded. "We have to keep moving forward you know." Chance chuckled. "We New Yorkers are a restless bunch. We really don't hate Rs up here . . . we just don't breed any. But a lot of us transplants still understand there's a big country out there that doesn't think the world revolves around the Clintons or Cuomos and New York City."

Blake examined the one-time high school band member and marveled at the man he'd become. Chance had founded a music internet company in his entrepreneurial studies class in college and sold it at a time when internet companies, even those with no sales or earnings, were gobbled up like umbrellas during a rainstorm. Chance had then parlayed his new fortune into building a small private-equity firm specializing in startup entertainment companies. Two short years later, the former band member cashed it all in, packed up his bags, and moved to New York City to live with Frankie, his life partner, in a friendlier environment.

"You're always welcome in my house," Chance added.

"I'm grateful for that," Blake responded.

"You know something, Blake," Chance said, handing him a drink, "I've always known you'd be playing in the big leagues. Even when we were in high school, I sensed it. That's why I've sent you contributions over the years. You're a born leader. Texas—hell, our country—needs more people like you."

Blake shrugged and felt himself color. "Thank you," he responded, "but you're giving me way too much credit." Blake remembered that he'd spent much of his high school life hanging with the *in* crowd, chasing accolades, actions hardly worthy of Chance's praise. But he liked that his old friend recalled him as one who hadn't joined in the juvenile slurs of his classmates and their tendency to ridicule those who didn't fit in.

"Well, that's all the time we have for our trip down memory lane," Chance observed. "The guests are about to arrive. My husband will be here, too. You'll like him . . . he's a Republican through and through." Chance shrugged. "The rest of the group is an assortment of Rs and Ds, but I think you'll be very happy with the haul from this event. We all want you to beat that woman down there. We've caught a glimpse of her aggressive pro-life positions on TV, which is cause enough to get this group activated, but it's her position on same-sex unions that has me most riled up. None of us can stomach her."

For the next hour, Blake greeted men and women he'd never met before and grew more and more impressed with the caliber of attendees—smart, decent, deep-pocketed. However, the one guest Blake kept looking for never appeared. Even as he finished his stump speech, Blake peered around the room hoping Cat had snuck in while he'd been talking. He was disappointed she hadn't made it and found it hard to hide his frustration as he continued working the crowd. About an hour later, as the last donor walked out the front door, he thanked Chance with a big hug and grabbed Rags by the arm. They headed on foot to their nearby hotel.

After checking in at the front desk, Blake said good night to his campaign manager and rode the elevator to the ninth floor. By the time he walked inside his room, he'd all but given up on his fantasy of seeing Cat before he left town the next day. It was only then that he noticed the blinking message light on his bedside phone.

CHAPTER 12

Rags retreated to his hotel room tired from the long day of hand-shaking and money raising. The event at Chance Mitchell's place had surpassed his expectations and he felt renewed by the seven-figure haul. Add in the upcoming announcement from Reverend Dodds, and the Buchanan campaign finally had some good news to build on. Rags sat down and kicked off his shoes, pleased with himself, ready to scroll through the messages on his iPhone. He immediately noticed that Faith Buchanan had called. Rags lost no time in punching the Call Back button, worried that something bad had happened in Texas. Faith rarely called him these days.

"Rags," she answered.

"Faith," he said enthusiastically. "Good to hear from you. Anything wrong?"

"Everything's fine but I wanted to talk to you before Blake got home. Are you alone?"

"Yes. What is it, Faith?"

"It's about the loan. I've told my father not to give the money to the campaign. I want you to tell Blake before he flies back."

Rags closed his eyes. One step forward, two steps back. "That's a little abrupt. You know we've been counting on that money. What happened?"

"I don't want to get into it, but you know Blake has no chance to win." She hesitated and Rags felt her anger brewing through the phone. "He's been saying that he doesn't want the money

57

anyway," she continued, "so I'm taking him up on his offer. I can't ask my father to waste his money any longer. I won't do it. You'll handle this, won't you?"

"Is there anything I can do to change your mind?"

"No."

"Okay then. You and Blake have been such a great political team for so long. I'm sorry you feel this way."

"Look, Rags, I told him this race was a fool's errand and the polls are proving me right. It's time he decided that his family is more important than some hopeless pursuit of the governorship. As if he's on some kind of quest like Don Quixote."

Faith's tone left no room for negotiation and Rags remained quiet. There was nothing he could say, since he was the primary architect of the so-called quixotic quest. He wondered if Faith was tipsy. Blake had refused to discuss her drinking with him, but Rags was convinced she'd shown signs of a problem over the past year. Rags told Faith good night. And with that, the best day for Rags and the Buchanan campaign took a major turn for the worse.

———— ★ ————

Ruing her decision to skip Blake's event, Cat headed out to Abrazo for the night, much earlier than she was expected or needed. But this way left less time for her to change her mind, and she'd be protected from her own wavering resolve. Cat tried to push all thoughts of Blake out of her head as she moved around her restaurant greeting patrons and supervising her staff throughout the evening. Still, she snuck a glass of wine into her private office for an occasional sip throughout the dinner hour, musing, then rejecting, the idea that perhaps, just maybe, he'd appear at Abrazo anyway, just as he had all those years ago in Asheville. As she'd hoped, the hopping activity at the restaurant kept her productively focused on her work, for the most part. Her romantic daydream about Blake was silly and unsettling anyway, and as the hour grew late and the last tables emptied, she'd almost tossed it aside entirely.

He arrived around eleven, right after Cat had run into the kitchen to say goodnight to her manager. When she spotted him at the bar, casually drinking a glass of wine, a soft smile on his face, she couldn't decide if it was a figment of her imagination or a fantasy. She gasped and trembled; there he was. He'd found her, just as he had twenty years earlier. But this was now, and so much had changed, they had changed, yet in so many ways they were still the same.

CHAPTER 13

Blake had the cabbie pull up at a dimly lit corner across the street from Abrazo, his drop-off spot obscured by the trees and bushes of Abingdon Square Park, which stood between him and the restaurant. Blake wanted the reality check of the evening air as he paced outside the now-locked gates of the small sanctuary of green space, and he couldn't ignore the parallels to his trip to Asheville years before. He remembered how his best intentions had escaped him the minute he'd seen Cat that night, and he wondered if the same might happen again. His better judgment told him the smartest move would be to turn back toward 8th Avenue so he could lose himself in one of the many bars in the West Village just powering up for the night. His better judgment lost.

Abrazo sat on the corner of Bethune and Hudson streets under a canopy of two tall, angular gas lamps that splashed light on a black awning and cozy outdoor seating area. Blake hadn't seen Cat when he entered, and creeping disappointment set in that she might have already gone home, although a waiter assured him she was still around and offered him a drink. Blake nestled into a seat at the bar, ordered a glass of the Torres Mas La Plana, and watched the last few restaurant patrons settle their bills. It didn't take long for Cat to emerge. She strode out of the kitchen confidently in a black dress, her blonde hair pinned in a tight bun, a light jacket draped loosely over her arm. A pair of gold hoop earrings dangled from her ears. Cat's face appeared flushed when Blake spotted her, but he wasn't sure if it was a reaction to

60

his presence or related to some kitchen crisis. She acknowledged him with a surprised smile and walked his way.

"Senator," she said warmly.

He drained his glass, stared at her, and asked, "Will you take a walk with me?"

She didn't answer for a moment, as though she was taking him in, all of him, but she appeared pleased with the invitation. Then she nodded and held up a finger before disappearing through a door to the back of the restaurant for what seemed like an eternity. When she reemerged, her jacket was on, her hair was down, and she looked refreshed. Blake's good intentions took a devious turn.

———— ★ ————

Cat knew her hair was a disaster, her light wool dress rumpled, and her eyes sagging from a long night of working the room and overseeing her restaurant. She dashed into the bathroom and within five minutes had touched up her makeup, shaken out her bun, and smoothed her clothes. Even then, she wondered how she looked given the late hour. But Blake was here and she was excited. Maybe scared. Maybe both.

Cat walked up to Blake a second time and he beamed at her. *God how she loved that smile.* "Why aren't you courting some big donor right now?" she asked.

"I heard you were rich," he answered with a laugh. "Was I wrong?"

"Hard to get rich with just twenty tables in this place. But you might get a free dinner out of me once you're governor. Will that work?"

"Deal."

"How well do you know this area?" she asked.

"Like most non New Yorkers, I think of Manhattan as a big maze of streets. I have no idea where I am most of the time. What do you have in mind?"

"C'mon, I'll give you a little tour of my neighborhood." She waved at her lone remaining employee, mouthed "good night," and led Blake out the door.

"So here we are again," she said once they were standing outside on the street corner.

"Yes, here we are again," he replied, as if he understood the subtext. "Where did those twenty years go?"

"You know we actually go a lot further back than that. Try thirty."

"God, I feel old." Blake sighed and turned to her. "What a great place you have. I can see you've accomplished everything you dreamed about. A quaint, five-star restaurant all your own. I'm very impressed. Abrazo?"

"Embrace," she said with a smile. She then grabbed his hand, in a familiar way that seemed to calm him, and led him down the street. She couldn't deny, as her fingers wrapped around his, the powerful force in their touch. A hint of romance that caused her to breathe more deeply as she directed him across the cobblestones that soon turned into the paved sidewalk along Hudson Street. As they strolled, hand in hand, she felt Blake absorbing the subtleties of the West Village, wondering if he grasped the same sense of community she'd learned to love in the collection of bars, bistros, and charming brownstones that dominated the Greenwich Historic District. The street lamps cast a mellow light across the tiny winding roads and she felt enthralled by the movie-like scenery.

After a couple of blocks, Cat stopped and turned to Blake. "You may remember, that summer I spent in Valencia during college changed me," she said. "I became obsessed with Spanish cuisine and that spurred my passion to create my own restaurant. What you didn't know is that I went to Valencia a second time after I left Asheville and took an intensive training course in cooking. Abrazo brought me back home or I might have stayed there the rest of my life. The restaurant wasn't much at the time, but we worked hard and eventually got there."

"I just saw the proof. Congratulations."

Cat squeezed his hand. "Well, thank you, sir." She then pointed to her left and said, "We're headed over there. It's known as the Meatpacking District."

Cat guided him left on Gansevoort Street, across Washington, toward a metal stairway that connected to a raised tree-lined platform sitting about thirty feet above the streetscape.

"Where are you taking me, Ms. Alexander?"

"The High Line. We have about forty-five minutes before it closes. It's time you learned a bit more about Manhattan . . . and about me."

Blake followed her up the stairs, still holding her hand, a willing guest to her guide. When they crested the stairs, Blake staggered, jolted by the cooler breezes energized by the Hudson River. He placed his arm around Cat's shoulders and asked, "Too cold?"

She looked at him and shook her head.

"This is amazing," he said. "I had no idea this was here."

"You don't get out enough." Cat smiled and nuzzled her head into his wool overcoat, a move that felt comfortable and familiar. "The High Line is part of an old rail system that was taken out of service back in the eighties . . . it was eventually converted into what you now see—an aerial greenway. The path is filled with trees, grasses, and all sorts of landscaping for about a mile and a half. Goes all the way through Chelsea. I walk it all the time. My favorite museum, the Whitney, is right over there." She pointed toward a building near the water's edge.

"Who would have thought?" Blake turned, gazed to his left, and asked, "What am I looking at?" He pointed across the Hudson at a series of light-silhouetted buildings in the distance.

"New Jersey. That's beautiful downtown Hoboken." Cat smiled, amused by Blake's lack of familiarity with the local geography. She followed him across the platform to the railing that overlooked the river. They leaned on the wooden barrier together, huddling their chilled bodies against the freshening winds, and he pulled her even tighter. Cat felt alive and invigorated, unfazed by the risk of running into an acquaintance while snuggling with another man.

"I understand Valencia," he said quietly, "but I lost some years after Asheville. How did you wind up in New York?"

"Once I'd finished my cooking school, I started looking for job opportunities back in the States. One of my culinary teachers knew the owner of Abrazo—it was called La Bodega at the time—and I sought him out. It wasn't much of a kitchen then; it was actually a lazy wine bar lost in the middle of Manhattan. But it intrigued me enough to take the job and I spent the next few years fixing appetizer foods and biding my time. I really believed the place could be a whole lot more."

Blake grinned. "I remember that determined streak in you. And based on your time in Valencia, you had a vision about how to transform the place. Am I right?"

She smiled. "Yes, I had to beg the owners to let me make some gradual improvements. We upgraded the décor, added a couple of entrees, and I eventually convinced him to change the name of the place. What you saw tonight was the result of many years of perseverance. I've grown up here, you see, and grown old here, too."

"Grown up, yes; grown old, hardly. You still look just like the young lady I knew in Texas."

She pushed her head against his shoulder in response.

"And how much time do you spend at the restaurant?" he asked.

"Every minute I can, but it can be a struggle at times. My family doesn't always agree with my schedule."

"I can relate." Cat sensed that Blake's words were both sympathetic and tinged with regret.

She didn't want to invite further discussion on their respective personal struggles, especially now that they were cuddled, shoulder to shoulder, in this beautiful setting, so she jumped past that conversation. "I want you to know I was the chef before Mitch was born," she explained while looking up to smile at Blake. "But I have to say the menu's gotten a lot better in the last few years. We have a real chef de cuisine back there now. You can probably guess I'm nothing more than a glorified hostess at this point."

"Owner, sole proprietor, toast of the town. You're a multitasker." Blake placed both arms around Cat and drew her closer into the warmth of his body. She slid her head into the fold of his chest and arm, in a place she remembered once fit her so well, and then rubbed her hands across his back.

"You're chilled," she said. "Let's sit down over there and get out of this wind. You wimpy Texans don't handle our weather very well."

Blake grinned. "Apparently not."

They sat on one of the wooden benches on the street side of the High Line parkway, nuzzling close together and holding hands.

"So, Senator, why'd you come to my restaurant?"

"Direct as always," he replied. "But honestly, I just wanted to see you."

Cat offered a comforting smile. "Well, I'm glad you did, but I'm not sure you've answered my question."

Blake looked temporarily confused and Cat could see his brain spiraling, formulating a better response, thinking through a variety of alternatives. "Being a politician always skews what I say to people," he started. "But let me see if I can be a little more straight with you. I think I told you back in Houston that I was never very smart when it came to you. Looking back, I can't figure out how chasing some fantasy of political office was ever more important than chasing you."

"It paid off," Cat interrupted. "Look where you are now."

She paused. "And you know I would've been a terrible political wife anyway." She chuckled. "Thankfully, everything's worked out just fine for both of us."

"Cat."

"Don't say it. We can't look back anymore. All we have is what's in front of us, and that's not too bad." She clutched his hand tighter, as if to say everything was all right. They remained silent for several minutes, huddling to warm themselves against the dropping temperature, perfectly together, neither wanting the time to end. Cat eventually poked him in the ribs and asked, "Don't you have an early flight tomorrow?"

"And I guess your husband will be wondering what's happened to you."

"My husband's fast asleep by now," Cat replied. "Sam used to wait up but time's broken him of that habit." She grinned. "But he's been great about staying home with the kids while I work. I couldn't have built the restaurant otherwise."

Blake nodded.

Cat's brief comment about Sam had opened a subject neither of them had ventured close to during either one of their conversations. While Cat had found it restorative to reminisce with Blake about their lives, she realized they'd carefully avoided tiptoeing into what these current encounters meant for their respective marriages.

"Will you show me those pictures of your kids before we get out of here?" Blake invited.

Cat pulled her iPhone out of her pocket and swiped her way to her photos. "That's Mitch right after his eighth birthday party earlier this year," she said, pointing at a picture of a boy standing next to a girl at the water's edge, with the Statue of Liberty in the background. "And this is Paige. She's twelve."

"They're great-looking children," Blake observed.

"Thank you," Cat responded with maternal pride, but at the same time her lower lip trembled. A mixture of anticipation, guilt, and fear. She realized something important was about to happen.

Blake pulled her toward him and said, "Cat . . ."

"Look," Cat interrupted, subtly nudging Blake away. "They're closing this place down. I think that attendant's coming over here to get us. We probably need to go."

Blake acted like he didn't want to move, but he followed her lead when she stood up and tugged him toward the stairway.

"I want to show you the outside of the Whitney," Cat said, "and we can have a couple of Ubers pick us up there."

They walked arm in arm, past numerous revelers wandering around the old meat-packing warehouses, and settled into an isolated spot, partially obscured by a thick column just outside the Whitney's glass walls. A curved streetlamp cast the pair's shadow against the aggregate pavement.

"Blake," Cat whispered while turning her head up to his, "what are we doing?"

When Blake looked into her eyes he offered no answers but instead leaned down and pressed his lips against hers, softly and tenderly at first, but when she didn't pull back, with a hungry force that swept her into the moment. She needed this, they needed this, and they kissed for minutes like overexcited teenagers. As the passion intensified, she felt his hand work its way inside her jacket, which seemed to shock him back into the present. He abruptly pulled back.

"Cat, I'm sorry."

At first, she wasn't sure why he'd apologized. She'd given him no reason to stop, even after holding back his advances on the High Line, but in some ways it felt like an apology for their unfinished romance, rather than his momentarily wandering hand.

Cat repositioned her stance, straightened her jacket, and stared at Blake, as she reached out her hand to take his. They stood for several seconds that way, looking at each other, as if waiting for a revelation, both seemingly wondering what came next. Finally, Cat broke the silence. "Let's go," she said. "I'll get us those Ubers."

CHAPTER 14

While they'd waited for their rides the night before, and he'd kissed her several more times, Blake had convinced Cat to meet him early the next morning for breakfast before he left town. She'd been unsure she could get away from her morning duties at home but promised to try.

Blake showered and prepared himself to head down to the lobby of the hotel, nervous that Cat might not appear, and wondered what about her was compelling him to take such risks. Cat was still very beautiful, and desire was a part of it, but Blake had turned away many opportunities for extramarital encounters in his life, many with younger and less complicated women. But Cat was different and, with their shared history, the attraction irresistible.

With uncertain expectations, Blake rode down in the elevator to The Pembroke Room in The Lowell. His heart accelerated when he spotted her waiting near the hostess stand, dressed in a blue pinstriped suit and a red scarf. She looked fresh and upbeat for a woman who hadn't had much time to sleep. He slid in next to her after they were guided to a booth in the corner of the room.

"How're you doing this morning?" he asked.

"It's not obvious?" Cat forced a laugh. "What do these saddlebags under my eyes look like?"

"A lot better than mine." He reached under the table and held her hand. "Thank you for coming. How'd you manage to get away?"

"I think I mentioned that to you last night," she answered. "Sam's good with the kids. He kicks and screams sometimes but he understands my schedule is less flexible than his. I occasionally have breakfast meetings I need to attend."

"I'm really glad you made it."

"Me, too." She scooched a little closer, but maintained a professional distance from him in the booth.

"I thought about you—us—all last night," Blake said. "That moment outside the Whitney reminded me of our days back in Austin."

"Ha," Cat laughed. "Except you're a much better kisser now than I remember. Did you go to kissing school since I last saw you?"

Blake squeezed her hand tighter, grinned, and then let it go when he saw the waitress approaching the table.

After they ordered, Blake started back up. "Last night was something I'll never forget," he said. He caressed her hand under the table again.

Cat didn't flinch and he sensed her shared excitement over their time together on the High Line. "I'm not sure what to say at this point," she replied, "and I have no idea what's happening or what this all means. It's just so surreal."

"I guess we're in the same boat on that." Blake's expression evoked empathy but also an anticipation about what lay ahead.

"As much as I'd like to give in to this moment," Cat advised, "you're leaving shortly and I've got to keep my head on straight. Care to help me?" Cat smiled while straightening up in her cushioned seat. "Maybe you can tell me about your campaign. What's next? How are you going to catch that woman?"

Blake understood Cat's need to avoid getting too caught up in the emotional pull of the previous night's events. "Well," he answered while releasing her hand, "that is the challenge. For now, I need money and they've scheduled a series of fundraisers for me all around Texas. Once those are done, my focus will be on puncturing some of the air out of my huge deficit in the polls."

"Good," Cat replied. "I've read up on that woman. She sounds like an opportunist who looks pretty on TV, but without the brains or gravitas to be governor of my home state. I've got to believe the public will see that."

Blake smiled. "What about these good looks? They're worth some votes, aren't they?"

"I'm a bit partial to them, but . . ." Cat looked up at the waitress, who dutifully filled their coffee cups.

Once they were alone again, Blake furrowed his brow and gazed into Cat's eyes.

"Is that the look you use with all your women voters?" she asked. "It could work for a lot of them. It's working right now."

Blake grinned and felt an even deeper attraction that made his body spring to attention. "Cat, I don't know what to say."

"Well, whatever it is, you better say it now because I think your campaign manager is walking this way. He may wonder what you've been up to when he sees me sitting here."

Blake frowned, knowing that the moment was lost with Rags stalking them.

"Good morning," Rags said. "Nice to see you again, Mrs. Alexander."

"Good morning to you," Cat offered, extending her hand. "And it's Cat."

"There's plenty of room," Blake suggested. "Why don't you sit down?" He made sure his tone reflected a lack of enthusiasm.

"No thanks, I'm just grabbing a cup of coffee and heading back up. Just spotted the two of you from a distance and wanted to say hello. Nice to see you again . . . Cat. Oh, there's my coffee. Enjoy your breakfast. Senator, see you in an hour."

Blake nodded as Rags turned around and marched out of the restaurant.

"Sorry about that," he apologized.

She brushed off the comment with a whisk of her hand.

"I think you've forgotten you're running for one of the most important gubernatorial offices in the country. If that campaign manager is worth a flip, he wouldn't want you spending your precious breakfast time with an ex-girlfriend. Not unless I was bringing you a sack full of money. Which, by the way, I told you I'm not."

Blake laughed, enchanted again by Cat's wit and grace. In their short time together over the past few weeks, she'd changed in ways that surprised him, and he stared at her with a strange sense of remorse, feeling like his ambition had cost him a chance to watch her mature into the compelling woman now before him. That reflection made it clear to Blake exactly why he'd taken so many risks with Cat Alexander. And why he might take even more.

———— ★ ————

Cat hoped she hadn't appeared too nonchalant about what had happened between them, but she knew Blake needed a graceful way out of New York. Discussing what the previous night meant, or why he'd kissed her, wouldn't do either of them any good, even if she wanted him to do it again.

"Blake," she said, "you know there's nothing but trouble if we keep this up?"

He placed his coffee cup onto its saucer. "I know that. You know that. But why do I think this is just the beginning?"

He'd done it again. Surprised her. She wasn't sure how to respond.

"I'm sorry," Blake continued. "I know what I'm saying makes no sense but damn I'm feeling some very strong urges."

Cat raised her eyebrows and gave him a look. Her body was sparking with the same sensations that had moved her the night before.

"What if one of these folks in this room takes our picture?" she asked. "Good Lord, you need to be more careful. I know I do."

Blake didn't back away, nor did she want him to. He just smiled as if he didn't have a care in the world.

"Cat," he finally whispered, "I understand the risks. And I know you're trying to protect me from my political enemies, but there's no need to worry. We can make this work."

Cat grimaced. "I wish it was that simple," she cautioned. "But we both have families. This moment is not ours to decide alone. No matter how good it feels to us."

"You're right. Of course you're right." Blake picked up his fork and stabbed at a piece of melon. They finished the rest of their meal in an awkward silence.

"You need to pack and I need to get out of here," Cat finally said.

Blake nodded with a frown.

"Let's not brood over this," Cat directed. "Time will clarify what it all means. Go back to your campaign and forget about me." Her pensive look suggested she wasn't sure that's what she really meant.

Blake sighed slowly. "Not going to happen," he responded. "The forget-about-you part."

"You did it once."

"Touché," he countered.

Blake paid the bill and then walked with Cat to the front of the hotel, where she asked the doorman to hail a cab. They kept a safe distance from each other in the more public setting and waited for the car to arrive.

"Off I go," she said. "Now the real work begins." Cat smiled ruefully as Blake acknowledged the impending New York City traffic.

As she stepped toward the cab, Cat felt Blake's hand gently turn her toward him.

"Love you," he whispered before she opened the door and settled herself against the scratched leather seat.

Her endearing eyes answered him, a look of sweetness, mixed

with hope and a touch of melancholy. She had no idea what to say but as the car pulled away she mouthed the words she wondered if she'd regret—"I love you, too."

CHAPTER 15

September 20

Striker headquarters buzzed with the news of Blake Buchanan's big money haul from New York City. That on top of Reverend Dodds's announcement had provided Marshall Phelps with plenty of reasons to knock heads. Tony observed the new urgency in the campaign manager's demeanor and swelled with pride that the complacency he'd complained about had transformed into a heart-rattling intensity. Despite the fact he'd received no credit for the newfound fire in the office, Tony's chest puffed out because today marked the moment he graduated into the big leagues of Texas politics. Phelps had invited him into the inner sanctum.

Tony strode into the closed-door meeting where Striker, Phelps, and a well-known third party waited.

"You're late," Phelps barked.

Tony looked down at his watch and saw that he was ten minutes early.

"Don't look at your watch!" Phelps ordered. "General Striker was here five minutes ago. She dictates your schedule, not your watch."

Tony looked to Striker for help, but she didn't respond. He grimaced, took his seat, and then turned his attention to Phelps. He wasn't going to like working more closely with this man.

"Let's get going now that Mr. León is here," Phelps commanded. "This is Stanley Braxton, also known as the Source . . .

75

the best pollster in the business." Phelps shot a dagger at Tony. "And needless to say," he continued, "everything we hear from the Source is confidential. No WikiLeaks bullshit in this campaign. Understood?"

Tony acknowledged Phelps's comment with a nod, his face reddening as the eyes around the table focused on him. Tony again furtively glanced toward Striker but she ignored him.

"Thank you, Marshall," the Source began. "And General Striker, thank you for allowing me to be part of your campaign. I'm very excited about where you stand right now. I've taken a large sample to give us a good base reading and I'm pleased that every number looks positive. You *will* be the next governor of this state! Now, if you'll glance at your handout, I'll speed through these numbers and then give you my recommendations. I've already shared them with Marshall."

"Let's get on with it then," Striker directed. She briefly looked toward her pollster, then returned her attention to her Android phone.

"Start with the most basic polling data," the Source responded, "name identification. General, you're known by about eighty-five percent of the Republican voters in our poll, carry a seventy-percent-favorable rating in that group, and have under ten percent negatives. That's a remarkable position, even for a front-runner. Buchanan, on the other hand, is known by only about twenty percent of the voters and has statistically meaningless favorable. And most who've heard of him haven't formed an opinion. I'll save my discussion on your likely Democratic opponent, Mr. Bowie, but he's not in much better shape."

Tony soaked it all in as the Source then walked through a series of polls on the hot-button topics of the day—border security, same-sex unions, transgender bathrooms, health-care mandates—but he grew uncomfortable with Striker's utter inattention to the presentation. Her head was so deep into her phone that he thought she'd missed every detail the Source recited.

Tony's occasional glances toward her went without apparent notice as well. That was, until the Source got to the one issue that interested Striker.

"Of course, the attorney general polls best on her stand for life," the Source stated. "The Republican primary voters overwhelmingly supported her actions at the Harrison County Hospital in East Texas last year, and in my estimation, we should focus a large part of our media campaign on that issue. It's a complete winner."

———— ★ ————

Grace Striker had first come to Tony's attention during a drama that unfolded with East Texas police officer Frank Blocker. The thirty-five-year-old Blocker, a native of Marshall, returned home one morning from his late-night shift to find his pregnant wife, Hermene, stricken on the floor, the victim of a pulmonary embolism. The clot had deprived Hermene of oxygen long enough that she'd suffered catastrophic brain damage, although her organs continued to function. Tragically, by the time she'd reached the hospital, the young woman had fallen into an irreversible vegetative state. Hermene and her twenty-two-week-old fetus remained technically alive but only through the life support provided by the hospital.

Within hours of hearing the news, Attorney General Striker had flown to the hospital to counsel and support Blocker. She'd prayed with him in front of the cameras and held his hand in the waiting room. Their pictures soon blitzed the mastheads across most of Texas. The photographs of Striker in a dark-and-curvy sheath dress embracing the police officer raised the A.G.'s profile faster than anything she'd done in her previous three years in office. Tony remembered how impressed he'd been with Striker's political instincts.

Striker's love-in with the grief-stricken officer changed the next day when Blocker announced he'd decided to terminate his wife's life support, which in turn would end—mercifully, in Blocker's view—the life of his unborn child. The politically deft attorney general seized that opportunity to solidify her bona fides with the evangelical Christian base of the Republican Party. She notified the County Hospital that it was legally prohibited from turning off life support for the pregnant mother while her unborn child remained "viable." According to Striker, God had to be given a chance to work His miracle.

While Tony and Texans across the state watched, Striker's frenzied campaign team transformed the Harrison County Hospital into a political cauldron. Officer Blocker became an innocent, heartbroken, and powerless bystander in the pro-life drama that ensued. The State of Texas, under Striker's order, filed a lawsuit to prohibit the hospital from turning off life support for the mother. During the two days that the parties waited for a temporary injunction hearing—and a brain-dead Hermene Blocker and her fetus were kept alive by machines—Striker became a star, interviewed on every conservative news platform in the country. The photogenic A.G. became a national symbol of the pro-life movement, and her electoral future galvanized in an instant. And even after the court ruled against her, and Hermene Blocker and her unborn child were laid to rest, the waffling, modestly popular, sitting two-term governor had known he was done. A month later, Governor Johnson decided not to seek reelection and Striker became the heir apparent to his job.

———— ★ ————

"I want to do a statewide tour of women's advocacy groups!" Striker announced while pounding her fist on the table. "Lots of pictures, lots of exposure, lots of press."

The Source shuffled his feet and pondered his response. "That's up to Marshall, of course," he said, "but your lead is too overwhelming to do anything but stay out of the crossfire. I like a very controlled and uncontroversial campaign."

Striker narrowed her eyes and glared at the Source. "Dammit, Stanley," she yelled, "I'm not going to sit on my butt and spectate." The attorney general stood up, waved her finger at each man in the room, and drew a deep breath. "You boys know this race isn't just about winning the governorship," she declared. "We've got a lot more ahead of us than that—and we can go all the way together—but you have to trust my gut on this one. It proved right in Harrison County."

It was the first time Tony had heard Striker allude to her aspiration as a potential presidential candidate, and her short speech chilled all further discussion on the subject. There was no question she had the look and momentum of a national candidate, and Tony understood she'd be regarded as a fresh face and an immediate frontline contender if she crushed her gubernatorial opponents. The stern look Striker fired at the Source told Tony everything he needed to know.

"General," Phelps said. "We don't need to decide any of this right now. I think we've seen enough polling data for one day. I have one other person I need you to meet with this morning before we move on." He paused. "Thank you, Source. Tony, please show our friend out. This next conference is off-limits."

Tony frowned. He wasn't aware that he was to be excluded from the guest-number-two meeting. In private conversations, Striker had assured him complete access to all matters in the campaign.

"Thank you both," Phelps said. "Source, we'll be in touch."

Striker dropped back into her chair and plunged into her phone again, too distracted to help with Tony's problem. He trudged out of the meeting with a long face, but his eyes scanned the hallway, searching for the mysterious person waiting to enter the room.

———————★———————

P helps's suspicions about Tony spiked during the meeting with the Source. Striker had protected the young kid, which meant Phelps had to make it work, but he knew trouble lay ahead. The handsome young Hispanic had ambition written all over him. He sensed another agenda at play, too, and that Tony's elevated position didn't originate from Striker's desire to placate big donors in San Antonio. Phelps recognized he'd have to keep a close eye on the hot shot from now on, making sure to shield him from all critical data, and protect the governor-in-waiting from herself.

But for now, Tony wasn't Phelps's biggest concern. His investigator was coming in to give him a full report on his candidate. And Grace Striker wasn't going to like what she was about to hear.

CHAPTER 16

Cat sprawled her mat on the floor next to her good friend, Abbie Corley, as they prepared for their opening movements. Yoga was always more intense when her best friend joined her. Accountability, a word now echoing in Cat's head for other reasons, was real with a girlfriend by her side. But once the series of upward and downward dogs began, Cat drifted off to the one subject a meditative state couldn't shake—Blake Buchanan. While she exercised and contorted her body in tandem with the instructor's commands, the thoughts that consumed her mind weren't those she typically associated with yoga.

"Okay," Abbie said as they sat down after a sweat-drenched workout. Abbie's ginger red hair glistened in the bright lights of the locker room. "What's going on with you? You were in another world in there. I thought I was going to have to kick you out of your stupor. Talk to me."

Cat wasn't sure that telling her friend about Blake was a good idea but Abbie had a no-nonsense approach to most issues and Cat hoped a conversation with her might lead to clarity.

"What version do you want?" Cat asked.

Abbie drank from her water bottle and sighed. "I'm not going to the shop until after lunch. Might as well give it all to me. What else do I have to do?"

Cat laughed and composed herself. "Please don't jump on me," Cat whispered, "but it's about an old flame . . . Blake Buchanan."

Abbie's mouth unhinged and Cat thought her friend might

spit up her water. "Damn, girl," she exclaimed. "I don't follow politics like you do, but I hope you don't mean the guy running for governor in Texas."

"That's him," Cat replied. She then revealed superficial details about her early years with Blake and how they'd recently reconnected in Houston. She described their exchange of messages on Facebook and Gmail, and recounted their long walk on the High Line, but selectively omitted the kissing part. *Full* disclosure was a little more disclosure than she wanted.

"I don't know what to say," Abbie interjected.

"Blake and I had . . . well, a history, you might say. We're just getting to know each other again. And he's different now . . . so much different."

Abbie's look of incredulity was more powerful than any verbal response she could offer. "So why bring him up then?" she asked. "Are you worried this is headed somewhere?"

"Headed somewhere?" Cat shook her head. "No, no." But she wasn't sure of that at all. "I guess something's happening," she conceded, "because I needed to talk about it. Maybe I wanted to hear myself say it out loud to understand how foolish it sounds."

"Well, sweetheart, you're right about that." Abbie reached out and grabbed her friend's hand. "The man's not going to have time to interrupt his campaign or his life in Texas for anything other than a flyby. You know that's right? I hate to be so direct, but this sounds like a John Edwards, Part Two."

"No, no, I'm not expecting to have an affair with him." Cat clenched her jaw. "But I have to admit I haven't felt this alive in a long time. And he did look rather scrumptious."

"Hold it right there," Abbie instructed. She squeezed Cat's hand tighter to emphasize her point. "I don't blame you for feeling that way because fifty and bored isn't much fun. But fifty and divorced is far worse. Not to mention what it would do to your kids. Think about what might happen if this blew up in the press."

"I know that," Cat replied, removing the levity from her voice. Abbie had hit a chord. Fifty was a special year and surely her life, while active, was missing the excitement Blake offered, but that wasn't it. She knew this revival of long-buried feelings was not some age driven flirtation; nor was she some clichéd version of the Spandex-clad moms hanging around her kids' school looking for a thrill. But if Abbie couldn't understand what Cat was feeling, who could?

Cat appreciated the need to cut the conversation off and move on. "Let's get out of here," she said. "You're right, the whole thing's stupid."

As she walked out of the gym with her athletic bag flung over her shoulder, Cat realized that from now on the Blake Buchanan experiment would be hers alone.

CHAPTER 17

Rags stormed into Blake's campaign office with his coffee cup teetering in one hand and a yellow pad squeezed in the other. He wore a white button-down shirt and mustard-stained khakis that looked as if he'd slept in them.

"What's got you so worked up?" Blake asked.

Rags thumped down into the metal folding chair across from Blake's desk. "I don't know if that woman's brilliant or just plain stupid," he started, "but she's giving us a chance. Striker's media consultant just released news of a statewide tour of pro-life organizations—from the Texas Alliance for Life to Save the Storks—and she's planning large rallies at each stop." Rags paused and sucked in air as if he was struggling to breathe. "I guess she's not too worried about making a mistake. She's decided to treat the primary as an afterthought and is accelerating full throttle to develop a national campaign." Rags inhaled deeply one more time. "I don't care what her motive is," he continued, "but I'm about to bust."

Blake grinned at his fired-up campaign manager.

"This tour," Rags said, "creates all sorts of possibilities for us. I bet Marshall Phelps is flaming mad. He'd never take this kind of risk with such a big lead. If it was up to him, I bet he'd have Striker locked up in a soundproofed room until March." Rags flashed a wicked smile. "I'm telling you, Blake, this woman thinks she's got Teflon around her, but I guarantee you she's no Ronald Reagan. Striker's fully capable of pulling a *Claytie*."

Blake chuckled at the reference to the Midland oilman, Clayton Williams, who'd run for Texas governor as a Republican in 1990 against Democrat Ann Richards. Political wisdom said Williams would win the race easily; that was, until he made a series of public gaffes—now popularly known as "Clayties"—that turned the election around. The most famous was an ill-considered comment that suggested certain rape victims should just "relax and enjoy it." Even in Texas, that quip was enough to torpedo his campaign.

"So how do we get one of those rallies to veer a little off course?" Blake asked.

"You're the candidate," Rags replied, "and I'm the campaign manager. There are certain things you don't need to know." They both laughed.

"Good enough for me," Blake said with a mock salute. "But you did promise me that the race would tighten by five points after we left New York . . . and you missed it. I just checked our tracking numbers and we've closed the margin by six." Blake smiled. "Good job, Rags. And Reverend Dodds is a one-man wrecking ball against any hope Striker has of tacking toward the middle. This little bump in the polls is renewing my spirits." Blake held up his hand for a high-five that Rags delivered with gusto.

Rags fixed his jaw as if to bring reality back into the room. "But, Blake," he insisted, "you have to keep raising money. We need that more than anything else. Reverend Dodds's announcement is going to help open up a few doors and we have to be ready. I need you focused and on point."

"Got it," Blake answered without acknowledging Rags's veiled message. "So where do I go next? Point me in the right direction and I'm there."

★

R ags stared at his candidate and wondered what was going on in the senator's head. For all the time he'd known Blake, the man in election mode was driven and locked on message. But not now. Ever since Blake had returned from New York with his pockets lined with Chance Mitchell's money, he'd appeared preoccupied, and worse, Rags had seen him surreptitiously punching out text messages on his new iPhone when he thought no one was looking. Blake had said the phone was dedicated to communication with his wife and kids, but Rags suspected something different.

The reason appeared obvious—Blake was carrying on with Cat Alexander. And Faith probably suspected as much. Why else would the candidate's wife have called him in New York about the loan, a message an emotionless Blake had accepted with only the curt comment, "No big deal."

Rags remembered being so flummoxed by what he'd observed that morning in New York at The Lowell hotel that he'd chosen to go back to his room rather than interrupt Blake's conversation with Cat. "Just rummaging through old memories," Blake had explained when they'd flown home that afternoon. But Rags had seen something more intense, and he worried that his friend and candidate had rummaged through far more than old memories. While Rags had spent time making sure young Kristen's infatuation with her boss didn't blow up in his face, Blake had forged a new, far more dangerous, liaison.

The worst might still be ahead. The candidate had scheduled an impromptu day off later in the week to recharge his batteries, or so he'd said. Rags interpreted that as evidence he was planning a rendezvous with Cat. This was territory Rags was least prepared to manage. His job was processing numbers and plotting strategy for a dedicated candidate, not advising him on how to conduct his personal life. But Rags no longer had a choice. He had to figure out a way to control the burgeoning problem.

Rags paced around the room, drew a deep breath, and then whirled around to face down his distracted candidate on the issue.

"Blake," he began, "I need . . ." But just as the words left Rags's mouth, Blake hit the Send button on his iPhone and looked up with a pleased smile.

"Yes?" Blake asked.

Rags's throat went dry and the conversation ended.

CHAPTER 18

As Tony León waited outside Striker campaign headquarters for his call, he thought about the rich history of dirty tricks in Texas politics. Over the last few years, as he'd inched past the practice of law toward a life pursuing elective office, he'd found himself captivated by the colorful accounts of secret backroom deals, inside fixes, and outright fraud in Texas politics. The stories fascinated him, and he devoured every one as a lesson in itself, tucking the details into the back of his mind, as if compiling a playlist to have at his disposal for future use. This reservoir of go-to strategies had prepared him for his expanding role in the Grace Striker campaign.

Tony hadn't been a great student in high school—he'd lost his father and his way at the age of thirteen—but he'd been lucky to find a mentor who'd helped him focus his life and career path, Cameron County Judge Rodrigo Canales. The sordid history of South Texas politics flowed through the veins of Judge Canales, who delighted in sharing his knowledge with his eager young protégé. "Tony," the Judge once said, "if you want to get ahead in business, do well in school, but if you want to know how the world really works, *prestame aténción.*"

The Canales family was an institution in South Texas and the Judge, as friends and foes called him, was the kingmaker of The Valley. For the four years Tony attended high school, he learned what was needed from his teachers during class, but from the Judge he obtained a master's degree on patronage and political power. Despite his admiration for his mentor's exalted position in the community, Tony believed he was made for brighter lights than Brownsville. In that search for higher purpose, Tony latched on to the stories of the most powerful Texas politician of the twentieth century—Lyndon Baines Johnson.

Every Texan knew bits and pieces about former President Johnson—how he'd risen to the presidency after JFK's assassination, the methods he'd used to advance the "Great Society," or why he'd failed under the pressures of the Vietnam War. In fact, the biography series by Robert Caro covering the president's career became Tony's political bible. He read each volume cover to cover, over and over. But it was not just the public acts that compelled Tony to dig into the young LBJ's career; there were the other stories, the private ones that were hidden in Judge Canales's brain and hadn't made their way into Caro's Pulitzer Prize–winning work. The old politico reveled in tales about LBJ's exploits.

"Tony," the Judge once said, "when Lyndon campaigned in South Texas, we didn't have reporters following us around . . . and we made things happen. If our friend needed money, we delivered it in brown paper bags. If he needed new supporters, we registered them at the Catholic churches around the region. And if he needed a few extra votes to get him over the top . . . well, we found them."

Judge Canales was proud and unapologetic that he'd spearheaded the effort to find the "missing" votes in Johnson's 1948 Senate race against Coke Stevenson that helped turn a twenty-thousand-vote deficit into a narrow eighty-seven-vote victory. The infamous "discovered" ballots from Precinct 13 were part of Texas political lore, and everyone knew that Canales and Duval County boss George Parr had provided the margin of victory for Johnson over Stevenson, which instilled in Tony the political truth that anything was possible, as long as a candidate was willing to do what was necessary.

"Hello," Tony answered when his phone finally rang. He'd positioned himself in a place where no one could hear his conversation.

"It's me," replied Phillip Connor, the investigator Tony had hired out of Houston. "It looks like your man is flying back to New York later this week."

"How do you know that?" Tony asked.

"That's why you hired me."

"You're certain?"

"He could change his plans but the flight's booked. I know that."

"And you've got folks covering the rest of the family as well?"

"The minute you sent me the money. But what about this New York thing? I'll need to hire another body to cover him up there."

"Let me think about how to play this," Tony said. "I'll be in touch."

"Got it."

Tony hung up the phone and reviewed the situation. Buchanan's trip could be nothing more than another campaign fundraising swing, but he dismissed that explanation with dispatch. No candidate would seek a second helping from the same donors this quickly. Tony realized the information from Connor could be used in many ways and he tried to summon up his hero LBJ to instruct him on his best and most ruthless option. One thing he did know—telling Phelps about the trip wasn't one of them.

CHAPTER 19

September 27

The night before he was to travel back to New York, Blake had an "off" political calendar, which allowed him to return home at a normal hour. When he entered the house, Blake was surprised to find Faith and the girls assembling for a rare family dinner.

"Hey, Dad, how's it going?" Fin greeted him as he dropped his briefcase and pulled off his jacket.

"Trying to scare up votes," Blake replied with a smile as he bent down to kiss his oldest daughter's head. He nodded at his wife, who stood near the cook at the opposite end of the great room. They were separated by a large, granite-topped island that bisected the space, the Viking stoves and other appliances on one side, the family room seating area and large screen TV on the other. The smell of an olive-oil-and-butter sauté filled the air.

"Dad," yelled Blake's other daughter, Shana, as she bounded toward him with open arms.

"What a treat," Blake said. "All three of my girls for dinner." He embraced Shana as Faith turned away and instructed the cook about the final details of the meal.

"How was your day, Faith?" Blake asked after letting Shana go.

"Fine," she replied, then took a sip from her wine glass. As usual, Faith presented herself smartly for Blake's arrival home. She wore a black, tie-waisted shirtdress and a pair of tan,

91

ankle-strap, lace-up sandals. Years before, she'd augmented her slight frame with plastic surgery, and her outfits now highlighted her figure despite her petite, angular body shape. Faith's favorite small, gold crucifix hung from her neck and she'd pulled her shoulder-length, blonde hair back in a ponytail. Blake's wife had always been strikingly beautiful. "You guys ready to go in the dining room?" Faith asked.

Blake's daughters—still dressed in their sports jerseys from field hockey practice—hugged their father on each side and escorted him into the more formal part of the house. As he clutched his girls around their waists, Blake again realized how thin they'd become over the past year. He held his tongue, but the girls' weight loss troubled him. In the past, Faith had sniped at him when he'd raised the topic, at one point arguing, "If you were around more, you'd understand the pressures they're going through." So he'd since grown gun-shy about taking on the issue.

Blake sat at his customary spot at the head of the table with Faith to his right and the girls next to each other on the opposite side from their mother. "Shana, will you please bless us?" he asked.

His youngest was eager. "Lord," she started, "thank you for bringing our family together today, bless those who are less fortunate than we are, and most of all thank you for our mommy and daddy. We ask that you help them as they work to make our state better. And we especially ask that you watch over Dad on his travels, and keep him safe from harm . . ."

Blake's brain shut off after the part about his safety, his shame over his next day's travel plan overwhelming the remainder of his young daughter's invocation. At the end, each member of the Buchanan family said "amen" and let go of the others' hands.

"So what did you do today?" Blake pressed Faith as his girls started chatting with each other, trying to draw her out but wary of provoking a confrontation.

"Had a few appointments . . . nothing important," she replied, before downing the remainder of her wine. "How's the campaign going?"

"We made up some serious ground this week, and the money from New York will really help. With the new resources, we should be able to open a full-time office in East Texas and start making some early media buys in Dallas. I'm going back tomorrow for a couple of follow-up calls. I hope they'll yield some more dollars."

"New York . . . tomorrow?" Faith asked, but she left the question hanging in the air. She turned to the cook, who'd entered the room and placed salad, green beans, and baked white fish on the table. "Thank you, Sophia," she said.

"This looks wonderful," Blake added. "Thank you, Sophia, we've got it from here." The cook nodded and ducked out of the room.

"Fin heard back from Texas today," Faith said with an edge to her voice. "Tell your dad about it, honey."

"I would've called you," Fin eagerly explained, "but I wanted to wait till you got home. I got early admission into the Liberal Arts Honors program! I'm very excited."

Blake turned to his high school senior, who beamed an ear-too-ear smile back at him. "That's awesome," he said. "I'm not surprised, but that's a huge accomplishment."

"Yay, Fin," cheered Shana.

"Thank you, thank you very much," Fin said while taking a bite of her green beans. "But it puts me in a weird spot. I won't hear from Stanford or any of the other schools for several more months, but I really need to let UT know something within the next two weeks."

Blake nodded. "I guess that's how these early admissions work now. It was a lot different when your mom and I went through. There was no such thing in our days."

Fin nodded but Blake could see she was distracted by her mother's despondent attitude.

"You applied for regular admission to all of the other schools, didn't you?" he asked.

"Yep."

"Well, I can't imagine any of them not taking you, but that's a tough call."

"No worries," Fin responded. "I'm not positive about what the deadline means yet. I'm going to meet with my college adviser next week and we'll figure it out."

"Is it still Ms. Martinez?" Blake asked. He then scowled at his wife who had picked up the wine bottle and re-filled her glass. Blake noticed his daughters' frowns while Faith poured.

Fin nodded in response to her father's question but glared at him as if to express her displeasure with her mother.

Blake studied Faith as she took a small bite of fish and washed it down with another gulp of wine. He realized that his wife's mood had grown even darker over the past month. According to what Fin had told him earlier, Faith was drinking every day, sometimes even starting in the early afternoon when her new tennis club friends would stop by their home. Even worse, Fin suggested these sessions were now extending into the evenings when Blake was out of town and women his girls hardly knew— like Meredith Simms, the tennis pro—would show up and hang out until all hours of the night.

The anxiety in Faith's pinched face grew as she drained the second and third refills of her wine glass while she picked at her food. The tightness in her lips, the rigidity in her cheeks magnified as the dinner hour wore on, and she eventually stopped even looking Blake's way. Shana and Fin attempted to fill the awkward silence with idle chatter, but nothing they tried altered the mood. Blake wondered how he and Faith had arrived at this agonizing impasse. He remembered a happier time when they'd sat around the dinner table with their doe-eyed girls chatting about every aspect of their daily lives together.

By the time Shana and Fin finished their supper and excused

themselves to begin their homework, Faith was wobbly and Blake was frustrated. Neither of them said a word for the next few minutes, and Blake watched Faith's eyes water with a sadness that he was helpless, or unwilling, to comfort.

CHAPTER 20

Blake bobbed his knee up and down as he leaned forward in his first-row seat on the plane to LaGuardia. He positioned his head toward the window in the hope of avoiding eye contact with any familiar faces boarding the jet. The last thing he needed was to explain why he was flying to New York.

"Howdy, pardner," drawled a burly, broad-shouldered man who placed his cowboy hat in the overhead compartment as if he were handling fine china. Blake didn't know the face.

"Morning," Blake responded, hoping the man didn't recognize him.

"You're that guy running for governor, aren't ya?"

Blake nodded, still wanting to dissuade the beefy fellow from further conversation.

"Jim Bob Tate," the man said, extending his arm as he plopped down in the aisle seat next to Blake. "I'm from Midland. What's taking you to New York City today?"

Blake shook hands and knitted his eyebrows. "Dragging the hat," he lied, which cemented the fib he'd told Faith the night before. "Blake Buchanan."

"I know who you are." Jim Bob chuckled. "Damn, all that money in Texas and you have to fly off to the big city. Doesn't make sense to me. You been to my hometown yet?"

"Many times," Blake replied. "But I'll be out there again in two weeks for my biggest fundraiser yet. Hope you can stop by."

"Thanks for the offer." Jim Bob smiled. "But I'm already

signed up with your opponent." He then leaned in to whisper. "Even though I don't think she's worth a warm bucket of spit."

"No comment," Blake said with a wink.

"Why you running?" Jim Bob asked.

"I like a man who gets to the point," Blake answered. "If I told you I've never gotten over losing my race for fourth-grade class president to Larry Cleaver, would you buy that?"

"You know," Jim Bob replied with a grin, "that's a more honest answer than I get from most politicians I hang around." Jim Bob stretched his arms and extended his legs to get comfortable. "I'd guess you're about the right age to be a Ronald Reagan boomer."

"Nice deductive work. It's no secret that Reagan almost single-handedly converted every college student of my generation into Republicans."

"That's my generation, too," Jim Bob added.

The flight attendant interrupted the conversation with instructions about safety belts and oxygen masks, and Blake thought he might have received a reprieve from his talkative seatmate.

"So you've been thinking 'bout politics your whole life?" Jim Bob started back once the announcements ended.

"I guess you could say that," Blake responded. "When Governor Clements began turning Texas red in the seventies, my dad saw a pathway for a young Republican in our state. He was thinking more about my future at that time than I was."

"Yep, that's when it all changed. Your father was a wise man. John Connally switched parties, then Phil Gramm, and the national Democrats kept picking libs like McGovern and Carter. Not many options left for us Texans but to join the Rs." Jim Bob smiled.

Blake felt himself drawn to the congenial West Texas chatterbox. He could see that Jim Bob's southern accent had a disarming quality about it. And the man had obviously given quite a bit of thought to the issues of the day. "Let me try to go back and answer your original question a little more seriously," Blake said.

Jim Bob nodded and turned toward Blake after taking a slug of the orange juice delivered by the flight attendant.

"My father was in a private securities firm when I was young and I spent a lot of time at his office. I'm not sure I ever heard him say one good thing about the government, especially when it came to his business."

"My kind of man," Jim Bob chortled.

Blake smiled. "I lost him several years ago . . . I think you would've liked him. He succeeded early in his career despite Jimmy Carter—do you remember the oil crisis and twenty percent interest rates? But sadly the bulk of his estate went to that same government he railed against his entire life."

"Damn estate tax," Jim Bob said. "I guess your mother had passed already?"

"No, but they'd divorced years earlier and Dad's estate was taxed at the maximum rate upon his death."

"That's a disgrace."

"So, to finally answer your question," Blake continued, "my father was the greatest influence on me getting into politics. When I first ran, I was idealistic enough to think I could help small businessmen like him and wanted to make a difference in the world. Believe it or not, despite everything I've seen, I still have that same goal."

"Good for you, Senator. That's a noble way to think. But you better watch out for that opponent of yours. She's not quite that good-natured. I think she'd sell her soul to gain that office. You best pay attention or you'll be pulling your guts off the pavement before you know it."

Blake recognized the wisdom in his folksy new friend's words. "Thanks for the warning but I know what I'm up against." He paused for a moment and focused his gaze on Jim Bob. "I really believe Texas can do better," he went on. "We're headed in the wrong direction in so many ways and politicians like Striker are the reason. Our state government doesn't need to spend all of its time dictating social agendas as policies of the state."

"I'm with you on that one," Jim Bob responded. "You're now talking about personal responsibility over government intrusion. I'm there . . . one hundred percent."

Blake fidgeted with his hands when the words "personal responsibility" came up. If only his fellow passenger knew where he was headed this morning.

"Well, let me tell you, Blake Buchanan," Jim Bob continued. "I think you're onto something important. Lots of Texans like me are sick and tired of being pushed into the gene pool with the frickin' Tea Party activists. We're looking for a change and Striker's just more of the same old . . . you know what I mean. You lead and show some balls on the issues, and you might even convince me."

Blake nodded. "Thank you, but I'd hoped to get you on my side before this flight is over!"

"Friend," Jim Bob laughed, "we'll continue this conversation later, but I can tell you need some rest. You look like you've been working too hard."

Blake watched Jim Bob pull out a spreadsheet and begin studying. "Presentation today," the big man explained.

"Good luck with it."

With his new friend now occupied, Blake laid his head back and closed his eyes. Jim Bob had given him much more to think about during his three-hour flight.

CHAPTER 21

After walking her kids to school, Cat anticipated taking it easy for a few hours—maybe a long bath followed by a visit to the salon—before meeting Blake in the early afternoon. Sam had left their apartment at daybreak, heading out around 6:30 to play golf with friends on Long Island. Cat's stress-free morning, however, changed when she found herself hustling to pick up Mitch at school, sick with a low-grade fever. After barely convincing her housekeeper to stay with him, she'd considered canceling her date. But nothing was going to stop her from seeing Blake this day. Not even an overtaxed conscience, filled with guilt for running out on her sweet boy.

Finally, at 1:30 in the afternoon, Cat hopped out of her Uber. The Plaza was undergoing renovations—again. She drew in a deep breath and headed to the lobby bar where Blake had texted he was waiting. She reapplied her lipstick, checked her hair, and straightened her blouse before walking in. The moment Cat spotted him her heart flip-flopped—she felt girlish and coltish at the same time—and she girded herself for this step into a new and dangerous setting.

Cat managed to stroll to the bar, where Blake smiled, stood up, and greeted her with open arms. His embrace was cautious—a political hug for the public setting—and the move temporarily quieted Cat's surging adrenaline.

How was your flight?" she asked.

"Nice and smooth," he replied, before looking around as if

he was distracted. "I had a talkative Texan sitting next to me but he kept me entertained." Blake glanced toward the stairs at the back of the bar. "Hey," he said, "there's a private upstairs seating area. It's closed till five, but the manager said we could use it. The candidate thing, you know. What do you think?"

Cat turned toward Blake and cocked her head. "The candidate thing, huh? What about the married woman thing?" She laughed but couldn't mask her apprehension. "What are you drinking?"

"Screwdriver."

"Make that two and we can go up."

It wasn't as if he'd invited her to his hotel room, and Cat had as much need to avoid being recognized as Blake did. The move to the closed mezzanine area of the bar was a good idea—safe, secure, and out of sight. However, that didn't stop Cat from shaking as she ascended the stairs.

Blake slid into a booth obscured from the lower bar and set his drink down. As soon as she followed suit, he was on her. Blake swept Cat into his arms, gripped his hand against her head, and pulled her mouth toward him. She had no time to react but in his powerful embrace, her body submitted, and time—twenty years of it—and all her reservations about what might happen next, disappeared. All that existed was Blake Buchanan and the kiss.

———— ★ ————

Why did he kiss her? He hadn't planned to do that. *Had he?* However, Cat's response assured him that she'd craved this moment as much as he did. The kiss was transcendent, removing all doubt that their bond was real and that each cherished the good fortune, the chance, that had lead them back together.

And then a near disaster. Blake had given her a key to his eleventh-floor suite and slipped away first to wait for her upstairs, Cat to follow at a safe, respectable distance. But as he began to make his way through the lobby bar, a voice cut through the room like an arrow slicing through open air. "Senator Buchanan?" was all Blake heard. The speaker's identity wasn't immediately recognizable but his tone sounded familiar, as if he knew Blake from the past. The candidate had no choice but to turn around, see who it was, and hope that Cat had waited before coming downstairs after him.

"It's Jackson Goodrich," the young man with the receding hairline blurted. "With the *Enquirer*. Remember? I interviewed you at Chance Mitchell's house." Goodrich was sitting at a table alone but jumped up when Blake made eye contact with him.

Blake veered toward the bar as he tried to divert Goodrich's sight line from Cat's exit route. His heart sped out of control, and Blake felt the familiar advent of a bout with arrhythmia, but he calmed when he peeked up the stairs and noticed that Cat hadn't begun her descent. Blake closed in on Goodrich's table, determined to block the reporter's line of vision so he wouldn't see Cat's movements.

"What brings you back to New York?" Goodrich asked.

"More fundraising," Blake lied. He avoided glancing too much toward the stairs because he knew Goodrich was watching his eyes. Fortunately, the reporter didn't turn around when Cat snuck her way down. Blake caught a glimpse of Cat hugging the back rail and turning her head away as she walked toward the lobby.

"More fundraising?" Goodrich asked. "You must have tapped a gold mine up here."

"Not exactly, I just ran out of time on my last trip. I needed to make a couple more personal visits." Blake realized he had to keep Goodrich engaged a while longer so Cat could flee the area. What he didn't want to happen, however, did. Cat hurried past the danger zone and nodded toward Blake, but rather than head to the elevator bank at the far end of the lobby, she motored straight to the revolving doors in the front of the hotel. In an instant, she was gone. Blake's shoulders slumped as she disappeared. He returned his attention to Goodrich but ignored his next few questions.

"Sorry, Jackson," Blake said. "I'm a bit preoccupied . . . I have a conference call in a few minutes. Nice to see you again." He then rushed to the elevators and rode to his floor, whipping out his cell phone along the way.

But the dreaded message from Cat was already waiting for him.

CHAPTER 22

"Let's get this thing started!" the attorney general boomed into the handheld microphone while flashing a wide grin to the hundreds of runners assembled near the starting line. Striker strode back and forth on the raised platform in a stylish, black-and-white jogging suit, which Phelps's assistants had spent two hours shopping for earlier that morning. She wore gold-framed, oversized Gucci sunglasses that accentuated her self-tanned cheeks. Her side-parted hair hugged her jawline and flowed gently over her shoulders. The "Ladies Right to Life" 5K run in Sugar Land, Texas, was the first stop on what was to be Striker's carefully choreographed eight-city, pro-life bus tour. "I know you're all anxious to start," Striker announced, "so I'll be short. But I want to remind you why we're here this afternoon. To save lives. You, and like-minded Americans everywhere, are the true guardians of liberty. You support the sanctity of life and hold the self-evident truths enshrined in our Declaration of Independence in your hearts. You believe, like I do, that unborn children have fundamental human rights. We must all do what we can to protect those who can't protect themselves. That's why we're here!" She paused as if the next line needed emphasis. "And you can count on me to make good on my pledge as your governor to defund Planned Parenthood, eliminate its diabolical clinics, and to support legislation to criminalize its horrific practice of selling fetal tissue. That is my cause; that is your cause. Thank you . . . all of you . . . for being here today. Have a great race!"

Marshall Phelps stood at the back of the stage watching the action and thinking through the manic events that had preceded this appearance. The chastened campaign manager had been in full damage control since he'd objected to Striker's barnstorming pro-life tour. Despite his advice, the candidate had bullied ahead and lambasted Phelps, saying his old-school view of *play-it-safe* politics was holding back her national launch. She was focused on "fifty states," she'd told him, not just the Texas governor's mansion.

That particular dustup had occurred before Phelps had been able to bring up the really bad news she'd needed to hear. Then again, once he'd started in on that subject, she'd closed him down like iron bars slamming shut on a death-row inmate.

"Are you kidding me?" she'd screamed.

"General," he'd pleaded, "you need to listen to our investigator before going ahead with this tour."

Striker had shot him a look, more a demonic stare. "Marshall," she'd growled, "I don't care what happened a hundred years ago, and neither will my voters. Your job's to bury that story. Quietly. Understood?"

Phelps had been about to respond when the candidate picked up a book from the table and slammed it down. "Dammit," she'd yelled, "this conversation's over . . . do you hear me? The tour starts next week!"

In his long career, Phelps had seen politicians like Striker become dazzled by their poll numbers and hype. Those candidates had decided they were immune from criticism and that their pasts were irrelevant to the rest of the world. Phelps had also worked with and observed more intuitive candidates over the years who'd successfully inoculated themselves early in a race to avoid fatal disclosures later on. Great politicians, those with instinct and feel, knew this was the only way to avoid trouble with the press. The most famous such pre-disaster disclosure had been Bill Clinton's *60 Minutes* interview with his wife, during which he artfully managed to admit and deny his reckless womanizing before the story could mortally wound him. But that semi-disclosure was only the most public of those Phelps had seen through his long career. He'd worked with many lower-tier candidates in similar situations, many with far worse resumes and needing more difficult "fixes" than Striker would require. He knew how to deal with problems lurking in a politician's past—disclose the subject matter before anyone was paying attention, then turn the focus on the accuser. Just four years earlier, Phelps had helped elect the new state comptroller in just this manner. The candidate, a little-known Tea Party activist named Florence Hickerson, had been prodded to self-disclose that she was under investigation for securities fraud, which had come well before her campaign caught fire and her name was popularly known. By the time the indictment had come down, at a stage of the race when Hickerson had assumed front-runner status, Phelps had already been ahead of the crippling disclosure, and had transformed it. The overzealous prosecutor then became the story, not the candidate. Phelps expected he could do the same with Striker's problematic background issues . . . if she'd let him.

But that wasn't going to happen today, or any day, because the candidate wouldn't permit it. Instead, Phelps found himself fidgeting next to his candidate on a makeshift platform in the Texas hinterlands as Striker fired a starter's pistol into the air and the flood of runners took off down the highway.

"Ready to go?" he asked the attorney general as she turned away from the front of the stage toward the small set of stairs leading off the platform.

"Give me five to say hello to some of these workers and I'll be there," she replied.

"Yes, ma'am." Phelps then hustled over to their waiting Suburban, climbed in the back seat, and began studying his phone messages. His mind, though, was on the words he was about to use with his candidate. He had to try again. He had to make one last attempt to help Striker see the light. Ten minutes later, she joined him.

"Did you see the power in that speech?" Striker exulted. "Did you see what it's like to have an army of women behind you? There's no better political capital. Every one of those ladies can multiply to bring in four, maybe five new voters. That's the power of my movement. Marshall, honey, get out of that dinosaur world of yours and jump in!"

Phelps squirmed, winding up to deliver his last shot at convincing his candidate to take a safer, wiser course. "I don't disagree," he answered, "but there are other ways to get your ideas across."

Striker rolled her eyes and waved at him.

"Listen to me," Phelps implored. "That's what you pay me for. If we found this information, others could find it as well. You know the risk."

"Don't start on me again," she chastised him with her arms crossed against her chest. "My God, I used a fake name and a fake ID. The only reason you found it is because I tipped you off. And it was over twenty-five years ago. The world's changed; so have I."

"All the more reason to disclose it now. No one would ever hold it against you. You were young. You're wiser now. It's the best form of protection." Phelps was running out of time.

"I want you to hear me," Striker warned, narrowing her eyes. "This is the last time this subject will come up. I've made my decision. Bury that story! That's it."

Phelps nodded, realizing he'd lost the battle. As disappointed as he was, he knew that despite his failure with his candidate, the war could still be won. What lay buried in Striker's past, dangerous as it was, might still stay hidden, out of sight, from the bloodhounds in the press. The political universe, the one he'd lived in for most of his career, was filled with game-changing secrets, many of which were never exposed to public light. No reason Striker's had to be, either. "Yes, ma'am," he replied. "I won't bring it back up. I understand your directions."

"Good," she said. "My God, did you see that crowd? It's happening! I can feel it."

"Yes, ma'am," he repeated.

And with that, the story of Grace Striker's decades-ago abortion was stuffed once and for all into a deep, dark closet. Marshall Phelps just hoped he could keep it locked up there.

CHAPTER 23

Jackson Goodrich sat in his small cubicle at the *Enquirer* sorting through the panic he'd captured in Blake Buchanan's eyes when he'd called out his name. The politician's ashen face and his exaggerated movements to block the mezzanine area nailed down his guilt. Too bad for Buchanan that he hadn't known the mirror behind the bar provided a perfect sight line to the stairway. The woman of interest had been crafty, hugging her body against the back rail to avoid detection, but no doubt she'd been with Buchanan . . . upstairs and alone. Busted. The Texas governor wannabe was frittering away valuable campaign time in an empty Manhattan bar in the middle of the afternoon, some fifteen hundred miles from home. Tony León had been right; there was a story out there. Jackson just wasn't sure what he wanted to do with the information—a byline on a second-tier politician's indiscretions was still small game—but he now had plenty of room to run. Rather than start down a path of helping the self-absorbed León, a man he'd never really liked, Jackson figured it was worth calling Buchanan at his campaign headquarters to get a reaction.

Senator Buchanan returned his message a short time later.

"Thanks for calling me back," the reporter said when he saw the number.

"I was expecting your call," Blake replied.

"Why's that?"

"I don't want to play games. I think you know why."

"No, what do you mean?"

"C'mon, Jackson, this is important to me. Can we talk off the record for a minute?"

"I don't know. Depends on what you have to say."

"I need your word on this. You'll get some facts on the record before we hang up. Otherwise, we have nothing to discuss."

Jackson didn't like Buchanan's attitude but saw little downside in taking his deal. He had the man from Texas hooked, the only question was how quickly he wanted to let the rest of the world know. He had good reason to be patient. Holding a public official hostage—especially, a politician in the midst of an election—could yield even more information if he played his hand wisely. "Fire away," Jackson said. "We're off the record. What do you want to tell me?"

"The woman you saw yesterday," Blake started, "and I know you saw her, is an old friend. She needed my help on a personal matter. I hope you will respect her privacy and leave her alone. Write what you want about me, but please leave her out of it. You'd be hurting an innocent person, and it's completely unfair. This isn't about her."

"What's her name?"

"You're kidding," Blake fired back.

There was blood in the water but Jackson wasn't feeling any real anger toward Buchanan. *Who else would call an* Enquirer *reporter in a similar situation?* But despite Buchanan's honorable intentions, he was still the most clichéd form of politician—caught in the wrong place at the wrong time. Exactly the kind of story the *Enquirer* thrived on. "So let's go on the record then," Jackson offered.

"If that's what you want."

"What were you doing in New York yesterday?"

"Personal business."

"Personal business of what kind?"

"Fundraising, primarily," Blake answered. "You know I was

here last week at Chance Mitchell's place and this was just a follow-up with a potential donor."

"But that donor isn't the woman I spotted you with, is it?"

"No, she's an old friend. I had to meet her on a personal matter. You know, Jackson, if a friend comes to me—no matter who it is—I'm always going to try to help. Being a politician doesn't change that part of me."

"I respect that, sir, but you can imagine that it's easy for a reporter to read your meeting a little differently."

"I understand, but I hope you'll avoid jumping to conclusions."

"Senator, you're not doing much to help me here. I know you were in New York without a public appearance scheduled and you met in a quiet bar alone in the afternoon with a woman who's not your wife. That may well be innocent, but it doesn't look that way from my vantage point. You know the *Enquirer* has to write a story."

"No, it doesn't," Blake challenged. "And no you don't. But even if you did, I'm just asking that you write it about me. That's all I'm saying. The woman's identity is not newsworthy."

"Very well, Senator," Jackson replied. "I'll give it some thought. I will. But please call me back if you have anything more to offer."

"I'm hoping that won't be necessary, and I'm sensing you'll do the right thing. Thank you, Jackson."

After clicking off his phone, Jackson Goodrich leaned back in his chair and contemplated his conversation. He wasn't sure where he'd go with it all, but he did know that any story he wrote might bury the obscure politician from Texas and maybe ruin lives around him. That was the career he'd signed up for with the *Enquirer*, but this wasn't a byline that would necessarily boost his own standing in the newsroom . . . unless.

Jackson looked down at his phone, opened up the Photos app, and stared at the picture. *Who are you, mysterious woman?*

Blake hung up, wondering if he'd made a colossal mistake. Calling a scandal-sheet journalist was never a smart idea and doing so without telling his campaign manager bordered on political suicide. But he didn't think he'd had a choice. Telling Rags or anyone connected with his team about the episode at The Plaza wasn't an option. They might all quit if they knew the truth. His staff admired and respected him, and this revelation would brand him as just another narcissistic, philandering politician. Blake didn't want that to be his story. Those thoughts took him back to the phone conversation he'd had with Cat from his hotel room right after he'd escaped Jackson Goodrich's scrutiny.

"Why'd you leave?" he'd asked.

"You're kidding," she'd replied.

Blake had sighed and then searched for the right words. "I don't think we have a problem," he'd suggested to her, "but I'll get it under control. I promise. Once I do, I'll get back to New York and we . . ."

"Blake!" Cat had interrupted. "Look, I was there voluntarily and I have some blame here too, but there's nowhere to go with this. Your whole election could be on the line. We have to end this!"

"Cat, I can't," Blake had implored. "Please, let's just get through this episode and figure out the rest later."

"Stop, Blake," she'd scolded, making every effort to correct the course of their conversation. "I have a life up here, too, and a family."

Despondent, Blake had wondered how he might appeal to Jackson Goodrich, a man he neither knew nor trusted. His insides had started to pull apart while he spoke. "I'll get it done," he'd assured her.

"Call me when you know more," Cat had said in a calmer tone. "And get your campaign back in focus. Screw your brain back on tight. Please, there's just too much at stake."

They'd hung up after that and Blake had realized Cat was right. The campaign had to come first and he had to get control of the *Enquirer* situation any way possible.

A knock on the door startled Blake as he was pondering his next move with Jackson Goodrich. He had a speaking engagement in less than two hours and had been expecting Rags to drop by and help him prepare. His campaign manager closed the door after he walked in.

"How do you like the speech?" Rags asked.

"Just getting into it. So far, so good."

Rags took a seat. The two men had always maintained a comfortable understanding between them and Blake sensed that his friend could see the worry painted on his face. This was no time to hold back. "I need to speak with you," Blake conceded.

Rags nodded and took a deep breath. "I've had a feeling there's been something on your mind," he replied. "Talk to me— there's no judgment here. Is it Faith?"

Blake shook his head. "No, that's not it. I'm helping an old friend through some personal problems, that's all. Sorry to keep you in the dark but I had no choice."

"It's that woman, Catherine Alexander?"

Although not surprised by Rags's conclusion, Blake still found it difficult to hear. Yet, as much as he needed to tell Rags the whole truth, he couldn't bring himself to do it. No matter how innocent he might make his meeting with Cat sound, Rags knew him too well and would never see it for anything other than what it was. Not to mention the public, the rest of his campaign staff, and his family. But he had to address the *Enquirer* problem. Jackson Goodrich might already be in the process of burying him.

"Rags," Blake said while rubbing his hands over his face, "you know I could give this speech in my sleep." He pointed at the papers on his desk. "Sit down. We have some other things to talk about."

———— ★ ————

Rags knew that immediate action was necessary—before the report went to print, or worse, into the internet blogosphere—to prevent Cat's name from being linked to Blake's. Negotiating a deal with Jackson Goodrich, and securing a get-out-of-jail card for his candidate, would require all the skills Rags had acquired over his lifetime in politics. The minute he'd finished talking to Blake, Rags dialed the reporter and headed off to the airport.

CHAPTER 24

Cat paced outside the Trinity School waiting for her son but her mind was locked elsewhere. The Blake Buchanan fantasy had morphed into her own private hell. They were guilty of nothing more than a serious flirtation at this point but whatever it had become—an affair of the heart?—had the potential to blow up both of their lives.

Given the uncertainty about what might happen with the New York reporter circling Blake, Cat now had to decide whether to get in front of the potential fallout by revealing the relationship to her husband. Why not explain it away as a friendship, harmless and inconsequential, rekindled after a random meeting in Texas? But she knew Sam probably wouldn't buy that explanation. At the very least, he'd question why she hadn't mentioned Blake earlier when he'd asked about her trip to see her mother. At worst, he'd become enraged and accuse her of sleeping with an ex-boyfriend. But she hadn't done that, and they were old friends—why couldn't she just look Sam in the eye, apologize, and move on? Her head pounded and her hands trembled as the consequences of her actions became more real. Indecision paralyzed her. She worried a damaging admission like that would undermine her marriage as much as revealing a full-blooded affair. Cat knew she was *in something* with Blake, maybe even in love, and no matter what she told her husband, he might read between the lines.

Cat's relationship with Sam hadn't always been this tenuous.

In their early days, when he'd enjoyed more business success than she had, Sam was full of confidence and their relationship had been anchored deeply enough to survive any Blake Buchanan type revelation. But that was no longer the case. Cat had never slowed down enough—maybe not even cared enough—to fully analyze why her marriage had deteriorated over the years, but she knew the problems had started as early as 2000. That was a time of huge changes in their respective business lives and in their futures. Sam had been in transition, having sold his insurance agencies for a multi-million dollar profit, and Cat had been bouncing off the walls, transforming her sleepy wine bar in the West Village into a trendy Spanish restaurant on the rise. As Sam's approach to work had slowed after his newly-minted success, Cat's had motorized. Her early pleadings with her boss at La Bodega had yielded dollars, plenty of them, and had kick-started the next phase of her career. Richard Saldano, the owner, had made her a minority partner and, eventually given her unlimited authority to manage the operation, which had included rebranding the restaurant as Abrazo. By early 2001, Cat had been hiring and firing employees, choosing the wine list, and picking the menu. As Sam had left his business suits and office life behind for a desk in their apartment managing his investments, Cat had turned a nine-to-five type job into a twenty-four-seven obsession.

———————★———————

Sam had tried to be subtle when pushing back on Cat's ambitions for Abrazo, but she'd sensed his negative attitude from the start. She remembered the first time they'd gotten into it as if it were yesterday. It was the spring of 2001, Paige was a newborn, and Sam had decided to use the freedom that came with the sale of his business to set up a private office in their freshly upgraded apartment on the Upper West Side.

"Cat, you can't keep up the pace at the restaurant with a baby in the house," Sam threw out while they prepared for bed.

"What's that supposed to mean?" Cat responded in an irritable tone. It had been another long but exciting day at Abrazo and she was tired and frustrated with Sam's lack of support. She was killing herself being a good wife and mother—and building her business—but that apparently wasn't enough.

"Calm down," Sam soothed. "I just don't want you to wear yourself out. I'm proud of what you've accomplished with the restaurant but Paige needs more of your time."

"Paige?"

"Okay, Paige and me. Now that I'm working from home, it would be nice to see more of you. Even the nanny goes home eventually. But not you."

That conversation, which devolved from there, was a telling sign that Cat's once active, confident husband would become more clingy and jealous over her time away at work. This subtle shift in his mood, and preoccupation with Cat's life, ebbed and flowed over the next months, but transformed into a true crisis after the devastating attacks of 9/11.

The terrorist drama in New York turned Cat's life upside down, leaving stress and anxiety as her constant companions, a poignant sadness overwhelming her. The friends lost, the lives ruined, and the devastation throughout the City kept Cat on edge every day. But the trauma was not only personal, it was also professional. Tourists, restaurant patrons, and city dwellers hunkered down after 9/11 and most small businesses in Manhattan, even successful ones like Abrazo, faced potential ruin. Cat worried every day about whether she could make payroll and if she'd be able to keep the employees she'd worked so hard to recruit and train committed to the restaurant's future. At this difficult time—with her business on the brink—Cat chose to double-down on her future, whether Sam came along or not.

"I need to talk to you about Abrazo," she said to her husband one morning in November while pouring a cup of coffee.

Sam didn't look up from his iPhone but mumbled, "Okay."

"This is important," Cat added. "I need you to pay attention."

Sam set down his phone and turned to her.

"It looks like Richard wants out. Business isn't picking up since we re-opened and he wants to shut Abrazo down."

"I can't really blame him. Who knows how long before this city gets back to normal?"

"I have more faith than that."

A knowing look spread across Sam's face, and just as quickly a frown replaced it. "You want to buy out his interest, don't you?"

Cat nodded.

"Do you really understand what this terrorist crap has done to us? All of my investments have been decimated. We're stretched financially and until the markets recover—if they ever do—I can't help you with the restaurant."

"I'm not asking for your help, Sam," she replied coolly. Cat's tone was indelicate but laid down a marker about her independence. "I just wanted you to know what I'm doing. With Richard out, the restaurant will be mine. I'm responsible, not you."

"Cat," Sam whined in frustration. "We've talked about this a million times. Is that what you think's best for our family? It's made a huge difference having you around this last month instead of running off to the restaurant at all hours. Why don't you rethink this?"

Cat hadn't changed her mind and, as she'd hoped and prayed, Abrazo and all Manhattan sprang back to life in 2002. Not with the same robust energy she'd known before the Twin Towers went down, but strongly enough to sustain her business. Sam's investments, however, did not share the same good fortune. Between stock-market declines and private-equity losses, Sam's net worth took a dramatic hit. The impact wasn't immediate—he masked his financial distress with a nonchalant attitude—but over time the effect became apparent. A lawsuit over a real estate investment on Long Island was the first sign, and then a move to a smaller, less expensive apartment the next, and soon the evidence was everywhere. Cat couldn't remember when she'd taken over responsibility for the family's budget—she thought it was 2008 when the huge stock-market correction occurred—but that ignominy had been the final straw for Sam. From that point forward, he'd withdrawn, choosing to sleep later in the day, rarely dressing in anything other than sweats and a T-shirt, and often times sipping on a Scotch in the afternoons when he was with the kids after school. While a blessing to the family's financial situation, Cat's success in that same time period ate away at Sam's self-worth, and she sensed that every positive accolade she received for Abrazo evoked a somber, negative reaction in him. From then on, Sam seemed comfortable dwelling in the dark place his business losses had taken him.

Two beautiful children and a love for New York City—plus Cat's empathy for the plight of her husband—held their marriage together over the years since. But even as she did everything she could to stabilize her family's future, Cat had felt herself changing, and she sensed that her diminishing respect for her husband had cracked open the door for a Blake Buchanan type to walk into her life.

Twelve years after 9/11, he had.

CHAPTER 25

October 7

A week had slogged by since his near-tragic exposure with Cat and no tabloid reports had blown up. Blake's magician, Rags, had somehow killed the story and saved Blake from joining America's infamous list of political philanderers. In turn, the candidate had followed his campaign manager's directive and stopped communicating with "the woman from New York" in order to focus his attention squarely on the fight with Striker. Nevertheless, Blake hadn't shaken the excitement still percolating from what The Plaza experience might have been for them, and he'd waited as long as he could to call Cat. A new burner phone, purchased the previous weekend, gave him the protection he needed to avoid detection from outside eyes and ears. Blake locked his office door and punched in her number.

"It's Blake," he said when she answered. "Can you talk?"

Did he hear an ugh? "Yes," she replied. "Unknown number . . . thought it might be you."

"It's good to hear your voice," he said. "Did you get my text?"

"Yes, I did. Thanks."

Cat's less-than-welcoming response troubled Blake. "I think we're past it," he revealed. "Rags went to New York and handled things. I'm sorry about all of the drama."

"That's comforting," she replied, "thank you. I was jumpy all last week but I'm better now. I'm still not sure communicating is safe no matter how we do it."

"I understand, but this number is clean. I'm the only one who knows about it. There's nothing to worry about."

"Blake . . ."

"I know what you're thinking," he responded. "But it's true. It's a throwaway."

"Don't you see yourself? You're acting like a kid hiding a *Playboy* from his mother. I'm flattered by your persistence, but I can't do this. One near-death experience is enough for me."

"Why did you come to The Plaza last week?" he asked.

"You know why, but what does it matter? We can't take these kinds of chances. Surely, you can't."

Blake had already made up his mind about what he was going to say to Cat. He'd thought a lot about the danger he was facing, the possibility of a humiliating exposure, but he'd decided it was a risk he could navigate. He just had to be more careful. "I'm scheduling another meeting with Chance in a couple of weeks," he said. "October twenty-first. I'm flying up and back that same day. I'd like to come in the night before and see you."

"No!"

"Don't answer me right now. Just think about it. That's all I ask."

"I really think you've lost your mind."

"Maybe," Blake replied. "But no one plans . . . life. Sometimes, it's beyond our control. In the meantime, text me every now and then on this phone. I assure you, I'll delete them, and it will be safe. Just don't forget to do the same."

"I don't even know what to say." Cat sighed.

"Don't give up too soon. The feelings we experienced last week don't come around very often. I don't even know what to call them. Overwhelming? Look, Cat, the genie's out of the bottle and I'm not willing to let you go."

"We'll talk later," Cat said in capitulation. "That's Sam calling on the other line now. I have to talk to him. Bye, Blake."

Seconds after shutting off the phone, Blake looked up as his campaign assistant Kristen entered the room carrying a stack of papers under her arm. The cut and style of her dress, while not flashy, revealed a shapely figure that couldn't be denied. Blake tried not to pay attention to Kristen's appearance but wondered if it was too attention grabbing for a campaign environment. The girl was quick—smart, personable and, yes, eager to please—but young, although perhaps not as naïve as he'd once thought.

"Here are the work-ups on your donor meetings this afternoon," the young woman said with a smile. "Do you need anything else from me?"

Blake heard the suggestiveness in Kristen's voice but ignored it. "Thank you," he responded. "That'll be all."

———— ★ ————

The meetings that afternoon at Buchanan headquarters were the most important in Blake's insurgent campaign for governor. He looked across his desk at Rags while scratching his chin.

"What do you think they really want?" Blake asked.

Rags took a deep breath before answering. "Well," he replied as he rubbed his fingertips together, "they're two of the biggest Republican donors, they have a long history of giving to Striker, and they rarely support underdogs. What do you think?" He chuckled. "Maybe they just want to personally evaluate the person dumb enough to oppose her." Rags stood up as if he was ready to leave. "I don't want to be too optimistic," he continued, "but this doesn't feel like a courtesy visit either. They don't make many house calls."

Blake nodded and smiled. "Guess I'll just have to dazzle them then," he said.

Rags rolled his eyes. "Finish reading that file. I'll come get you when they arrive."

Blake turned back to the papers in front of him. Frank and

Barney Jarrett—aka the Booze Brothers—had made a fortune selling wine, beer, and spirits in Texas. For the past twenty years, their political organization, BB PAC, had spent more money on politicians than any other political action committee in the state, and they were unapologetic about their willingness to pay to play. The public officials they supported took care of their business, and the Booze Brothers in turn protected their politicians. Rags had carefully steered Blake away from them up to this point in his career.

"They're here," Rags announced through Blake's open office door. "Meet you in the conference room."

Blake took the measure of the two heavyset men in their mid-sixties. Both wore pinstriped suits that looked snug, maybe uncomfortable. Blake recognized Frank as the taller of the two, Barney the more squatty. Chunky would be a kind description for either man. Both were as bald as the globe in the corner of the room and a faint whiff of Scotch clung to their bodies.

Blake reached out to Frank. "Blake Buchanan," he said. "Nice to meet you. Thank you for coming."

"Hello," Frank grumbled. "We were in town and thought coming over here was safer. You show up at our offices and lots of tongues start wagging."

Blake shook hands with the even grumpier Barney before they all hunkered down around the small modular conference table. "Yes sir," Blake said, swiveling in his chair, "I understand the tongues-wagging thing. Glad this worked out."

The brothers looked impatient. Neither Blake nor Rags was sure where to start. Rags jumped in to fill the void.

"Here are our latest numbers," Rags opened, handing Frank and Barney single sheets of paper. "General Striker's lead is down to the mid-teens and we think there's a chance we can take it to single digits by the middle of November. That gives us plenty of time before the holidays to force a second look."

Barney wheezed and waved his hand. "We're not here to deal

with hypotheticals," he interrupted. "You guys have very little chance of winning, short of a miracle."

Blake glanced at Rags but held his tongue.

"Frank and I," Barney continued, while pulling out a cigar that he proceeded to chomp without lighting, "have seen models of your race that show without a Claytie Williams you're dead. And Phelps is too smart to let that happen. So tell us the real story—why're you in this thing?"

Blake directed his eyes right at Barney and didn't hesitate. "To win," he declared. "And because I think Texans will see clear through Grace Striker before it's over. The state's ready for a change. I'm confident of that."

"How're the people going to see that," Barney interjected, "when all the media covers is a pretty woman in short skirts on the stump? Does anyone really pay attention to what she says? Hell, she doesn't even know your name yet."

Frank nodded.

"You didn't come to my office to tell me that," Blake replied.

"You're right," Barney said.

"We don't like the woman," Frank chimed in. "She seems to have forgotten what all good candidates understand—that no matter how well funded or momentarily popular they are, they still need friends like us. But we need a candidate we can believe in, too. One who loves Texas, has the balls to take her on, and understands our role in the economy."

"I want you behind me," Blake stated with enthusiasm, "no matter what your polling data shows or your political whizzes say. Tell me how I can win your support." As soon as the words left his mouth, Blake regretted his comment. It was a loose one that vultures like the Booze Brothers would pounce on.

For the next ten minutes, Frank covered a series of statutory protections that could be under assault if the next governor wasn't willing to stand up to aggressive activists who wanted to chip away at the power of Texas liquor heavyweights like the Booze

Brothers. Blake listened closely and periodically nodded but took no notes. His briefing papers already covered most of the subjects they discussed. The overall message, and the price for securing the Booze Brothers' support, became as clear as the alcohol emanating from their pores.

"Striker's not listening," Blake suggested.

The shorter brother shook his head. "That moralizing woman thinks she's already been elected. And bulletproof."

"I understand," Blake responded.

"Are you loyal to your friends, Senator Buchanan?" Barney asked.

"The Jarretts will have a governor who will listen," he replied. "That much I assure you. I think I understand your concerns—I really do—but I need to study up a bit more on a few of your issues."

"That's not the answer we're looking for, Senator," Barney expressed with a frown.

"Gentlemen," Rags broke in. "We've had a good meeting. Senator Buchanan appreciates your interest. Thanks for coming by."

Frank didn't take the bait. He simply leaned forward in his chair, as though he had all the time in the world. "We have a few more things to say," he announced.

Blake looked at Rags as if to tell him to stand down. The power duo was in the room, and Blake needed to show them respect and hear them out, even if they were crude and offensive. With Blake's encouragement, the brothers then cut to the chase about what they wanted.

"We need to kill any bills put forward to hurt the Texas liquor industry," Barney said. "I've already seen one proposal that will allow out-of-state wine merchants to sell in Texas without going through a local wholesaler. That's absurd. Senator Buchanan, if you get on board, you'll have money to run this woman. At least enough to fight the media onslaught that's coming your way. Is that direct enough?"

It was the kind of deal-making Blake had promised himself to stay away from, the type he'd avoided throughout his career, but now that Faith's money was gone, he realized that being his own man might not be enough to put him over the top. When Barney finished talking, the brothers had dangled a network of donors in front of Blake who could bring in one to two million dollars in a flash, with a chance for a great deal more later on.

Blake felt invigorated about the offer—but at the same time, disgusted. As the brothers filed out of his headquarters, Blake paid homage to the mighty moneymen, smiling and shaking their hands, but what he really wanted to do was shower and clean himself off.

CHAPTER 26

Marshall Phelps surveyed the swarm of people at the third stop of the Striker pro-life bus tour, the Waco Convention Center, and inhaled the intensity of support that only a charismatic leader could generate.

"The right to life," Striker declared into the microphone, "is not a political issue . . . it's not a policy issue." She paused, took a deep breath, and turned away for a moment. "It's a definitional one," she roared, "that defines us as human beings. We who believe in a just and benevolent Creator understand that protecting life is a basic core issue and that our society must answer the call here. Because we know that how we protect life will distinguish who we are . . . and the society we choose to live in."

The crowd cheered and Phelps watched a sea of red, white, and blue "Striker for Governor" signs bob up and down in the convention hall.

"This is an issue," Striker continued, "that we in the public arena cannot back away from or cower to the evil on the left, or to unholy influences like Planned Parenthood. We must stand by our convictions as children of God."

Phelps always grew uncomfortable at this point, when Striker extended her planned remarks into grand overstatements, but he couldn't deny the fervor of her audience. He understood that for all her limitations on substance, her inchoate incoherence, and her unwillingness to consider the deeper implications of her grandstanding policies, Grace Striker could light up a crowd.

She thrived on attention, ate up the camera, and had a magnetic quality that few politicians could match. So why did Phelps still worry so much?

Those worries, of course, included the festering Tony León problem. By now, Phelps was certain that the young man was attached to his candidate by more than ambition and the promise of a plummy patronage job down the line. To save his candidate from herself, Phelps had to find a way to end their cozy relationship, even if the attorney general didn't like it, even if she threatened to fire him . . . again. As a single, divorced woman, Striker was entitled to her freedom, but Texas was too conservative a state for a boy-toy scandal.

Phelps eased over to the pack of workers milling around the side of the small platform where Striker was speaking. He noticed Tony bustling from place to place as if he were in charge, directing members of the staff on lighting, camera angles, and numerous other details, all of which Phelps had covered before the event started.

"Tony," he yelled, "I need a minute."

Tony waved his hand as if to put him off.

"Now," Phelps barked.

Tony stomped over to Phelps with a harried look on his face. "Lots to do," he huffed. "What's up?"

"Walk with me," Phelps ordered. He marched off without waiting for Tony to respond.

The young Hispanic appeared to sense Phelps's attitude and dropped the pretense of being too busy to pay attention. He followed Phelps to a location behind the stage and out of the vision of the reporters, camera crews, and crowd. Phelps glowered at him when they reached a safe spot.

"This conversation's between you and me," Phelps directed. "Understand? You repeat one word of it and I'll rip your tongue out."

Tony's lack of surprise suggested to Phelps that he knew what was coming. "What's the problem?" Tony asked.

"I know you're fucking her," Phelps growled. "And, as of today, that stops! Got it?"

Phelps watched Tony attempt to remain calm when hit with the news but he could see the momentary sense of unease in the trapped gigolo's eyes. "I don't know where you get your information," Tony answered, "but you're wrong."

"Pay attention, son. I don't like you, but I know you want a future in politics. Fucking the next governor is the quickest way to kill your plans. You're too stupid to see that right now, but I assure you she'll fire your ass the minute she tires of you."

Tony looked away from Phelps as if formulating his response. "But I have . . ." Tony stopped himself and Phelps could see that his brash aide had shared more than he intended.

Phelps narrowed his eyes and glared at Tony. "Do we understand each other? And if you have any recordings, pictures, or other sick shit in your possession, they best disappear. If you don't handle it, you can be damn sure I will. Got it?"

Tony's brown skin turned white and Phelps thought he had his man temporarily scared straight. Even then, Phelps could see it was going to take more than harsh words to rectify this dangerous situation for the long haul.

"Tony," Phelps continued, "you have a future in politics, but the next twenty-four hours will be the most important in your life. Lose the pictures and cut off the fuck sessions. If you don't, I won't ask politely again."

"So this is polite?" Tony snipped. Phelps could see the brash young man's fear now turning into anger.

"No," Phelps responded. "This isn't polite; it's very polite."

———— ★ ————

Tony watched his campaign manager storm away after his condescending smack-down. The exposure stung, but Tony knew he still held the cards. Phelps might not understand it, but the attorney general had tired of him and his medieval political strategy and had already talked about jettisoning the veteran politico. Tony hoped that today's power play, once reported, might be the catalyst for that action. Striker would never permit Phelps to intrude into her personal life or speak to Tony like he was a two-bit political groupie.

However, Tony also recognized that Phelps wasn't a man to trifle with. The campaign manager still had the power, the position, and the contacts to undermine his future, and Tony couldn't allow that to happen. For that reason, he had to be very careful before taking the man on and had decided to hold back using the latest piece of oppo research he'd uncovered for the campaign. He planned to store that one away for another day, for if, and when, it was needed.

Truthfully, Tony was tired of banging Striker and almost wished he'd never let her pull him into her bed. Political women, he'd discovered, provided far fewer advantages than the society women in San Antonio he'd been with before joining the campaign. Those ladies spoiled him, tucking rolls of cash into his jacket pocket while he slept, and showered him with gifts in appreciation of his many talents. And discretion. Striker, on the other hand, just demanded he perform when called upon and then sent him around on errands like a teenage cabana boy. In hindsight, Tony wished he'd never called the private number she'd slipped into his pocket at the fundraiser where they met. He'd been seduced by her status as "governor-in-waiting," but in reality the rich donor class of women had far more potential to promote his political career. But it was too late to turn back now. He'd sold out as Striker's lackey and had accepted all the duties, sexual and otherwise, that status entailed.

Striker came off the stage following a final flurry of smiles and waves, gliding by the press and backstage workers as though she'd been crowned Miss America. Phelps hastened to her side. Tony acknowledged the attorney general as she walked past him but they didn't speak. One of their rules was to never communicate in a public place where even the slightest look might be picked up by a random camera phone.

Once the A.G. had exited the building, Phelps drifted back and stood next to Tony.

"We good now?" he snapped.

"Yeah, Mr. Phelps, we good," he answered. Tony cracked a wicked smile once Phelps turned away. The man had no idea what "good" meant.

CHAPTER 27

Cat's dinners with only Sam were rare these days but he'd surprised her on her night off with an invitation to Quistos. Cat's immediate concern was that her husband had heard about Blake and wanted to confront her over the rumors. Then again, she hoped this might be nothing more than some much needed alone time. Months had passed since they'd gone out to dinner as a couple, and maybe Sam sensed they needed to re-connect and recapture that dim, elusive something in their relationship.

After they sat down, Cat excused herself to use the restroom so she could check her iPhone in private. Even in the midst of her worries over her husband, she needed to know if Blake had sent her an email. A senseless urgency about him still possessed her, and her heart accelerated when she noticed her Gmail icon showed one new message. Cat dropped her purse onto the vanity, entered her password, and touched her way to her inbox. The sender was Valerie Wilson, aka Blake Buchanan.

Had a great day today. Very pleased with the way the race is going. Sensing real momentum, finally. Wish you could be part of it. I'm excited about seeing you again. Please let me know when we're a go. Can't wait.

Cat smiled as she punched in a quick reply. Again, like Blake, she used a fake identity, Sterling White, and kept the message as generic as possible—no names, no places, no identifiable information. There was a feverishness to her response, a rush of energy, as she brushed the keys. Then, the moment she hit Send, she remembered Sam sitting alone at the table waiting to share a romantic dinner with her.

Sam was staring at his wine glass, seemingly lost in thought, when Cat eased back into the chair across from him. "This is nice," she said. "We should do this more often." Cat's stomach churned as she smiled across the table and tried to hide the guilt she feared showed on her face.

He reached for her hand and paused for a second. "Actually, Cat, I wanted to talk to you about something. It's a new deal I've been working on."

Sam hadn't brought up his investments in some time. Cat wasn't sure whether to be pleased or worried. She took a quick sip from her glass of pinot grigio in hope of settling her nerves. "Tell me about it," she said as a waitress approached their table.

Sam took a deep breath, drank some wine, and stared at his wife. "This isn't easy," he began. There was almost something boyish and shy in his manner.

Cat offered a soft, encouraging smile.

"I've made some mistakes over the years," Sam acknowledged, "and I know it's not always been easy for you while I've been more down than up."

"Sam."

"No listen," he said, cutting her off. "I've been waiting and waiting to find a chance to turn things around and it looks like I've finally found *the one*."

The one? Cat didn't want to put a damper on her husband's enthusiasm but his penchant for riskier, bigger-return deals, had been the primary reason for his early investment failures. Sam had cured himself of his speculative habit over time—at least that's what he'd told her—but she wondered if his shrinking resources, and maybe her success at Abrazo, had pushed him back into the world of the get-rich-quick types. Cat hoped that wasn't the case.

"I can see you're already questioning me," Sam griped.

"That's unfair," she replied. "Why do you say that?"

"I guess I know you too well."

"My God, Sam, don't make me into the villain. What's with you? All I've done throughout our marriage is support you in every way."

"There it is again," he fired back. "You supporting me! How many times am I going to have to hear about that? Forget I brought up the new deal. You've already ruined it."

Cat took a deep breath to contain her frustration. Despite her building anger, she didn't want to confront Sam for fear of the truth spilling out. She had in fact grown very weary of his repeated refrain that he was only one break away from being back in the chips, and she'd never accepted his unwillingness to return to the real work force to provide for his family. It had been far too easy for him to ride Cat's success, style himself as an entrepreneur, work from their study at home, and keep his financial situation shrouded in mystery.

"Good Lord," Cat said while shaking her head. "I've always been proud of you and I've encouraged you in all your ventures. Why can't you just tell me what's on your mind without trying to read every twitch on my face?"

"Let's not ruin our dinner," Sam grumbled. "The waitress's coming over. Let's order."

After an edgy, tension-filled quiet, they moved on to an awkward discussion about their kids while they waited for their meals. By the time Sam's osso buco was finally placed in front of him, Cat hoped her husband had reconsidered his peevish behavior. She waited patiently for him to open up about the new deal again but eventually decided she'd have to make the first move. Sam's pride, his stubbornness, or just his plain unhappiness with her, was holding him back. "So please tell me about this new opportunity you mentioned," she said.

Sam coughed and stared at her a moment before responding.

He then took a big slug from his wine glass. "Cat," he started but then his voice locked up again.

"Please, Sam. Tell me what's on your mind."

"It's a real estate investment," Sam reluctantly answered. "It's much like the Canouan prospect I passed on several years ago, which I'm told made a fortune. It's a little farther south on a tiny island called Mayreau. You can only get there by boat and the closest air service is the Canouan airport. Very exclusive."

Cat nodded, pushing Sam to continue.

"It's five or six beachfront lots," he explained. "The island's so tiny that it's taken years to acquire the land. Jax Hendrix—the guy who did the Canouan development—is the lead partner. He's going to build two of the properties right away and then decide on the rest. I might even be able to keep one for our family if you like it."

As much as Cat loved the thought of spending time in an exclusive Caribbean getaway, she was taken aback by the thought of bulldozing the pristine beauty of another tiny island in the Grenadines. She tried not to show her concern. "Why Mayreau?" she asked.

"I knew you wouldn't like it." Sam's mouth twisted into a scowl.

Cat took a sip of water. "I didn't say that." She felt relieved when the flabby-armed waitress walked over to check on them.

"That's what I was talking about," Sam argued as the waitress hovered over them. "I bring up a deal I've worked to get involved in for over a year and you react like this."

"What do you mean, 'like this'?"

"Your facial expression says it all."

The uncomfortable waitress scurried away.

"I brought this up," Sam went on, "because this investment is going to require a lot of travel. I would need to leave in a couple of days for a week and I may be spending up to seven days a month down there for a while. I hoped you might be excited about this for me—it could change my . . . our . . . lives—but I guess that's too much to ask."

Cat's body went numb upon receiving the news. It was more of the same with Sam. He'd already made up his mind to do the deal and his offer of a potential new vacation home for his family was his way of coopting her support. She would have preferred he'd taken on the job as a consultant and earned a fee for his work, not parlay whatever equity he had left in his bank account into a luxury home they probably couldn't afford. But it wasn't just these issues that knocked Cat on her heels; it was also the red carpet Sam had unwittingly laid out for Blake to come visit if Sam did in fact go to the Caribbean.

Cat leaned back in her chair, as if Sam's announcement was rolling around in her head, before pulling forward and looking him in the eye. "Sam," she said, "I'm sorry you feel I don't appreciate how hard you've worked to create this opportunity. That makes me very sad." Cat steadied herself because she knew her next comment would have real consequences. "But I've never tried to pass judgment on your investments or interfere with anything you do. Even when I don't agree with your decisions. You've done the same for me with Abrazo and I've always appreciated that. So as far as Mayreau is concerned, if that's a project you believe in, I say go for it."

Sam didn't reply but a tentative smile creased his lips. And with her approval, Cat had opened the door to a new world of possibilities. One that scared her to death.

CHAPTER 28

Rags paced the floor of his Dallas hotel room before Blake's speech to the local chamber of commerce, wondering what he was going to do to crack the impenetrable lead Grace Striker had again opened up. The attorney general's insane pro-life tour was playing to all the right crowds in the Republican Party and Striker had made none of the mistakes Rags had hoped for. Without a break soon, nothing else would matter. The primary campaign was only a month away from losing all voter attention to the Thanksgiving and Christmas holidays, and if the lead wasn't cut in half by then, the race for the March nomination might be over.

Rags again landed on the one strategy he still found plausible. He picked up the phone and called the chairman of the Texas Republican Party, Oliver Nightlinger. The first black chairman of the Texas GOP was an old friend who'd let slip once that he didn't trust Grace Striker, although as the Republican leader he'd never share that publicly. He was the only person who could make Rags's dream of a series of debates a reality.

"Rags," Oliver answered after the call went through two secretaries to get to him. "How's it going out there on the trail?"

"I think you know the answer," Rags replied. "Now tell me when we're going to get these debates going."

"You know I've tried, Rags. But I can't get Striker on board." The chairman sighed. "She's intractable."

"Oliver, you're the head of our party, dammit. Tell her she has to do it." But Rags knew Nightlinger was powerless to force the front-runner to do anything. And truth be told, if the tables had been turned, Rags would have made sure his candidate avoided debates as well. That hadn't stopped him, however, from shaming Striker in the media for hiding from Blake, although his efforts hadn't moved her one inch closer to a shared stage.

"That's a good one." Oliver chuckled. "You know as well as I do there's an advantage to carrying a double-digit lead. They're not about to give you all that free publicity and an open shot at them."

"We have to change that," Rags countered. "You're a clever lawyer. There has to be a way."

"Look, I couldn't agree with you more. But there's not much I can do. Phelps isn't going to budge."

"Maybe I have an answer for that," Rags hinted. The battle-tested campaign manager had hatched a plan, but it could only be pulled off with Nightlinger's help.

"Of course you do." Nightlinger laughed. "I'm all ears."

"Ego!" Rags shouted. "Go to the big cable networks and get a commitment to broadcast the debates in prime time. Striker's got her sights on national celebrity and I know she'll jump at that kind of attention."

"You're dreaming. Phelps will stop her."

"Bypass him then. Go straight to the candidate. Find a way to get to Striker before Phelps has a chance to get in the way. You're a resourceful guy, Oliver. You can do it."

"That's a tough one—maybe impossible—but I don't mind trying. There are a lot of Republicans across this state who'd love to see some of Striker's ideas debated with your man and our buddy Dodds. I'll give it another shot and get back to you. Talk to you later, Rags."

Feeling better, Rags turned his attention back to his candidate. For all of Blake Buchanan's personal charm, his message wasn't getting through to voters, and Rags needed him to break character and throw out a few bombs. Rags had been working hard to assemble the weapons his man needed. The whispers had been out there for years about Striker's past, and his team had devoted many hours to following leads to unearth the stories, but so far they'd come up with little more than unconfirmed rumors. That needed to change.

A knock on the door startled Rags and he turned around to see his assistant Kristen standing in his doorway. Her fitted pantsuit and attractive new haircut caught him off guard. As much as she'd followed his directions and maintained a professional attitude at campaign headquarters, he still couldn't change the one undeniable fact about her appearance. The young woman was jaw-droppingly beautiful, and that still made him very uncomfortable.

———★———

As Blake left the stage after delivering a vigorous attack on Striker's policies to a small group of Dallas business leaders, he felt the weight of another frustrating day bear down on him. He tried to keep a positive attitude as he mingled with the sparse group of supporters who'd stayed behind for the post-speech reception, but he felt many of their questioning eyes boring into him: *What are you doing? Don't you know you're beat?* Blake had been pleased to gain the support from several prominent Dallas businesspeople at the event, and he believed his message about conservative-but-responsible government had resonated, but his attendance still wasn't large enough to fill half the room. At this point, Striker's campaign looked like a juggernaut with no weaknesses. Voters gravitated to winners, and Blake's campaign, by comparison, already had the smell of a rotting corpse.

This wasn't how Blake and Rags envisioned it when they'd first begun planning his run for governor five years earlier.

"The Republican Party in Texas has gone over the edge," Blake had said at that first meeting. "And only a courageous candidate, with money behind him, will turn this state around." It was a strategy Blake's father, the formidable Walter Buchanan, had endorsed over dinner-table conversations many times in the past. Rags had immediately seized on it and devised a way to put it into practice.

"We won't be tiptoeing into the Tea Party," Rags had enthused. "We'll be going headlong at them with guns and knives. That's the only way to win. We challenge every one of their statements on gay marriage, gun control, or any other wedge issue. Expose their positions to light, make the candidates discuss them intellectually, not emotionally, and demand people listen. Republicans are the only game in this state and we might bring independents, and some Democrats, over to our side. It's not a foolproof plan but it's never been tried."

And now, five years later, here they were trying to gain traction with the unconventional plan. But at this point it felt as if they were constantly spitting into the wind.

Blake strolled back to his hotel room after the Dallas reception ended and flung himself on the couch exhausted. He looked down at his iPhone at the roughly thirty text messages waiting, the first one time-dated 7:12 p.m. He read them one after the other until the hotel phone interrupted him.

"Yes," he answered.

"Senator," his aide Kristen started, "Mr. Beckham wants you to come down to the lobby bar for a brief follow-up. I was supposed to catch you before you got on the elevator. My apologies."

Blake was weary but understood his relentless campaign manager needed him to plan the next day. "Be there in a minute," he told her.

Blake hung up and returned to a text message from Cat's alias. It was simple but caused him to smile:

Someone's going out of town for a week starting Saturday. We should talk.

Blake's heart rate jumped as he banged in his response.

Yes, yes and YES!

His energy miraculously revived, Blake threw on his jacket and hustled off to the lobby bar. When he arrived, he observed the normal group of traveling business types clustered at one end of the room and couples paired up at small cocktail tables elsewhere. From his vantage point, no one seemed to recognize him. He scanned the area, looking over and around the small crowd, before spotting Kristen sitting alone at a table in the corner gabbing on her cell phone. As he approached, Blake realized he'd failed to notice earlier that his assistant had cut and restyled her hair into a mature, tight bob.

"Rags on the way?" Blake asked when he sat down.

"I was just talking to him," she answered while dropping her phone into her purse. "He said he's got to take a call and will be down momentarily."

"Do you want something, Kristen?" Blake asked. "I'm going over to the bar."

"Yes, thank you. A Moscow mule, please."

Blake knew that sitting alone in the dark bar with a beautiful young woman wasn't a good idea, even if she was his aide. He hoped Rags would hurry down and get their business done. For twenty long minutes, Rags no-showed and Blake drifted into an uncomfortable conversation with Kristen about her life on the campaign trail.

"I miss my boyfriend but love the work I'm doing," she said while sipping her drink. "I get up every day fired up about helping you win."

"Thank you," Blake said quietly. "And I'm sure your boyfriend will be there waiting for you when this is over."

Kristen rolled her eyes as if it didn't matter. That gesture, along with several inquiring glances from nearby tables, cued

Blake in that it was time to leave.

"Let's meet for breakfast and get our business done then," Blake directed. "Rags must be locked in." He drained the remaining Scotch from his glass.

"Yes, sir," she answered, "that's fine."

"Enjoyed the visit. Thanks for all that you're doing for me." Blake stood up to leave and reached out to her.

"I'd do anything," she replied while staring into his eyes and shaking his hand.

Blake nodded and hustled back to his room, relieved that he'd maintained a proper distance from the young woman. He dismissed the idea that darted across his brain and went back to his iPhone to see if Cat had sent a reply. He was about to call his wife to check in, a conversation he knew would be short and perfunctory, when he heard a knock on his door. Figuring Rags had freed up from his business, Blake flung the door open without looking through the peephole. "About time."

Blake gasped at the vision before him. Kristen, the top button of her shirt undone to display a hint of cleavage, stood there with a suggestive look on her face.

"May I come in?" she asked.

Blake stared at Kristen and knew sexual depravity, but he couldn't give in. "What are you doing here?" he followed up.

"May I come in?" she asked again.

Blake had no doubt what the young girl wanted and, while tempted like a starving man at an all-you-can-eat buffet, realized how foolish he'd been to give life to this embarrassing scene.

Kristen edged toward him and Blake wasted no time. He stepped outside the door and confronted her.

"Kristen," he stated with a fixed jaw. "You can't be here."

The expectant woman looked at him with her doe eyes and Blake knew he was being tested. "You need to go back to your room," he continued without a trace of equivocation in his voice. "Whatever you need to discuss can wait till morning."

"But Senator," Kristen pleaded. "I thought?"

"If I left you with an impression downstairs, it was unintentional. Let's get some rest and work this out tomorrow. We'll forget this ever happened." Blake fixed his eyes on his assistant and motioned with his head for her to leave. "Good night," he said.

Kristen's shoulders fell, betraying her disappointment, as she turned and walked away.

Back inside, Blake slammed the door with more force than intended. The Kristen moment made him realize how close he was to spinning out of control. Because of Cat, his tightly choreographed life was derailing from its storybook script, yet, even then, he was determined not to allow himself to slip into the caricature of a philandering, unrepentant politician. Cat was a different story, however, and he realized that was the danger with love, *real* love. The powerful emotions he shared with Cat couldn't be so easily shut out—no closed door could turn them away—and Blake felt hostage to their increasing attraction. As if on cue, Blake's iPhone chimed, startling him back to reality. He recognized that chime. It was the one he'd reserved for Cat.

CHAPTER 29

October 18

Tony had refused to follow Phelps's directions about ending his relationship with Striker and knew a showdown with his boss loomed. He'd wondered how long it would be before Phelps took his shot. But when Tony realized Phelps had spotted Striker giving him the *look* when they arrived in Tyler, the code she used to signal she wanted a "private" rendezvous, Tony sensed the moment was near.

Tony read his morning briefing from Phelps while sitting in the coffee shop across from the Magnuson Grand Hotel and Conference Center. The daily message discussed the upcoming events, summarized new issues of importance on the Texas landscape, and reviewed the VIPs for that evening's fundraiser (with a special emphasis on the whales who needed extra attention). The clogged schedule explained why Striker requested to see him after 11:00 p.m., a time he knew created flexibility in case her political work stretched into the late hours. As Tony continued reading, he noticed that Striker had agreed to debate her two Republican rivals twice over the next few months, a decision made without even his slightest input. His face flamed red as Tony wondered how and why Striker would make such a decision without consulting him. The obvious answer was Phelps.

When he spotted the campaign manager coming toward the diner from across the street, Tony stormed outside to intercept him.

"Walk with me," Phelps instructed as he approached.

Tony wanted to shoot him the finger but instead followed the campaign manager to a park bench farther down the road, where they both plopped down. The area was separated from the busy pedestrian corridor nearby. "This won't take long," Phelps said.

"Okay, what's up?" Tony asked. Then a bad thought streaked across his mind. Was he about to get fired? Had Striker betrayed him? Suddenly, Tony didn't feel quite as full of himself.

"Let's be straight with each other," Phelps started. "You're here for one reason . . . to build your political resume. But the only way you do that is if this woman gets elected." Phelps pulled a handkerchief from his pocket and mopped his brow. "And the only way I get what I want is if the woman gets elected. So we have the same goal. Isn't that right?"

Tony nodded but his face remained implacable. He was confused by Phelps's pleasant tone.

"The fact that we don't like each other is irrelevant. Do you agree?"

Tony remained silent.

"The bottom line is our lady fucked up," Phelps declared. "She agreed to these debates with Dodds and Buchanan without even running it by me. You'd better not tell me that was your fool idea."

"I thought you'd done it!" Tony fired back. "It's a terrible plan, political malpractice! But the first I even heard about it was in the briefing paper that I just read."

"I believe you," Phelps replied with a wry smile. He spit into the flower bed behind him.

"Then who got to her?"

"I don't know but I think it was the party chair. That shitbag Nightlinger. He went around me and I assure you I'll cut his balls off for that. For now, I have to fix this situation before she signs off on the specifics—dates, venues, format. I need your help."

"Yeah?" Tony was listening. The role reversal had him scratching his head.

"You need to talk her into letting me plan the details. Debates are a bad idea but I can manage the risk if she lets me. Problem is . . . I know what will happen if I bring up the subject again."

Tony understood what was going on. A mischievous smile flashed across his face. He tried to keep his tone neutral as he asked, "And what's in it for me?"

Phelps stood up, paced for several seconds, then stared down at the young aide. "It's very simple. Help me on this one and I'll take care of you once she tires of fucking you. And you know as well as I do that day's coming."

Tony narrowed his eyes and stood up as if he was about to leave.

"Sit down," Phelps demanded. "We're not done."

"You better sweeten your offer then."

A knowing look spread across Phelps's face; Tony realized he was prepared to deal. "I can clear the deck for you in a House district in San Antonio in the next cycle," Phelps remarked. "You won't survive that long with her anyway. From there, it will be up to you."

Tony wondered if it was time to deploy one of the secrets he'd compiled during his campaign research. "And I suppose that's when you get your money, too," he snarked. "When she wins, you pay off your gambling debts."

Phelps glared at Tony. "You little punk," he snarled. "I'll pretend like you didn't say that. What's real is that neither of us can afford to risk this woman going rogue. She's nowhere near as smart as she thinks she is, and this whole campaign could come apart. We need her to manage this. Do you understand?"

Tony shook his head. He recognized as much as Phelps did that Striker's arrogance was her Achilles' heel. The entire staff saw it, too. "If I help on this," he responded, "how can I trust your word on the House race?"

Phelps glared at him again. "I'm Marshall Phelps."

The real Phelps didn't ask for favors, he demanded them. But Tony figured he didn't have much choice anyway. They both needed Striker to win. With a nod, he agreed to the deal, then stood up and marched back to the hotel. He had work to do.

———★———

Tony snuck out about 10:55 p.m. to carefully thread his way to Striker's suite. Small hotels in small towns were particularly difficult to navigate for his clandestine encounters. At least Phelps was giving him a pass on his sexual services this evening. As usual, the candidate had left the door open a crack so he could push it forward. Tony checked both directions before edging his way inside.

"Hurry up, darlin'!" she called out. "And lock the door!"

Tony had dealt with Striker in many different moods over the course of the campaign but her most common one was impatience. Tonight, her voice carried its normal demanding edge, the one he disliked the most. The room was dark but enough ambient light spilled through the closed drapes that he could still make out the contours of Striker's naked body on the bed.

"Take your clothes off and come here!" Striker ordered. She opened her legs and Tony knew what she wanted.

"Can I talk to you first?" he asked.

"Sure, honey, but after we're a little more . . . relaxed. Now get over here. I've been waiting all day for this."

Tony stripped off his clothes and reached down with his arms to spread Striker's legs farther apart. He knew what he had to say would be much better received once the attorney general was pleased. He lowered his head and went to work.

CHAPTER 30

Cat was still dressed in her nightgown and robe when she handed her husband his briefcase. Sam leaned down and kissed his children on their heads before getting into the car where his driver waited. "Be safe," Cat said, patting him on the back.

"We love you, Dad," Paige and Mitch chorused.

Sam blew his family a kiss as the black Town Car pulled away from the curb and headed to the airport.

Once the sedan turned the corner, a wave of guilt engulfed Cat. Yet, she couldn't help feeling her whole body levitate off the ground as a smile slowly spread across her face, and her stomach began to unknot. Blake was arriving later that morning.

———————★———————

Blake stared out the plane's window as the wheels of the 757 touched down at LaGuardia. He'd taken the 6:00 a.m. flight from Houston, so it was still early when he landed. He'd tried to stay calm throughout the flight, but his anticipation was overwhelming. Somewhere between Kansas and Missouri, he'd ordered a Bloody Mary to take the edge off. He never drank this early in the morning, but then again he'd never planned a day like the one he had ahead.

While waiting for his plane to come to a final rest at the gate, Blake's mind shifted back to his earlier conversation with Rags. He was relieved he'd told Rags the whole story—almost—about Cat, but he'd nonetheless kept his colleague in the dark about today's trip, and that misdirection weighed heavily on his mind. His campaign manager would never have let him go to New York City. "Cut it off," Rags had demanded when Blake had finally told him the truth, "or say goodbye to the governor's race." Their talk, however, had only made the candidate more secure in his decision about one thing—protecting Kristen. The story of her flirtation might have unglued Rags altogether.

CHAPTER 31

With Blake out of town chasing a huge donor in Midland, Rags had decided to use the day to convene his campaign team in an effort to sharpen his man's strategy ahead of the coming debates.

"Good morning, everyone," Rags said to the four participants assembled around his conference table. Rags stood near a large whiteboard, pen in hand, ready to go. "We have a single agenda item today," he announced. "We need to create some movement for Blake, and it needs to start today. I thought we could run a *different* kind of campaign, but the polls are demanding a new direction. My first question is—do you agree these are the issues we should focus on?" Rags gave the group a moment to read the materials in front of them:

Buchanan Debate Strategy

Participants
Kristen West (scheduling and campaign coordination)
Susan Wilde (fundraiser and adviser)
Rich Franks (communications director, political strategy)
Taylor Brooks (opposition research, policy)

Issues
1) Abortion
2) Border security/the Wall

3) Health care
4) Infrastructure needs
5) Morality/Religion
6) Tort reform
7) Water and natural resources
8) Environment
9) Property taxes
10) Transgender bathrooms

There were many other subjects to discuss, but before the debate Rags wanted to build immediacy in Blake's public appearances on a couple of vote-moving issues. The polls showed that the original strategy to run against Republican orthodoxy wasn't working so far. Rags felt like he had to redefine Blake's campaign, even if it meant pushing his candidate into taking more traditional Republican positions and praying those changes would breathe new life into the candidate's events.

"You all remember George W.'s strategy in '94 against Richards," Rags began. "Drive home a few key issues and never let up on them. Then let the debates be the stage to reinforce those themes, the platform that reinforces the message. And maybe even coax the opponent into a mistake or two."

Rags had seen both scenarios play out on a national scale during presidential debates and had studied many of those tapes until he'd memorized every line. In fact, Rags had listened to Senator Lloyd Bentsen's famous retort to eventual–Vice President Dan Quayle dozens of times. "Senator," Bentsen had stated, "I served with Jack Kennedy. I knew Jack Kennedy. Jack Kennedy was a friend of mine. Senator, you're no Jack Kennedy." Rags had never forgotten the look in Senator Quayle's eyes when he'd taken that missile to the chest. He needed Blake's comebacks to be just as blistering, and he had only two weeks to get him prepared. And yet, Rags also knew that even Bentsen's brilliance hadn't saved his presidential running mate, Michael

Dukakis, and memorable lines alone wouldn't be enough to derail Striker.

"Morning, Rags," said Rich Franks. The number-crunching, thirty-three-year-old whiz kid had a pencil behind his ear and a grim look on his face. Franks was one of the fresh-faced breed of boy strategists who reminded Rags of himself at that age—all analytics, all the time. "Our man is so far behind in the polls right now," Franks stated, "that normal debate strategy is out the window. Shouldn't we get into Taylor's oppo right away?"

Rags had expected to go through the checklist of Blake's positions with the team, but he sensed the whole group agreed with Franks. "What do you think, Taylor?" Rags asked. He looked at his old friend and gave him a nod while sitting down in one of the conference chairs. "Go ahead, then."

Taylor Brooks, a former small-time investigator in Dallas who'd once made his living sneaking around philandering husbands' windows, owed most of his success—and a substantially increased bankroll—to meeting Rags decades earlier. Rags's candidate at the time, a straying husband from Houston, had been the target of Brooks's opposition client, and the rest was history. Brooks had delivered very damaging photos to Rags of his candidate with another woman, and the embarrassed father of two had promptly pulled out of his race. "You have to be pretty good to get those shots," Rags had told Brooks at the time, "and I don't much like my guy anyway." From there a partnership was born. Over future campaigns, Brooks became Rags's go-to investigator and Rags had never been disappointed. Brooks now employed a small shop of associates, had almost more work than he could handle, and commanded fees that even shocked Rags at times.

Brooks had the group's attention because they all wanted to hear more about the attorney general's risky sexual appetite, rumors about which had dogged her for years. Brooks had been hired to unlock that story. Rags's investigator nodded to the eager gathering, pulled out a pad from his slim briefcase, and set it on the table. He drew a deep breath and looked at each face around the room. "This woman's covered her tracks well," he started. "Or Marshall Phelps has done it for her."

"That sucks," Franks blurted out.

"Let's never underestimate our man Phelps," Brooks responded with genuine respect in his voice. "He's been at it a long time and seen a lot of undisciplined candidates in his day."

Everyone in the room knew that to be true. Rags, more than anyone, respected Phelps as a worthy opponent and recognized nothing would come easy when battling a man of his talents.

"Got any good news?" Franks asked.

"I'm not finished." Brooks started to grin. "They can't hide everything . . . not even Marshall Phelps. And you know how hotel personnel love to talk."

"Well then," Franks said.

Brooks had told Rags, on the phone, a little about what he'd found out, but not *everything*.

"She's boffing one of her campaign aides," Brooks revealed. "And he's a kid . . . about twenty-eight-years old."

Susan Wilde pounded her fist on the table as if to say "Of course!" Franks leaned back in his chair.

"What can we do with that?" Rags asked. "She's been divorced forever. Who's going to care?" Rags's question was rhetorical because everyone knew it was his job to make people care.

Brooks held up his hand. "There's more. The second piece, however, isn't quite as straightforward as the first. It's going to take me a while to explain."

Brooks hadn't tipped Rags off that more was coming, and Rags saw a twinkle in his friend's eyes. Everyone in the room leaned forward in their chairs as Brooks turned his notepad to a second page.

"Grace Striker has always had a voracious appetite when it comes to men," Brooks began. "And this goes back a long way."

Twenty minutes later, Brooks had laid out a clear pathway for

Rags's team to rip into Striker's impenetrable lead. It wouldn't be easy, and the strategy depended on a focused candidate doing his part, but Brooks's research offered fresh hope—as long as Rags could finish the job.

CHAPTER 32

Jackson Goodrich hadn't thought much more about Blake Buchanan since he'd made his bargain with Rags Beckham. The deal had been acceptable, and he'd moved on to other stories, but in time, he expected some payoff for his forbearance. Giving up a back-page article about an obscure gubernatorial candidate in return for a promised front-page exclusive on a nationally known political figure had been an easy trade. It remained possible that Rags had misled him about a potential scoop to buy the *Enquirer's* silence, but Jackson had been willing to take that chance because Blake Buchanan wouldn't have moved the needle at all with his readers, with what, yet another story about a philandering politician caught in an embarrassing situation. But a headline on a potential *presidential* candidate . . . now that would garner national attention. Even then, Buchanan's campaign manager had better come through with something soon or Jackson would savage his man solely out of spite.

It had also helped his decision that he wasn't doing any favors for Tony León. Jackson had grown more and more ticked off every time he considered Tony's brazen attempt to use him. The men had never been close in law school and Tony's transparent attempt to stay in touch once Jackson had landed his *Enquirer* gig still bothered him. Truth be told, Jackson relished the thought of dumping Tony's candidate in the grease.

Now Jackson had a dilemma. Buchanan had reappeared in New York and he couldn't turn away from the obvious conclusion.

Was the man that stupid? Didn't Buchanan understand that Jackson and his *Enquirer* colleagues had eyes everywhere? Especially at the airport. A casual comment of no apparent significance had tipped him off—"Hey, Jackson, that guy you wrote about from Texas is back in the City." But Jackson had found it too inconceivable to be true. *Did Buchanan have a death wish?* The simplest response was to call Rags Beckham and see where they stood. If the campaign manager couldn't control his man or deliver on their deal in a hurry, then Jackson had a new story to write.

CHAPTER 33

Blake didn't have to turn around to know Cat had entered the room. The first sensation he felt was a gentle hand on his shoulder. He reached back, grasped her fingers, and spread them between his.

"Here we are," she said, swinging around into the chair across from him. They lowered their locked hands under the table.

"Are we safe?" Blake asked. "From what I can tell you've found the most secluded spot in the City."

"Can't be certain, but I've never set foot in this little pub, nor has anyone I know. That's why I suggested it. The good thing is that door over there connects directly to the hotel."

Blake caressed Cat's hand as he studied her eyes, looking for any sign of reservation. He steadied himself and admired the woman before him. Cat's white satin blouse, navy knee-length skirt, sapphire earrings, and floral scarf were all choreographed to perfection, draping the soft curves of her still lithe body. He didn't need a reminder of Cat's beauty, but despite his effort to remain calm, seeing her in this setting, in this way, crippled him. He moved closer to the table and asked, "May I kiss you?"

"Blake," she objected, holding him off.

"I'll go up first," he whispered. "It's room 322."

Cat sighed and squeezed his hand before leaning back in her chair. "I'll wait about fifteen minutes and then follow you up," she said. "Now go on before I change my mind."

Once in the room, Blake threw his jacket on a chair, brushed his teeth, and pulled off his tie. He and Cat hadn't been intimate in over twenty years and his mind wandered over the landscape of their past. The memories—once distant, but now so present—intoxicated him. He yearned to hold her again in his arms and longed to rest his head against her breasts. Yet, Blake wondered what had happened to the man he used to be. The one who'd been so dedicated and disciplined, devoted to his home and family. For now, that guy no longer existed—not in this room at the Hudson hotel—his wife and their mutual disappointment in one another had seen to that. But still, shouldn't he feel indecision, some guilt, at least some trepidation? What about the risk he was taking concerning his relationships with his girls? The potential decimation of his campaign? What about all those things?

The door edged open and a barely audible knock followed. Cat peered in from the hallway and Blake no longer worried about anything.

"Come here, you," he greeted her while opening his arms. Cat sprang into his embrace.

"Oh my God," he said, smoothing her hair and pressing his lips against her neck.

"I've missed you," she whispered.

And then they kissed, but this time without pause or the pressure they might be interrupted. He bathed in the delicacy of her lips, the warmth of her tongue, and inhaled the distinctive smell of her skin that had lodged in his memory. He guided Cat toward the bed but their mouths never lost contact, their tongues revolving around like dancing butterflies. He backed off when they bumped into the mattress and she impatiently yanked his shirt out of his pants. The sight of her sliding his leather belt from his waist, loop by loop, pushed him toward the edge. She then sat down on the bed, unclasped his pants, and slowly guided them past his hips to the floor.

Blake staggered momentarily as Cat trailed her fingers across his legs and gently tugged at his briefs until they fell to his feet.

She didn't hesitate, gliding her tongue up his inner thigh in a way that he'd never forgotten. His eyes rolled back in his head as she performed her magic, which left him dizzy and short of air. Blake couldn't bring himself to watch as Cat moved up and down, fearing he'd lose all control. But it was too much, too fast, so he forced her to stop. Blake took a deep breath and pulled Cat up for a long, lingering kiss, then lowered her onto her back and unbuttoned her blouse to reveal a lace, blue-silk bra. He slowly slipped her pants down her legs.

Blake remained motionless for a second to admire Cat as she removed her bra. "You're incredible," he said.

She smiled up at him, waiting for his next move.

━━━ ★ ━━━

Had she just done that? She couldn't understand her actions or the wild energy that surged through her body—she was twenty again—but she had no desire to slow it down. At this point, she was committed, even if just thirty minutes earlier the very idea of being in Blake's room had made her crazy with fear. But none of that mattered anymore; the only thing that did was how he made her feel. As Blake removed her panties while she lay on the bed, his remarkable naked body in full view, she had nothing on her mind other than the next few minutes.

He stood in front of her, strong and magnificent, and pushed at her knees, spreading her legs. She hadn't experienced this kind of pleasure in such a long time that her body trembled when he knelt, leaned in, and tasted her thighs. Cat's belly began twitching in anticipation. He worked his way up to her chest, then back down to her stomach. He was slow, patient, and then hungry. The uncertainty that had troubled her on the trip to the hotel melted away.

"Quit teasing me," she said in a breathless voice once Blake raised his head.

"Should I get protection?" he asked.

LANDON WALLACE

Cat suppressed a laugh. "I'm almost fifty years old."

"I love you," Blake said.

"Oh my Lord, Blake." Cat moaned with pleasure. "I love you too. I guess I always have."

160

CHAPTER 34

Blake waited at gate C35 to board his plane after an unforgettable afternoon. Lovemaking, laughs, old stories, more lovemaking, more laughs, and finally, exhaustion. They'd held and consumed each other as if they'd had just five hours to live. Neither of them had wanted it to end. Politics and all its related problems had disappeared for Blake when he'd lain beside Cat, and he'd almost forgotten the rest of the world existed outside their hotel walls. But reality eventually asserted itself and Cat had raced off to attend her son's soccer game. When they parted, they'd looked at each other with confused expressions, having no idea what to say or do, but with an understanding that their lives would be different now.

Then he'd received Rags's message about the *New York Enquirer* reporter having spotted him at the airport. The ensuing conversation hadn't been pleasant.

"Blake?" Rags said in a raised voice. "What the hell's going on?"

"I'm in New York," Blake answered. "On my way home, boarding any moment now."

"Are you fucking crazy?"

"I know, Rags. I wasn't honest with you earlier, and I'm very sorry. I really am. I should have told you about my trip, but I couldn't." Blake felt panic-stricken that his friend and his entire campaign staff might resign immediately if word of his whereabouts leaked beyond their conversation.

"I don't know what to say," Rags scolded, "but I couldn't be more disappointed. We'll hash this out when you get home, but for now I need to make sure no one has followed you, or worse, taken photographs."

"No, I'm sure that hasn't happened. I've been very careful other than my walk through the airport."

"Get your ass on that plane and we'll figure this out. I just hope that damn *Enquirer* reporter wasn't tipped off to anything more than you think." Rags paused. "And your wife, of course. God knows what will happen if Faith finds out about your jaunt to New York."

"She won't. Rags, I'm very sorry I've put you through this. I know it's not what you signed up for."

"You're just lucky that reporter hates Striker and León more than you. But I'll deal with him. See you *mañana*."

"Rags, thank you . . ."

"Just get on the damn plane."

With the luster now wiped away from his inspiring reunion with Cat, Blake realized he had more than a little thinking to do as he headed back to Texas.

━━━ ★ ━━━

Blake landed around ten after his presumed trip to Midland, stopped for fast food on the way home, and found his wife's bedroom door already closed by the time he'd climbed the stairs. He was glad he'd caught the last flight out of LaGuardia and made it to his house the same night. Director of College Counseling Tanya Martinez had scheduled a conference at 9:00 a.m. the following day about Fin's future, fitting it around Blake's calendar, and he'd told Faith he'd be there.

Blake and his wife barely spoke before getting into their separate cars and heading out to the school the next morning. They needed their own transportation because Faith had a tennis clinic as soon as they finished, and Blake would be in a hurry to get to campaign headquarters to huddle with Rags. As Blake whipped through the entry gates of the eighty-acre St. Joseph's K–12 campus, he wondered whether he'd made the right decision sending his girls to a private school. There was little debate that St. Joseph was the finest high school in Houston, maybe in the state, and most students graduating in Fin's class would find their way to the college of their choice or a close second. Still, the school was so protective and homogenous. Blake worried all the time that his girls hadn't seen enough of the real world in their young lives.

"Senator Buchanan," the director greeted him when he walked in her office.

Blake smiled and shook hands with Tanya Martinez. She guided him to the small conference table and they exchanged pleasantries while they waited for Faith.

"Hi, Tanya," Faith said when she walked in. "Sorry, I'm running behind the Indy driver over there." She pointed her finger at Blake and cast a cynical smile.

To Blake, Martinez appeared less than comfortable when Faith arrived, the director's body posture suggesting a nervous tension. "Hello, Mrs. Buchanan," she replied. "Your husband and I were just catching up."

Blake had stood up when his wife strolled in. He leaned toward her, and pecked her on the cheek.

"You seem chipper this morning," Faith observed. "I hope all of that positive energy is a result of our girl's performance." Faith forced a smile and gathered around the table with her husband and Tanya.

"Your daughter's a wonderful young lady," Martinez started. "That early admission into Liberal Arts Honors at Texas speaks volumes about her intelligence and work ethic. But that's obviously not why I invited you here today. Fin's other applications are all out now and a couple of things popped up that I thought you might want to know about."

Blake looked at his wife and cocked his head. Her blank reply suggested she had no idea what Martinez was talking about.

"I'll get right to the point," Martinez followed up. "Some of these applications ask for demographic information that the applicants don't need to fill out. It's become a more common trend these days to allow students to voluntarily self-identify certain aspects of their personality."

"I'm not following you," Blake said.

"Like I mentioned, your girl's an incredible young woman," Martinez offered. The college adviser's hand trembled as she set a small stack of papers on the table.

"What are you telling us?" Blake asked.

"Senator Buchanan, I do recognize you're running for governor and that some of this information, while private, could leak out. That's why I've asked you here today. It's unusual not to include Fin, and I'm uncomfortable with that, but given your candidacy and the potential for exposure . . . well, everything is so public today."

"What is it, Tanya?"

"I'm a little embarrassed to even m-mention this," Martinez stammered.

"Please, don't worry," Blake said, trying to calm the woman's anxiety while shuffling through the documents in front of him. "My political life's of no importance when it comes to Fin's future."

"I know, I know," she replied, but her twisted expression suggested trouble.

"Faith, look," Blake directed. He pointed at a gray box marked "Optional" in the corner of one of the pages.

"LGBT?" Faith turned to Martinez. His wife acted confused about the designation but Blake saw her face flush as she read the initials.

"Yes, that's it," Martinez explained. "Some of the applications today have optional sections for transgender and LGBT students to identify themselves. And given . . . "

"Ms. Martinez," Blake jumped in, "may we have a minute?"

The embarrassed college counselor scurried away as if relieved to avoid further discussion of the subject. The Buchanans had apparently found what she wanted them to see.

The minute Martinez exited, Blake turned to Faith with a confused look on his face. "Our daughter's gay?" he asked.

Faith's complexion had transformed into bright crimson at this point. "What do you think?" she responded in a halting voice. Faith fidgeted with her fingers, tapping the table several times.

"I don't know," Blake answered. "She's never mentioned it, and . . ." Blake stopped and reconsidered his words. "I couldn't care less if she is. Still, she's my baby, so I guess we should talk to her. Why would she have kept this from us?"

"This is very disturbing," Faith mumbled while looking away from her husband.

"Disturbing?" Blake questioned. "There's no reason to feel that way. Confused maybe, but I'm confident Fin has been mature about her decisions."

"I'm not so sure about that."

"What's that supposed to mean?"

Faith squirmed, as though she was not sure how to respond. "Let's not act too precipitously about all of this," she finally answered but it was clear to Blake that his wife was upset by their daughter's disclosure. Perhaps, it was justifiable frustration that Fin had hidden such an essential piece of information about herself from her mother, but Blake sensed it was more than that. Was it that Faith's prominent standing in the Houston community would suffer if the world learned she had a gay daughter? Or, that Faith's socially conservative parents would be embarrassed by such a revelation? Whatever it was, that was a topic for another discussion.

"Tell Tanya to come back in," Faith continued. "We can talk to Fin about this later."

CHAPTER 35

November 1

Tony twirled his pen as he walked toward the conference room for Striker's debate preparations. He was more than a little worried. The attorney general hadn't communicated with him in days, she'd excluded him from several work sessions, and he'd rarely seen her in that time. No furtive messages, nothing. They'd gone for longer periods without getting together, especially when she'd been on the road or preoccupied with her official duties, but Tony sensed this was different. He was beginning to wonder if Phelps had duped him, laid a trap at their recent meeting, and turned Striker against him. "Honey," she'd responded to his suggestion that she turn the task of prepping for debates over to him, "stick to what you do best." Striker had then marched out of the room without another word. From that point forward, Tony had perceived a shift in the candidate's attitude. And for the past few days, Phelps had almost been pleasant, even smiling at times, which was the greatest indicator of all that something was up.

The first debate was set for Friday, November 15, in Austin, just weeks away. Clever timing, which suggested Phelps had gained control of negotiating the dates and debate rules. With the primary itself still over three months away, high school football owned the autumn Fridays in Texas, and thus only senior citizens and political junkies would likely be watching that night. A decided advantage for the front-runner. For Blake Buchanan to score a knockout blow, he would need to land one from Brooklyn in Striker's face, and even if he did, few would probably be paying attention. The possibility of a surprise, more than any other factor, troubled Tony. The one haymaker that might be available to Buchanan was the disclosure that Striker had been banging a half-her-age staffer. Maybe that's what had Phelps smiling lately.

When Tony walked into the room, Phelps and two men he'd never met before waited. He recognized the brilliant consultant Michael "Tuffy" Meadows, a chunky twenty-something brainiac with Tea Party connections, but the second operative, a stooped-over, gray-haired man, didn't register. The unknown visitor walked toward him with Phelps. "Meet Tony León," Phelps said. "He's our policy director and head of Hispanic outreach."

The mystery man opened his hand and offered it to Tony. "Fred Zinger. Nice to meet you. I've heard good things." Phelps smiled like the cat that ate the canary, which further set Tony on edge.

"Nice to meet you as well," Tony replied.

"Freddy's run many national campaigns," Phelps explained, "and he's here to steer General Striker on big-picture issues. He has no official role, at least not yet, but he'll keep an eye on Iowa for us." Phelps grinned.

Tony nodded, a bit taken aback that he'd never heard of the man who was to have such an important role on Striker's team. In fact, there were few important names in politics he hadn't heard about, but this Fred Zinger was a new one altogether. The man had the steel-gray eyes of an experienced sharpshooter and Tony could sense he and Phelps shared some history. Meadows, on the other hand, was a more recent addition to the inner circle, and a different type of political animal altogether. As Tony had learned from numerous sources, Meadows had grown the reputation as the human form of the Microsoft Cloud. The flabby-cheeked man from Muleshoe, Texas had an uncanny recall of voting data from every one of the two hundred and fifty-four counties in the

Lone Star State, and was a master at messaging the base with relevant facts and figures. The consultant was awkward in public, often hugging the backs of rooms when major donors arrived, but his intellect was a political treasure. Every position Phelps had adopted for Striker over the last few weeks had apparently blossomed in some way from Tuffy Meadows's brain.

The door to the conference room flew open and Grace Striker strode inside. She was dressed in a perfectly tailored charcoal pantsuit, with a breezy white blouse and a gold Byzantine necklace. With her jaw fixed in place and her eyes narrowed, she had the look of a focused candidate.

"Are we ready, gentlemen?" she asked.

"Yes ma'am," Phelps answered.

"I guess I'm going to have to hear from the whole bunch of you." Striker smiled at each face in the room. "So let's get rocking."

A positive sign for Tony. He noticed an ever-so-slight wink from Striker as she gave her directions.

———————— ★ ————————

The meeting was thirty minutes deep into facts, figures, and mind-numbing boredom before Tony got his chance.

"Let's talk about motivating millennials," Meadows suggested.

"Yes," Zinger added. "We'll need that voting block as much as any on the national scale. Much like Obama excited the youth, we'll need to do the same with her base. Let's start with the young Christian conservatives."

"So what's your plan, Marshall?" Striker turned to her campaign manager.

"General, you're winning every demographic in the state right now. I don't think we need a different plan for younger voters. The millennials as a group will be on to other issues by the time Iowa rolls around."

"Damn, Marshall," Striker said in a raised voice. "There you go again. I'm not worried about beating Blake effing Buchanan. Fred's here to start setting themes for a fifty-state campaign. And I don't want to wait. Let's form a plan for young voters *now*."

"May I offer my thoughts?" Tony asked.

"We'll call on you when needed," Phelps retorted.

"No," Striker interjected. "I like hearing from these younger guys." She looked over at Tony and smiled. "Tell us what you think, Tony."

Meadows nodded as if to cede him the stage.

"Millennials across the country," Tony started, "are dying under mountains of student debt and low expectations. They mortgage their futures to pay for college, can't find jobs when they graduate, and don't believe in politicians of either party. But, if we can find simple answers that address these questions, frame answers you can articulate in repeated messages, I think the college-age demographic will take notice."

"Tough to do, Tony," Phelps replied with a frown, "when you're a fiscal conservative."

"I'm not talking about giving things away," Tony followed up, his voice warming to the spotlight. "What if we take back the free tuition already provided to illegals in Texas and promise to use that same money to help college students with their loans? It's revenue neutral but also shows kids we understand their biggest concern. And it's a nod toward the white minimum-wage earner who's frustrated about losing his job to a guest worker from Mexico. Plays well in Texas but also across the red states between the coasts."

Tony looked around the room and saw a mix of reactions. Phelps looked unhappy, Meadows mildly interested, but Zinger nodded. And Striker's face broke into a wide smile.

"Now we're talking!" the attorney general exclaimed. "Marshall, put the team onto this idea. I like it. We can capture the border nuts by fighting free tuition for illegals, plus we can offer free shit to our real voters without spending new money. And you know young voters love free shit." Striker laughed.

"I'll study it," Phelps grumbled, "but we need to move on now; there's lots more to cover."

After another couple of hours, Tony felt pleased he'd handled his role in the meeting with the command of a veteran operative. He'd never spoken out of turn, and he'd answered all the questions directed at him with relevant facts and figures. He thought he'd even seen a couple of admiring glances from the more experienced strategists. Striker's reaction, however, had been the most important. During the last break of the meeting, she'd slipped him a note while the other men were getting fresh coffee. It read:

Good job here today. Last week was tricky. Lots of eyes on me, but I don't care. Come fuck me tonight.

CHAPTER 36

Cat scurried around her kitchen prepping dinner as she waited for Sam to get home from his trip to Mayreau, but her mind wasn't on the fancy dish marinating on her counter. She was fixated on the emotions gnawing at her insides, a painful mix of conflicted feelings—joy and longing for Blake, sadness and guilt about her husband. Blake was sweeping her away again. Following that dream of an afternoon at the Hudson hotel, her safe and coded emails had now cascaded into risky and more frequent texts, and these communications had become the crack cocaine of her existence. Cat recognized it was stupid, and very dangerous, especially because of her inquisitive children, but she couldn't help herself. She had no idea how Blake was controlling the eyes around his messages but he'd assured her it was all safe. Cat struggled to get herself right before Sam walked in the door.

About 4:30 that afternoon, she fired off a text to Blake to notify him of her night ahead:

H coming back soon. Dinner with fam tonight. No more communications today. Hope your event went well. Xxxxxxxx

Cat hit Send and turned back to the stove to work, first plugging her phone into the charger tethered to a wall socket under her plate cabinet. As she always did, Cat swiped her text to Blake and punched the red Delete button. Then she tucked her phone behind the paper-towel dispenser. Cat dove back into her food preparations, working on a special meal for Sam and the kids, hoping a family dinner at home would prove to them—maybe to herself—that she was still committed to her marriage. Cat had called in to the restaurant and let her employees know that with Sam just back she'd be taking one more night off.

Twenty minutes later, Mitch sprinted into the kitchen.

"What's for dinner?" the eight-year-old asked as he slid across the hardwood floor in his socks.

"Your dad's favorite, red snapper." Cat smiled. "How does that sound?" She nudged her wine glass behind a large bowl to hide it from her son. Paige followed her brother into the kitchen.

"Why the fancy meal tonight?" the young girl asked.

"Your father will be home in a few minutes," Cat replied. "I thought it would be nice to surprise him."

At that moment, the front door opened, and seconds later Sam entered the kitchen, looking weary but undoubtedly pleased to be home. The kids bounded immediately to his side to embrace him. Cat held back, now feeling exposed about her infidelity, as if there were a video, hovering in the Cloud, of Blake kissing her. She waited a moment, then walked over and brushed her lips against Sam's.

"Welcome home," she greeted.

Her husband gave her a half hug and gazed at her. "Smells great," he mumbled, "and I'm exhausted and hungry. Let me wash up and get comfortable. Back in a few."

Mitch followed his dad out of the room but Paige stayed behind.

"You're really not going to the restaurant again tonight?" Paige asked.

"No, you're stuck with me one more night. That okay?"

Paige half smiled but Cat could sense that her daughter was holding back a smart-aleck reply. In that instant, terror struck. Just as Cat began tossing the salad, she noticed Paige eyeing her cell phone on the counter.

"I need to make a call," Paige said while disconnecting her mother's phone from the charger.

"Why don't you use your own?" Cat replied, her hands now trembling as her heart rate accelerated.

"C'mon Mom, yours is right here. Won't take a minute." Paige disappeared into the dining room and Cat felt the panic of a skydiver in freefall with a broken parachute. Despite all the precautions she'd taken in her messaging with Blake, Cat never felt comfortable when her phone was out of her control.

——————★——————

Blake leaned on his desk and sent a simple *K,xx* in response to Cat's text message about her family night before returning to his briefing book. He'd spent most of the late afternoon in his study preparing for the upcoming debate and working hard on the wedge issues Rags had scripted for him. He was doing his best to honor his commitment to Rags to keep his head down and grind forward but it wasn't easy; thoughts of Cat kept zipping into and out of his mind.

He looked up as the door opened and his wife stepped into the study. Faith locked herself in position and braced her arms tightly across her chest, staring at him.

"Have you spoken to her yet?" she asked.

"What do you mean?" Blake answered, his patience already worn thin over the familiar subject.

"You know *who* I mean." Faith's voice rose in agitation. "Our daughter, if you could pull your head out of your campaign long enough to pay attention."

"No, I haven't," he replied, letting out a long breath. Blake stood up from his chair to face his wife. "But if you're asking me if I will talk to her . . . of course I will."

"You should do it soon," Faith insisted.

"I'll handle it."

The discovery that his oldest daughter was a lesbian had

shocked Blake. Finley hadn't dated much in high school, few of her age group did for that matter, but he'd never seen any signs that she was gay. Then again he'd been gone a lot and, despite his close relationship with both daughters, he recognized he wasn't always in tune with the girls' lives as they'd matured, and there was no mistaking that Fin had grown more private.

Blake left Faith behind and walked upstairs to his older daughter's bedroom. He tapped on her closed door before pushing it forward.

"You dressed?" Blake called out.

"Come on in, Dad," Fin responded.

Blake stepped inside and saw Fin on her stomach, sprawled out on her bed with her laptop in front of her. "I'm Face-Timing with Jackie . . . hold on a sec."

Fin had grown up so much in the last year. Blake was astonished by how she'd gone from a gawky, gangly teen to a young woman with the model-thin figure and porcelain features of her mother.

"I'm done. What's up?" Fin straightened her body and crossed her legs in front of her.

Fin's bubbly mood made it even more difficult for Blake to approach the awkward subject.

"Your mother and I met with your college adviser the other day," he began.

"Really?" Fin acted surprised. Blake felt bad for catching her off guard this way.

"Yes," he replied with a slight smile. "Nothing's wrong . . . but something came up during our conversation that I need to talk to you about."

Fin's look turned more serious as she studied her father's face. "What do you mean?" she asked.

"It has to do with one of your applications."

A look of recognition spread across Fin's face and Blake knew she was already there. "You saw the Penn app?"

Blake nodded, almost embarrassed he'd brought it up.

"It's not what you think," Fin explained.

"What do I think?"

"Dad, I know you're running for governor, but I didn't expect anyone to see that app but the admissions folks. Who told you about it?"

"Forget my running for governor. I just wanted to talk to you."

"Stop!" Fin held up her hand. "And calm down. I'm not gay, if that's what you're asking."

"I don't care if you are," Blake responded with a set jaw as he positioned himself next to his daughter. "You know I'll support you no matter . . ."

"That's enough," Fin interrupted. "Please, Dad, slow down! No speeches. Listen to me. It was a prank, that's all." She sighed. "I know I shouldn't have lied on my application—and I'm sorry about that—but I don't have a girlfriend, I promise." Fin tucked her long lean legs under her. "My bad, but I never thought you'd see the stupid application. I'm not going to Penn anyway. It was dumb . . . just a way to test whether filling out that optional section mattered."

"I-I don't understand," Blake stammered.

"I was surprised, but a couple of the colleges included an optional section on their applications that give students a chance to check off their gender identity and sexual orientation. Apparently, it's permissible as long as it's not mandatory."

"Okay, that's new, but . . .?"

Fin patted her father's arm. "Very new," she agreed. "But the question was does it really create diversity. They already have boxes to check for race and ethnicity. I was more interested if it enhanced my chance of getting accepted. Not a very scientific test, and also pretty lame, but I never expected you, or anyone other than the folks at Penn, to see it." The young girl leaned over to hug her father. "I'm sorry, Dad. But even if I was gay, I wouldn't out myself right before your election!"

Blake's mind bounced from place to place and he didn't know whether to believe Fin or push deeper. One thing he was sure about was that he couldn't believe he was having this discussion with his little girl. It was only yesterday she was wearing pigtails and braces. "So what should I tell your mother?" he asked.

Fin rolled her eyes. "Tell her I'm gay! It would serve her right." She laughed, but there was an edge to her voice.

Blake cocked his head. That answer left him certain that Fin had told him all he needed to know.

"Give her any story you want," Fin continued, "but don't fret. I plan to have babies one day—with a man—just not for a long time."

"Well, I guess you've put me in my place."

"I know you wouldn't care if I was gay, even if you *are* a Republican. That's why you're the best and I love you. Now are you going to win this stupid election?"

Blake looked at his daughter and smiled. "Maybe I will."

CHAPTER 37

Several minutes passed after Paige left the kitchen with her mom's phone, and Cat moved from concern to full terror mode. She switched off the stove and stormed after her daughter.

"Paige," she yelled.

There was no reply at first but then Cat heard a crashing sound from the other side of the apartment and a muffled yell, and she realized something had gone horribly wrong. She raced to her bedroom and confronted her worst fears. Sam sat on the corner of their bed, her phone in his hand, his face red enough to explode. Pieces of a broken lamp lay scattered across the floor.

"What's wrong?" she asked.

Sam wouldn't look at her but held out her phone as though it were made of kryptonite. Cat wondered if she'd somehow missed the Delete button in her haste in the kitchen.

"Where's Paige?" Cat was terrified by Sam's expression, but she had to hold it together for her children.

Sam pointed toward the hallway and collapsed, head in hands.

Cat sprang out of the room before Sam launched into an assault. Paige and Mitch were the priority now and she needed to see them before the walls came crashing down. She raced across the hardwood floor and banged open Paige's door. She was relieved to find her daughter playing a game with her brother on his laptop. The wall-mounted television blared, which had apparently drowned out most of the noise coming from Sam's explosion.

"What's happening?" Paige asked without looking up from the computer screen. "Sounded like something broke in your room." Mitch didn't appear to be any more alarmed than his sister.

"It's nothing," Cat answered in the calmest voice she could muster. "Your dad accidentally knocked over the lamp when he was unpacking." Cat's heart was pounding. Fortunately, there was no sense of crisis in the room. She needed to keep it that way.

"Whatever," Paige said. "By the way, Dad has your phone now. I handed it to him after I tried to make my call."

"I was looking for it," Cat replied. "Thanks." A waterfall of relief cascaded over Cat's body. "I'm going to help Dad clean up the mess," she continued, "so we'll push dinner back about fifteen minutes. I'll call you when it's ready."

Buoyed by the notion Paige had likely missed the texts Sam had apparently seen, Cat now readied herself to deal with whatever her husband suspected—or knew.

She jumped back to her bedroom and found Sam slamming clothes into his suitcase. He'd dumped those from his trip all over the floor. "Sam, not this," she pleaded.

"What in the hell's wrong with you?" he screamed.

"I don't know what you've seen, but please give me a chance to explain. And I beg you, please keep your voice down. I told the kids you knocked over a lamp by accident."

Sam lowered the rage in his voice to a hoarse whisper. "Explain away. What lie can you spin about these texts?"

"I don't know what you're talking about," Cat replied.

Sam cocked his arm as if he was about to wing the phone at her, but instead pitched it underhanded across the floor. "Really? You've got to be fucking kidding. 'Husband's coming back soon.' Damn you, Cat!" Sam continued spiking clothes into his bag, his movements growing more violent by the second.

"Sam, please help me with the kids," Cat implored. She knew he was right to come apart, to be furious with her, but those emotions had to wait. "Please . . . Mitch and Paige don't need to hear any of this."

Sam paused for a minute. He glared at Cat and rubbed his hands through his sparse hair. "Go on, talk to the kids and I'll wait here. Since you appear to be so good at lying, you can come up with an explanation about why I'm leaving. Now get out of my sight."

Cat picked up the phone and left the room, so overcome with panic that she couldn't counter Sam's harsh words. She looked down at the text icon and saw Blake's return message—*K, xx*—along with her earlier one from the kitchen. Not explicit, but very incriminating.

Cat then fired off a short text to Blake—"*red alert, don't send me any other messages . . . it's over . . . no more communication*"—and then carefully deleted the short chain of messages as she reentered Paige's room. The kids were now lying on the bed watching television.

"Almost ready for dinner?" Cat asked.

Paige appeared to sense something was up but waited for her mother to say more. Mitch barely looked up.

"So Dad just got a call and he's got to run an errand on that new deal of his. I'm sorry, but it's just the three of us now." Cat forced a smile.

The children just looked at her and the pit in Cat's stomach grew deeper. She couldn't hide the fear spreading across her face. "Give me another minute to help him get ready," Cat followed up. "I'll be back in a sec."

Cat closed the door to Paige's room before the two of them could follow her out. She'd stemmed the tide, if only temporarily.

Cat raced back to Sam, where he waited with resentment steaming from his pores. He'd stopped packing his bag but his look could have burned a hole through his wife. "You've got one shot to tell me the truth," he growled. "And that's it."

Cat realized it was do-or-die time to save her marriage and she was determined to save it. Even if she and Sam weren't perfect together, he was the father of her children, and she'd do whatever it took to protect them.

———— ★ ————

Blake read Cat's incoming text and banged his head against his desk. Whatever earthquake had struck in New York, the tremors had spread all the way to Houston. Fear gripped him in a way he'd never known. How could he have been so stupid to text her? Until the past week, they'd exchanged secure emails only, but now their excitement after their recent liaison had made them reckless. His thoughts reached out to Cat—he wanted to help her in some way—but his mind vaulted back to his family and the campaign. *What had he done?*

Blake stood up and staggered to the bathroom across the hallway, bent over the toilet, and threw up.

CHAPTER 38

The debates were less than a week away and Marshall Phelps had somehow managed to get the Striker campaign back under his control. The pro-life bus tour had come to an end without incident, he'd regained the A.G.'s confidence after constructing a hip, young voter's theme called "Striking Forward," and he'd kept the dangerous Tony León away from important decisions. Phelps still didn't think much of his candidate—she remained more enamored with magazine covers than policy—but he could do little to change that. His job was only to get her elected and then hand over her oversized ego to the citizens of Texas. Now that he'd received inquiries from the cable television shows about post-election work, he had an even bigger financial incentive to get Striker to the finish line. Phelps had just one last task to accomplish, and it would be the truest test of his "new relationship" with the candidate. He'd waited several days to get her attention and she'd finally agreed to stop by his office before heading to a dinner appearance at the Houston Wildcatters Club.

Striker walked in to see him at 6:00 p.m., her usual look of flushed importance painted on her face. "Why do you need to see me, Marshall?" she asked.

"Please sit down," he responded. "This won't take long."

Phelps's smooth baritone appeared to reduce Striker's anxiety and she slipped out of her black jacket and eased into one of his chairs. "Okay, you've got my attention," she said.

Phelps walked around his desk and sat in the chair across

from the attorney general. Striker's eyes looked noticeably tired tonight, and her makeup was caked and uneven, a departure from her typically immaculate appearance. While Striker remained a very attractive woman, the tired version would not do. She needed to look rested and fresh for appearances like the Wildcatters Club. "You sleeping enough?" he asked.

Striker twisted her head and half-frowned. "Marshall," she protested. "Cut the bullshit. What's wrong?"

"General," he started, "the polls look good and these upcoming debates should cement your lead . . . as long as we play it smart." He handed her a sheet of paper with the latest field research.

"I know, I know," Striker responded without even looking down at the report. "We've been through all of this. I'm ready—you know that."

"But we still have that lingering vulnerability."

"I'm ready there, too. C'mon, Marshall, you approved the damn strategy." She smiled and began to rise.

"That's not the vulnerability I meant."

Striker paused, sighed, and dropped back into her chair. "Not again. So you want me to get rid of him?"

It was the response Phelps had hoped for. His persistence had finally paid off—she wasn't biting his head off this time at the mere suggestion. "Yes, like yesterday."

"God, you're a pain in the ass."

"Just tell me he doesn't have anything compromising on you."

"Hell no," Striker declared. "There were a couple of photos that I made him delete, and I'm sure he doesn't have anything else. He would never take that kind of risk anyway."

"Don't be too sure of that," Phelps responded.

"I'm sure of it."

"So we're in agreement?"

"Yes," she answered. "I'll tell him first thing in the morning. That satisfy you? Get the little shit a job somewhere. Okay?"

"Yes, ma'am, I will."

———————— ★ ————————

Tony arrived in the office extra early and was surprised when Striker texted him at 6:30 a.m. She rarely communicated in the morning, and the attorney general offered no clue about what she had in mind, except that she wanted to meet with him outside the office, in a public place, around nine. The next few hours were torture as Tony waited for the meeting.

Grace Striker arrived at the park outside their campaign headquarters about 9:15. She dismissed her security detail with a curt wave of the hand and stared at Tony. Her sour expression told him she was carrying bad news.

"Let's move to that bench over there," she suggested. Tony looked to his right and saw an area with no people around.

"What's going on?" he asked once they sat down.

Striker fumbled through her purse for a minute, pulled out a cigarette, and lit up.

"Smoking again?"

"No, just today."

"That sounds cryptic."

"Tony, I have to take you off the campaign," Striker blurted out as she took a deep drag off her Virginia Slim and exhaled.

"Why?"

"You know why. The closer we get to this election, the more I'm being scrutinized. You're just too big a risk right now."

Tony wasn't shocked—this outcome had always been a possibility—but he hadn't expected how vulnerable he'd feel upon actually hearing the news. "Phelps behind this?" he asked.

"Of course he is, but I'm in agreement. It's best if you leave today. I don't think I could control myself if you stayed around." She forced a smile before taking another drag off her cigarette.

"So what do I do? Box up my shit and live on the street?"

"This isn't a public execution," she explained. "We'll just

184

announce you took a new job. Say the offer was too good to pass up."

Tony wasn't sure what the right move was at this point. He valued Phelps's promise to set him up in San Antonio, but he still wasn't sure he could trust the man. "The world's going to believe I was canned," he complained.

"Marshall will find you a job . . . I promise. A good one may take a little time but he'll get it done. And once I'm governor, there will be other things I can do for you. Just keep quiet for now. This will all work out."

Tony tried to control his emotions but he felt himself panicking in spite of his resolve to stay calm. The truth was he was being banished, fired like a stock boy, after everything he'd done for her. "I can't believe this," Tony whined with a pained expression.

Striker glared at him without a trace of sympathy.

"Can't we just cool it for a while?" Tony pleaded. "I've done all that you've ever asked of me."

Striker's body language transformed as her patience, the little she had, expired. He knew what was next.

"Tony," she said with a piercing gaze. "Just accept it. This has been coming for weeks and I've told you that I'll take care of you. That should be enough. I can't afford any mistakes right now." Striker then sprang up as if she was ready to leave, reached over, and patted him on the shoulder.

Tony sat frozen in place.

The attorney general extinguished her cigarette as if she was stomping on a bug. It might as well have been him. "Be a good boy," she advised, "and I'll make it up to you at some point." She turned and strutted away.

CHAPTER 39

Jackson Goodrich popped open a beer, manipulated his TV remote, and punched in the number for one of the stations broadcasting the debate. He hadn't followed the progress of the Texas gubernatorial campaign, and according to his newsroom, the race was still not competitive. Grace Striker carried a fourteen-to-twenty-point lead and the two scheduled debates would likely be inconsequential in reducing that spread. But Jackson had a reason to watch the television this night. Rags Beckham had promised to finally pay off on their agreement. The minute the debate was over, Beckham was to fire off an exclusive on Grace Striker that would turn her campaign—and maybe the political world—upside down. Rags provided no details, but he'd promised that the attorney general would cover herself with lies and contradictions during the debate and those would make the forthcoming disclosures even more compelling.

In exchange for that promise, Jackson had agreed not to reveal Blake Buchanan's relationship with the married woman in New York. Of course, Jackson understood that his agreement to bury his story made his "threats" to Beckham less valuable every day, but in truth, he didn't care about Buchanan's affair. Deep down, Jackson didn't value an exposé about an obscure politician's personal life, but capturing an emerging national figure, like Striker, in a web of lies was altogether different. And now that he'd heard his old "friend," Tony León, had parted ways with the Striker campaign, most likely because he was fired, the reporter saw the potential for a headline-spinning scandal before him.

Jackson placed his beer on the side table, kicked up his feet, and grabbed his pen and pad.

CHAPTER 40

November 15

Blake sat backstage at the conference hall at the University of Texas campus and rehearsed his debate lines. Tonight was his last best chance to ignite his campaign and he had to be perfect if he was going to effect Rags's strategy. But even amidst his swirling thoughts on this, the biggest night of his political career, Blake's mind continued to fixate on Cat Alexander. He wondered if she might be watching.

The fact that his campaign, his marriage, and his world had survived Cat's husband's discovery of their affair still amazed him. Miraculously, in his orbit, only Rags knew the truth, and somehow Cat had convinced her husband that whatever had happened wasn't serious enough to merit a divorce. Cat's voice mail message from the day after the incident had been direct.

I can't communicate with you at all. If I do my life's over. I'll lose my kids and Sam will destroy your life as well. I couldn't live with either of those two things. Don't call me, text, or try to reach me in any way. Good luck my darling. I wish you every happiness with your life . . . and with the election. Cat.

That had been it. Not another word, not another email, not another message of any kind followed. Despite his grief, Blake buried his disappointment in policy papers, rehearsing his debate lines, and spending every other waking minute talking to voters in coffee shops, manufacturing plants, and rotary clubs.

Rags thundered through Blake's door with an exultant look on his face. "You ready?" he asked. "It's show time."

"Yep." Blake smiled, trying to sound more confident than he felt. "Let's go see if we can make a race out of this thing."

———— ★ ————

Over an hour into the debate, moderated by local television anchor Roger Patman, Blake still hadn't laid a glove on Striker. She'd used her time as if she was running out the clock, rarely engaging or tussling with him (or the even-more-distant third candidate Dodds), and she'd perfected the classic front-runner strategy of bobbing and weaving. She'd smiled and charmed, and never gotten too far over her skis on any answers. On the other end of the stage, Dodds was his normal windbag self, pontificating on morality at every opportunity and smiling for the cameras but never seriously attempting to knock Striker off her game. Blake was beginning to feel deflated, even though the debate had twenty minutes left. That's when the question he'd been praying for finally came up.

"General Striker," the moderator began, "you've made life, and the rights of the unborn, a central theme of your campaign. Why have you done so, and what will you do as governor to further limit abortion in Texas given *Roe v. Wade* remains the law of the land?"

Striker straightened her back, pursed her lips, and stared at the camera. Blake could tell the woman had been waiting for this softball. "Today," she opened, "we live in a world where the most basic human liberty—the right to life—has been taken away by those in positions of power within our government. My bus tour around this state confirmed to me that Texans believe that life at any stage is sacred, and they want their leaders to protect the unborn, any way possible, through any—legal—means available. Anyone can see by my record as attorney general that I've taken aggressive action to limit and constrain the impact of *Roe v. Wade*. I've prosecuted unlicensed abortion clinics throughout the state and shut down two Planned Parenthood centers where my investigators found evidence of fetal tissue sales. I've spent my entire life fighting to combat the pernicious stain the *Roe* opinion has branded on our country's history. Many innocent women, convinced abortion is their only choice, then go through life regretting that horrible decision. You have my promise to support those women who make the right choices . . . and I'll continue my crusade as governor of this state."

Next it was Dodds's turn to respond to the question.

"God," he intoned, "has spoken to me many times on this subject. We, as Texans and Americans, must build a culture in our state and country that protects the rights of the unborn, where every single life is valued and protected, and where we as individuals stand up as God's warriors. We must speak from the pulpits both inside and outside of our churches and be cognizant to remember our Lord and Savior's words at all times—that He formed us in the womb, and before we were born, consecrated us in his image, and that He wants all of his creatures, great and small, to be sanctified in life."

Blake found himself mesmerized by Dodds's booming eloquence. The man could flat out preach. Yet, Blake focused on something Striker had said during her remarks. He wasn't sure what it was about her tone or inflection, but he was almost certain she'd foreseen his coming attack. Was it possible she knew?

When Dodds finished, Blake pivoted toward Striker. "General," he began, "you say you value life and have staked your career on that principle. And yet, we live in a society where unwanted pregnancies are common and real-life decisions must be made every day by women, many times in desperate and tragic circumstances. So my question to you is simple—can you tell the voters of Texas what you would do if faced with an unwanted pregnancy?"

The crowd murmured as if confused by Blake's departure from the debate format. Up to this point, none of the candidates had directly confronted their opponents, following the rule announced at the outset by the moderator. Blake could see his deviation from protocol had startled Striker.

"Mr. Patman," the attorney general responded while resting her hands on each side of her podium, "are we asking questions of each other now? With all due respect, Senator Buchanan is out of line."

"Direct questions," the intimidated moderator politely admonished, "are not permitted by our rules, that's true. Mr. Buchanan, you should respond to my original question on *Roe v. Wade*. You're not to direct questions at General Striker or Reverend Dodds."

The moderator had assisted Striker, at least temporarily, so Blake had to adjust and hope Patman did his job. "My question to the attorney general," Blake explained, "has everything to do with my answer. Abortion, and the question of whether a woman has the right to control her own reproductive rights, is profoundly personal. What I think as a man, or even as governor, is irrelevant to what an eighteen-year-old rape victim, or a twenty-two-year-old pregnant college student, or a middle-aged mother with health risks thinks about it. Life doesn't come wrapped in perfect boxes. Yes, our culture values human dignity—and life—and yes, we should defend the most vulnerable in our society, but we must also value women and their right to control their bodies. We can embrace life, as I do—but *Roe v. Wade* is the law of this land. Women have the right to an abortion in the narrow, protected circumstances presented by our Supreme Court, and as your governor, it won't be my priority to undermine that decision. But I'd still like to hear General Striker's answer to my question. Her answer may enlighten us all."

Patman paused, tilted his head as if considering his options, and then hesitantly asked, "General, what would you do if faced with an unwanted pregnancy?"

The crowd in the small auditorium went silent. A tension gripped the room and Blake watched as Striker calculated her thoughts. His campaign team had anticipated she had two options—one, a Michael Dukakis moment, where the candidate showed no emotional reaction to the dramatic question, or the second, hoped for response, an outright lie. To Blake's chagrin, neither happened. Striker crumpled; she dabbed her eyes with a tissue, and then she stepped around the podium to address the audience from the front of the stage. The viewers collectively held their breath.

Striker glanced at the microphone on her lapel, then turned toward the sound man, and he signaled she was live.

"Mr. Patman," Striker started, "there's something I've been waiting to talk about with the people of Texas for a long time. Senator Buchanan's now given me a chance to reflect on a very dark place in my life. This may be the most difficult two minutes I'll ever go through." Striker shuffled her feet, looked down for a moment, then raised her head to reveal watery eyes. "I was raped as a young woman," she declared. A collective gasp rippled across the crowd. "And I became pregnant. At the time, I was on my own, and had no idea what to do or who to turn to—I was so young." Striker hesitated and drew a deep breath. "Shame prevented me from telling my parents and fear stopped me from going to the police. I made the decision to abort the pregnancy." Tears streaked down her cheeks, and Blake realized that Striker had transformed the damaging disclosure into a transcendent moment. "I've lived ever since with that horrible decision," she continued, "the shame, the guilt, the loss of life. And I've regretted it every day since. Abortion isn't just the physical death of an unborn child but the emotional death of the mother." She paused again and dried her wet cheeks. "That is why I've dedicated my life since that dreadful day to erasing that stain from my past, by preaching, praying, and fighting for the sanctity of life. And to try to help others avoid the same mistake." She walked slowly back to the podium, then stopped and clutched her chest. "That, Mr. Buchanan," she whispered, "is my answer."

Without thinking, Blake rushed to Striker's side to console her. In that moment, as his back shielded the audience from the face of his weeping opponent, Blake briefly locked eyes with the flushed woman. It came in a flash—imperceptible to all but Blake—yet it was unmistakable. Striker winked at him.

CHAPTER 41

Marshall Phelps couldn't believe what he'd witnessed on his backstage monitor. Yes, he'd discussed the possibility of a disclosure with Striker in the past, even practiced it several times, but he'd never expected her to go through with this type of come-to-Jesus revelation. The risk was too high, the potential scrutiny too intense, and the timing suicidal. But she'd pulled it off—a virtuoso Clintonesque turn that even Phelps had to admire. Striker had transformed a ruinous situation into the defining moment of her political career. The candidate appeared so authentic, so human, so real, that the weepy confession—although untrue—had the potential to transform her image overnight, garner her huge national press, and light up the internet for days. She'd be booked on every important news outlet in the country by morning. Phelps shook his head. He'd underestimated the woman.

As directed, Striker bypassed the press after the debate and returned to the private dressing area she'd been assigned. There Phelps waited and greeted her with a grudging smile. She plopped down in front of him and kicked off her pumps. "What'd you think?" she asked.

"You pulled it off," he replied. "Fucking masterful."

"You act surprised."

"I'm rarely surprised in this business. You surprised me."

"Buchanan knew something," Striker posited. "I'm sure of it. I felt him setting me up like the weasel lawyer he is. He was positioning himself the whole debate for that question. I don't know how much information he has, but he's got his sniffer pointed my direction. I couldn't take a chance."

"You've got good instincts. I thought the same damn thing. Maybe they found someone willing to talk."

"Hard to find someone to contradict me since there never was a rapist." Striker's ease with embracing the fake rape story worried Phelps more than he let on.

"Yes, ma'am, I understand. But we need to practice your responses right now. There are reporters out there who will have questions. We can't keep them waiting too long. And my phone's already buzzing for interviews tomorrow morning. We need to be ready. Your story needs to be perfect."

"Then let's get on with it," she said.

———————— ★ ————————

Rags dialed Jackson's number before the debate was even over. He figured the itchy reporter had seen the dramatic confession and might already believe he'd been double-crossed.

"I guess you're going to tell me this rape confession was a surprise," Jackson said without even acknowledging it was Rags calling.

"I don't have to answer that question," Rags replied.

"She's very resourceful, that woman. I presume you were going to tell me about the abortion so I could scoop the world."

"That was the plan . . . after Blake set her up in the debate."

"But she played you with her teary confession."

"Something like that. As you can tell, my candidate's mortally wounded, if he wasn't already. I'm the one to blame for sitting on the story, not him."

"I understand your strategy. You wanted to catch her in the big lie. I get it. What will appease me now is the evidence. I may not get the story first, but I might still beat the *Times* on the details. What do you know about the rapist, or should I say alleged rapist?"

"Is our deal good if I give you that? You understand we'd heard rumors about an abortion but we had no idea about the rape."

"I believe that," Jackson responded. "And no, I'm not interested in your man, or Catherine Alexander, if that's your question. I don't have any plans to run that story."

"In that case, I'll give you what I have. Get your pen out."

CHAPTER 42

Alone in her restaurant office, Cat turned on the *Fox News Channel* and watched the debate on her computer. She missed much of the broadcast—work had pulled her away for part of the evening—but she'd shut the door and taken in the last forty minutes without interruption. Although impressed with Blake's steady confidence and debating style, Cat recognized the devastating impact of his opponent's stunning confession. Yet, while Striker's act had been brilliant in many ways, something didn't sit right with Cat. A politician who'd spent all her public life moralizing about the sanctity of life while hiding a secret teenage abortion didn't have much credibility, in her view.

Then the irony slapped Cat across the face. She was having an affair—or had just finished one—with Striker's opponent. He had no moral high ground to stand on, even if Striker was a bald-faced liar.

Cat's memories of Blake had been the one good thing about her life since the *incident*. Sam had made a show of avoiding her since then, burying himself in work on his new deal in Mayreau, which from the little he'd shared, appeared to be going well. She, in turn, had found herself spending even more hours at the restaurant, if only to avoid the suffocating silence that surrounded her time with her husband. She'd reached for him one night in an effort to start repairing the damage, but had received only a turned shoulder and a hostile attitude. And even when they'd finally made love, Sam was a punitive and detached partner. He hadn't forgiven her, and she feared he never would. When Sam had confronted her a second time over the details of her relationship with the *adulterer* from Texas—this time without the anger or accusations—the ensuing conversation done nothing to remove the cloud hanging over their marriage.

"Did you sleep with him?" Sam had asked, as if starting to compile the facts he'd need for his divorce lawyer.

"No," Cat had lied. "I saw him in Houston when I was down there visiting Mom. I went to his campaign event, out of curiosity, and we spoke for a couple of minutes. I shouldn't have gone; I understand that. And then we communicated a few times after that by text and over a period of weeks I obviously—I don't know—started thinking we were more familiar with each other than we really were. I'm ashamed of my messages and wish I could pull them all back."

Sam had never said a word while she went through the humiliating disclosure again, as if he was comparing her answers to the ones she'd given the first night, and the repeat story only seemed to exacerbate their estrangement. Cat wasn't sure how long it would take for her home life to be normal again, but she was committed to making the frustrating effort, no matter the personal toll.

Cat went back and forth to the restaurant floor several times after watching Striker's theatrics on her computer but she was still thinking about Blake when she returned to her office about an hour after the debate was over. At that point, her office phone rang, interrupting her thoughts. No one but her manager and business advisers ever called this line so she jerked up the receiver and answered, "Sharon?"

"Nope," Blake responded. "It's me."

"You have to be kidding. How did you know I was here?"

"Took a chance," he explained. "I figured this was the only safe place to call." His voice sounded totally deflated.

"That's true but nothing's safe anymore. You know that."

"Yes, I do, but Cat I've felt so horrible since that text. And after tonight's fiasco, I just had to call."

"Fiasco. I don't think that's fair."

"Forget that," Blake interrupted. "How are you?"

"It's good to hear your voice," she conceded. "You can imagine things haven't been very good here, but at least the kids don't seem to be affected. Sam's going to take a lot longer but that will improve, I hope. He's not leaving me, at least I don't think he is."

"I'm grateful for that," Blake replied.

"It's tough right now and I sometimes wonder why he's staying. I hate to think it, but in some ways it feels like our finances are holding us together as much as the kids are."

"What do you mean?"

"No, forget that. Sorry, I shouldn't have brought that up." Cat felt bad, maybe even disloyal again, for inserting this deeply sensitive layer of her relationship with Sam into her conversation with Blake. "All I should say is that Sam's struggled for a number of years with his work and just recently latched on to a new deal he thinks will turn things around. The timing's ironic. That's all I meant."

"This is completely my fault. I'm so sorry, Cat."

"You aren't to blame for my problems. I did this to myself. At this point, nothing really matters to me other than Paige and Mitch anyway. They've been my comfort through all of this and I'm fighting to save them. Whether Sam forgives me or not is secondary to protecting my children."

"I don't know what to say."

"There's not much to say, and I don't want to talk anymore about this. But I did see the end of the debate. How's the press reacting?"

"I just finished a group of interviews and it wasn't pretty. Striker's the star. I'll be lucky to even get a mention in the stories tomorrow, although some will ridicule me for helping her on the stage. I'm not sure what else I could have done."

"I don't have much time—neither do you—but I believe you did the right thing going to her side. You were reacting as the decent human being you are to another person's suffering. No one will penalize you for that."

"Thanks for the encouragement."

"By the way, just in case you didn't notice, that woman's a liar."

Blake imagined Cat's knowing gesture. "The liar bit me pretty hard," he said with a halfhearted chuckle. "But I have to say you're quite perceptive. The phony winked at me when I was helping her on stage."

"Why am I not surprised? Hang in there . . . you'll get through this."

"Cat, it doesn't have to be the end."

"You know my answer to that."

"I guess I do. But I'm still going to stay in touch."

"I told Sam I was cutting off all contact. This phone, too, is off-limits after tonight. Maybe a note every now and then on our secure Gmail accounts but nothing more. We have to protect ourselves. At all costs. Do you understand?"

"When this race is over, I'm going to . . ."

"Blake, stop! No more loose talk!" A frozen moment passed as both hesitated. "I have to go now," Cat said, breaking the standoff. "Go dig into that woman's story. There's a hole in it somewhere. And Blake, this has to be it. We can't take any more chances."

"Yes, I know. But promise me, and I mean promise, you'll call if you ever need me. For anything."

"I don't have much choice about loving you," she answered in a softer voice. "Now go win your election. Someday all of this will make sense. Goodbye, Blake." Cat set the phone down, and an overwhelming emptiness filled her heart. Tears welled in her eyes just as she heard the hostess call her name.

CHAPTER 43

Rags paced around the small stacks of files that dotted his office floor like anthills before lighting on a spot and calling Taylor Brooks. Rags had a day, maybe two, before the political news cycle permanently sanctified Grace Striker's confession. He needed something from Brooks, and fast.

"Hey, Rags," Brooks answered.

"What's the latest?" Rags asked.

Brooks and his crew had spent almost all of their time searching for evidence of Striker's secret abortion, but his men had struck out time and time again. Rumors had leaked out of Abilene for years about Striker's teenage pregnancy, but confirming them had been impossible. The identity of the man—the now-alleged rapist—was unknown, and records of the clinic where Striker said the procedure was performed had supposedly been destroyed. The tidbits Rags had used to interest Jackson Goodrich appeared to be dead ends now, and the fawning mainstream media had quickly drowned out Goodrich's initial piece, which had proven vague and inconsequential. Rags feared it was over for Blake and his campaign, unless Brooks could pull out a miracle for them.

"They didn't just plan this weepy confession yesterday," Brooks replied to Rags's question. "Phelps knew this might be coming one day and that's why he cleaned her story up early. Rape, my ass. Reporters are crawling all around Abilene but there's nothing to be found."

"It's my fault," Rags said. "I should have got this out there sooner. I waited too long."

"Bullshit," the investigator replied. "You did what any professional would do. We needed to catch her in a lie first. We had no real proof and still don't."

"So what about your work? Anyone new pop up now that the story's out there?"

"Nope. The rapist angle has a lot of folks interested but Striker claims she never knew the rapist's real name, and the clinic where she had the procedure was shut down long ago. Hell, as A.G., she may have shuttered it herself. There are no records to be found. And no one in the press appears willing to challenge her on the details anyway. About the only thing we do know from her interviews this morning is that she pinned the date of the abortion to her early years in college."

"That's something, isn't it?"

"It might be if we had a name or if the clinic was still around."

"Shit," Rags replied. "And there's no other source for records about the abortion?"

"Any that Striker's folks have are locked up in a vault somewhere in Siberia. You know that."

"You're not doing much for me here, Taylor."

"I did have one last thought," Brooks offered. "I talked to an old college classmate of Striker's last night who said our A.G. had a sometime boyfriend in the early years at Abilene Christian. From what the friend described, Striker was dating him in the general time frame of the so-called rape. The guy lives in Tennessee now. Not sure he knows anything but I thought it might be worth a trip up there. That's my best shot."

"Hell yes," Rags shouted while stomping his foot. "Get on a plane right away. And please bring me some good news." Rags hung up, looked at the ceiling in exasperation, and resumed pacing. His phone beeped again just as he dropped it in his pocket.

"Rags Beckham," he answered, unfamiliar with the number

showing up on his digital display.

"Mr. Beckham, my name's Tony León. We haven't met before but I'd like to talk to you, in private. I have some information you might find helpful to your campaign."

Rags stopped dead in his tracks as a surge of adrenaline coursed through his body. "I know who you are," he said. "But why should I trust meeting with you? You work—or did work—for General Striker."

"Things change, Mr. Beckham. Thursday afternoon, I'll be at the Hampton Inn on Sage at three. Come in the hotel lobby. I know what you look like."

CHAPTER 44

Cat's mind meandered as she walked the few blocks between her apartment and the yoga studio. She wondered if Sam would show up for the class, something he'd begun doing more of late, in his not-so-subtle way of needling her. He didn't trust her, and if she was being honest with herself, he didn't like her either. She could tell he was enjoying these random "meetings." Yoga had always been her time, her private space with girlfriends, and she hated it when Sam forced himself into her group. He was an unwelcome presence among the women, and Cat's friends, Abbie included, now chose to scoot off after class rather than staying behind and visiting with her over a cup of coffee. But Cat knew that Sam's awkward appearances were her fault and there was nothing she could do but endure them until the Blake episode faded away.

A block from the studio, Cat heard a loud crashing sound behind her and wheeled around to find two cars interlocked by bumpers. Traffic snarled within seconds, and a taxi driver vaulted out of one car and began yelling at the offending motorist in a language only a cabbie could understand. Every car within earshot blared its horn and a classic New York traffic pileup quickly engulfed the area. In that brief moment, she spotted him again. A tall, bald-headed man in sunglasses who appeared to be hanging around a storefront some fifty feet behind her. The same man she'd seen several times over the past week.

———— ★ ————

Blake flicked on his Bluetooth application and connected his iPhone to the small speaker on the corner of his desk. He scrolled through his playlists and chose a collection of eighties tunes, starting with one that struck his mood—"Faithfully" by Journey. As the music began to relax him, Blake thought more about the aftermath of Grace Striker's stunning announcement. No fewer than five national news programs had interviewed the attorney general to discuss her "confession." In every case, the reporters had avoided asking tough questions, either worried over viewer pushback if they were to question a rape victim's story or too enamored with Striker to confront her. Instead, they'd lobbed softballs focusing on Striker's anguish in coming forward with her secret. Any hopes that a backlash might form over her gamesmanship were dashed when a post-debate poll showed her lead swelling to a gluttonous twenty points. And that was before the ever-flexible Reverend Dodds had piled on by announcing that God had told him to withdraw from the race and throw his support behind the A.G.

The beeping light on his phone pulled Blake out of his musings and he grabbed it off his desk.

"What's up?" he asked.

"You need to get over here right now," Rags snapped.

"What's going on?"

"Get here and I'll explain. And please hurry. This can't wait."

———— ★ ————

"What's got you so worked up?" Blake asked as he entered his campaign headquarters.

Rags ushered the candidate into his office, locked the door, and closed the blinds. "Guess who wants to come in from the cold?"

"You've got me."

"Tony León."

"The young kid Striker was boffing?"

Rags nodded. "Striker fired him. I guess he became too big a liability for her."

"And?"

"He's looking for a home . . . and a little money."

Blake knew what that meant. "What kind of money?"

"Enough that his information has to be game changing. That's all you need to know."

"Do we have the resources?"

"That's my job, remember?"

"So why am I here?"

"Because no one knows about this but Tony, me, and now . . . you. I can't tell you any more, but I do need to get your blessing. It's a risk, for sure, but we don't have many options now."

"And we won't know what this information is until after we've bought it?"

"Something like that."

"I don't know, Rags, maybe he's a Trojan horse. Didn't our pollster say a sex story about Striker would backfire this late in the game? I thought we'd given up on that angle."

"I'm not sure that's what he's peddling. Listen Blake, she's a fraud. We both know it. That rape story is total bullshit. I need to find a way to expose her. It's all we have."

"This is the kind of politics I was going to stay away from. And it sounds desperate."

"I know."

Blake looked to the heavens and wondered how it always came back to this. Politics was such a sordid business. It was almost as if the unseemly money he'd accepted from the Booze Brothers had been parked in his campaign account waiting for a Benedict Arnold from Striker's camp to parachute in. But virtue be damned. Blake was tired of having his teeth kicked in every day and he needed something to give his troops hope.

Blake stood up and walked to the door before turning back

to Rags. He drew a deep breath and ran his fingers through his hair. "Do it," he said.

CHAPTER 45

"We own it now," Marshall Phelps announced to his staff at their morning meeting at headquarters. "We've earned all the positive spin we're going to get, and remember, no one comments about the story. No one. Not one damn peep. Direct any further press to me. Everyone clear?"

The young staffers collectively nodded and chorused, "Yes, sir."

"Get to work then," Phelps barked.

The seven men and women in Phelps's office dispersed like their pants were on fire and the campaign manager then slid behind his desk and picked up his cell phone. He punched in Grace Striker's private line.

"Marshall," she answered.

"Free to talk?"

"I'm alone in my room practicing. I leave in thirty minutes. What's the latest?"

"The story seems to be contained. No one is questioning the rape allegation and your pain in those interviews convinced everyone . . . including me. That's all good. But I have one other concern. Our friend Tony went to see Beckham. You certain he doesn't have any information to peddle?"

"The little bastard. Damn him. I assure you he doesn't have anything from me. I'm positive."

"I hope so, but we'll keep watching him. My guess is he's been telling them about his extracurricular role in your campaign."

Phelps paused as if to say *I told you so.* "I just need your approval to handle him my way."

"Want me to call?"

"No, he's my job."

"Okay, handle it. What else?"

"We need to start our prep for the second debate. I'll get you a new briefing book in the next couple of days. You'll have over a month to get ready but I want you to commit all of the data to memory over the holidays. When this rape story finally dies down, you'll need to be crisp and tight on your policy positions and the financial numbers. It's time we show the state what a real governor looks like."

"Maybe Buchanan will drop out before the next debate," Striker mused. "The sanctimonious bastard can't have much money left except what those bloodsucking Jarrett brothers keep giving him. I can't wait to fix those assholes."

"Yes ma'am," Phelps replied. "You'll have plenty of time to rip them a new one after March fourth. And yeah, their booze money is keeping Buchanan alive. But remember, at this point, he's little more than a gnat on an elephant's back. Your focus is Iowa, and that begins the day after this election. The race is right where we want it to be. Just tell me again there's nothing I've missed on this rape story. We can't leave any angle uncovered before we get to the national stage."

"There's nothing else," she answered.

Phelps wondered if he'd heard hesitation in her voice or if he was just giving in to his deepest fears. "That's what I wanted to hear," he exclaimed. "We'll talk again soon."

Phelps clicked off his phone and walked into the busy exterior room set up with rows of tables and cubicles for volunteers. He spied the burly Farrukh "Boots" Ali sitting alone and signaled to him. The Pakistan-born Ali, with a deep-treaded face and blacksmith's hands, hustled across the room. Phelps had first met Boots years before in one of the poker houses where only the most serious of gamblers played, and they'd struck up a useful business relationship. Boots had worked for Phelps a handful of times since, and their ventures had always been successful—and discrete. "Investigator" was on Boots Ali's business card, but cleaning up was his specialty.

———— ★ ————

Tony decided to give Phelps one last chance before cashing in with the Buchanan campaign. He fidgeted with his hands as a cooling breeze eased through the trees surrounding the secluded area in the back of the cemetery where he waited.

Tony knew Phelps had been watching him; that was the crazy campaign manager's style. As much as he now despised the man, Tony had developed a grudging respect for the crusty politico. Phelps's experience and network had won out, at least for now, and he'd proven too valuable for Striker to discard. With the candidate behind Phelps, Tony's banishment had become inevitable. But Tony wasn't the fool Phelps played him for—he'd kept his eyes and ears open and now he had a trunkful of secrets to use if Phelps didn't come through.

Tony watched Phelps march toward their rendezvous point with a scowl painted across his face.

"Bad fucking idea," Phelps griped as he approached.

"I never trusted your boss would live up to our deal so I held on to some insurance," Tony said, launching right into his business. He hoped he looked more confident than he felt. "They're willing to pay me a lot of money," Tony bragged.

"My word wasn't good enough for you?"

"Probably would've been if I didn't know your candidate so well."

"Tony, I told you I'd find you another campaign. And you're smart enough to know that trading inside information isn't going to enhance your reputation in our business. You'll be iced out by all factions of our party. Is that what you want?"

Tony shuffled his feet but didn't answer.

"As for your so-called information, you have two options." Phelps glowered before reaching into his pocket for a handkerchief and blowing his nose. "One, rethink my offer and accept what's about to happen, knowing that it could get worse. Or, two, continue down your current path and I guarantee it will get worse. Got it?"

The cold look in Phelps's eyes assured Tony the negotiations were over and no handshake was coming. "I've protected myself," Tony countered. "If something happens to me, my files go to the police."

Phelps didn't bite. Frowning, he explained, "Tony, I'm going to pretend that we aren't having this conversation. Our deal about San Antonio is still on, but I don't want to see or hear from you again until this election's over. Do you understand?"

In that frozen moment, Tony recognized what was about to happen. The crumpling of leaves nearby caused him to lurch to his right, but Tony was too late as a heavy presence emerged to his left. For a brief flash, he caught a glimpse of dark skin and movement, but then the sweeping fury of Farrukh Ali's giant fist blocked out all light.

CHAPTER 46

A demoralized Blake hadn't been home in several days and he expected little comfort from his wife as he pulled into his garage about 7:30 p.m. Blake hadn't spoken much with Faith while on the road, except the night of the debate, when she'd called to gig him about how much she admired his "gallantry" in consoling Striker on-stage. That biting pile on hadn't sat well and their conversation had ended abruptly. Based on a couple of texts since, Blake believed his wife's sole fixation now was on Fin's sexual preference, even though their daughter had debunked the lesbian story to her father several times. For whatever reason, Faith couldn't let the subject drop and she continued to push Blake to become more direct in questioning Fin about her sexuality.

The campaign's disastrous week made coming home even worse. Although the unexpected León contact had created some hope with Rags, even Blake's most optimistic followers, including his daughters who'd stopped their daily supportive texts, seemed to question the viability of his listing ship of a campaign. Before getting out of his car, Blake scribed a quick email to Cat to divert his mind from the grim reality in front of him:

I'm sitting alone right now wondering what I'm doing. The race is floundering and hope is wavering. I miss you.

Should he hit Send? Delete? Blake recognized he was

violating the directions of Cat and everyone around him, but he could hardly help himself. He drew a deep breath, paused, and then punched the Delete button.

Blake hadn't called Faith to let her know he'd canceled his dinner meeting so he doubted she'd expect him home this early. The fact the house alarm wasn't on when he entered the back door suggested a presence there, but no greeting party awaited him. Blake walked quietly up the stairs and turned toward the children's side of the house, where he heard raised voices from behind Fin's closed door. As he drew closer, Blake realized Fin and her mother were arguing. There was no sign of Shana. Rather than announcing his arrival, Blake decided to listen from the hallway. It didn't take long for him to figure out that Faith was prosecuting their daughter on the lesbian subject again.

"I still don't understand why you checked that box," Faith screamed.

"Mom, stop! Are you kidding me?" Blake could hear the exasperation in Fin's voice.

"I'm sorry," Faith countered, "but we haven't finished this conversation."

"What? Yes, we have! And this is stupid. Why do you keep bringing it up?"

"You're not telling me everything. I know it."

"That's wrong; I've actually told you way too much. C'mon, Mom. Why are you making this such a big deal?"

"Fin, talk to me. Please, talk to me, dammit."

"This is crazy," Fin fired back. "Listen, I'm about as gay as you are."

A pregnant pause followed, and then a violent crashing sound reverberated through the walls.

Blake lunged forward and pulled the door open. Shards of what appeared to be a shattered drinking glass were scattered on the floor. "Good Lord, Faith," he yelled while rushing into the room.

Faith ignored her husband and stormed past him red-faced and frowning. She hustled away.

Blake hurried to his daughter's side. She'd recoiled against the headrest of her bed and was trying to breathe through a fit of tears. "Are you all right?" he asked.

Fin looked at him and buried her head in his shoulder. "What's happening?" she whimpered.

Blake comforted his daughter, placing his arm around her back, and wondered the very same thing.

CHAPTER 47

For all Taylor Brooks knew, Grace Striker's long-ago boyfriend had left his past life behind in Abilene after settling with his family in Nashville, Tennessee. It was entirely possible that Luke Gresham no longer remembered Striker or even knew she was running for governor in Texas. Yet Brooks's instincts told him something different. He'd always reveled in the pursuit of difficult investigations, ones where all hope seemed to be lost except for whatever information he could dig out, and this one had him energized. With the stakes as high as they were for the Buchanan campaign, Brooks wanted to believe his intuition about Gresham was right. From his Nashville hotel room, Brooks plotted his strategy with great care and read all he could find on the real estate broker from Nashville, his wife, and their three boys.

Based on his research, Brooks learned that Gresham was outgoing, well established in the community, a church regular, and successful in his business. His wife was a native Tennessean and his boys attended a private Christian school called Bernard Academy. He was a Titans fan according to his Facebook page but it appeared his big passion was fishing. Although the Davidson County Election Commission showed Gresham was a registered Republican, Brooks noticed he voted sporadically and showed no connection to the local party. With this and other information gleaned from Gresham's LinkedIn profile and other social-media outlets, Brooks believed he could engage the man in conversation.

Brooks waited at the corner near Gresham's office building

to intercept the middle-aged real estate professional on what Brooks had established was the man's regular afternoon walk to Starbucks.

"I'll buy his as well," Brooks said to the barista while coming up from behind and pointing at the man in khakis in front of him.

"That isn't necessary," Gresham replied, turning to face his unknown benefactor.

"It's no big deal," Brooks explained. "I do this every time I come in for coffee. It's just my thing."

"Then I guess I should thank you." Gresham smiled.

"Taylor Brooks." The investigator offered his hand.

"Luke Gresham. Very generous of you. Thank you again."

"Like I said, no big deal. When I'm traveling, it gives me an opportunity to meet a new person. I'm going to sit for a minute—can you join me?"

"Uh . . . yes." Gresham smiled. "For at least a few minutes. Thanks for the coffee." The two men carried their cups to a table in the back of the store.

"Incredible weather," Brooks said after sitting down.

"But winter's coming," Gresham warned. "We get some nice days this time of year, but this isn't the norm. Where you from?"

"Texas—born and raised. Up here on business. But I expect to get a little fishing in too."

"I'm from Texas," Gresham replied. "Moved here years ago but I still have a few family members near Abilene. Where you planning to fish?"

"Got a friend with some frontage on Percy Priest Lake. Says they have plenty of bass up there."

"Great place," Gresham commented while slurping his coffee through the small opening in his cup. "I take my boys up there all the time."

"Cool. Then I'll have to make the stop. I'm from Dallas, by the way, but I've spent a fair amount of time all around Texas."

"What do you do?" Gresham asked.

"Commercial real estate. Looking at an office complex deal here in Nashville. What about you?"

"Another coincidence." Gresham chuckled. "I'm in the real estate business as well, but I'm in the industrial space."

"Well that is some coincidence," Brooks fibbed. He wondered if he'd overdone the similarities in their stories, but he was pleased with Gresham's enthusiasm. "How's your business these days?"

"Pretty good. Tennessee's booming and industrial space is at a peak right now. Can't complain at all."

"Good for you—commercial's not quite that hot but it's incredible compared to what we saw a few years ago."

Gresham nodded in agreement and the two men launched into a brief discussion about the financial meltdown of '08 and its devastating impact on their business. Having primed the pump, Brooks felt ready to turn to the true subject of his interest.

"You follow politics at all?" Brooks asked. "We've got a big election for governor back in your old home state."

"Oh yeah, I'm familiar with that one." Gresham's tone suggested more than a passing interest in the subject.

"Really? I guess we Texans never get away entirely?" Brooks flashed the familiar Hook 'em Horns' sign. "Did you happen to see the end of the debate that got splashed all over the national news recently?"

"Yeah, I did," Gresham replied.

Was there a trace of attitude in his response? Brooks cocked his head as if waiting for Gresham to continue, but the man didn't offer an explanation.

"So you saw that dramatic confession by the attorney general?" Brooks pushed. "Some of my buddies thought it sounded a bit contrived."

"Contrived or not, she pulled it off. I have to say that woman's very resourceful."

Brooks paused a moment, for effect. "You said that like you know her."

Gresham hesitated. A look away to the ceiling and a nervous peek at his cell phone for messages suggested he was holding back. The investigator had seen this type of reaction before.

"Well, don't make me beg," Brooks pleaded.

"Sorry," Gresham responded while gathering his coffee cup and standing up. "I really didn't mean anything by that. It was just an observation."

"Well, I guess you're going to leave me hanging," Brooks said in his friendliest tone.

"Guess so. Thanks for the visit, Taylor. And good luck with your deal. Time for me to get back to the office."

Brooks camouflaged his excitement over his visit with Gresham, but the smile he suppressed stretched all the way back to Houston. He shook hands with his new acquaintance and wished him well. "Nice to meet you," Brooks said. "Enjoyed the visit. Look me up if you ever get to Texas." Gresham gave him a thumbs-up and bounded away from the table as Brooks sank back into his chair and contemplated what had just happened.

The minute Gresham cleared the Starbucks' door, Brooks dialed Rags Beckham.

"Taylor," Rags answered. "Give me some good news."

"He's the ex," Brooks reported. "I'm certain of it. He's keeping track of the election and I sensed some resentment when I brought up the rape story. Put all of that together, and you know where we have to go."

"Good work, Taylor. I'm with you."

Brooks hung up the phone and realized Rags's candidate would be very unhappy with the moves he and the campaign manager were plotting. But he also knew the campaign was dead if they didn't give them a try. A narrow pathway had cracked open for the Buchanan team, admittedly with risk of more disappointment, but also for the first time in months, filled with real hope.

CHAPTER 48

Two days into his hospital stay, Tony León felt his senses finally returning. The stabbing pain in his ribs, the throbbing contusions on his face, and the bruises covering the rest of his body had left him immobile and wincing even when he blinked. A morphine drip remained threaded into his arm and the button in his hand that connected to the drug-infusion pump had become his best friend.

The excruciating pain had also prevented Tony from formulating a response to Phelps's assault, but for the first time since the beating he was clearheaded. He was glad he'd been unable to speak to the police when he was admitted into the ER because that break had given him the chance to craft any story he wanted. His mind raced with possibilities as he attempted to scooch up in bed.

Commotion outside his hospital room diverted Tony's attention toward the hallway. Seconds later, the door flew open and Grace Striker entered . . . alone.

"How are you, my dear?" she asked while locking the door behind her. "I've been sick with worry about you."

Tony closed his eyes and grimaced while he tried to straighten his body. "That's heartfelt," he responded. "I'm sure you're concerned."

"You know I am," Striker cooed. "I was on the road when I heard the news but came as soon as I landed. I got you this private room, you know."

Tony appreciated that Striker wouldn't admit to any knowledge about Phelps's attack but couldn't believe she had the nerve to show up like this.

Striker closed the blinds and then edged up to Tony's side. She reached down and held his hand. "Let's forget about what happened," she said seductively, in a voice Tony had never heard on the campaign trail or even in their late-night visits. "I've missed you," she continued, "and I want you back as part of my team."

"What does that mean?" Tony asked weakly.

Striker moved her hand under the bedsheets, tickled her way up his leg, and began massaging his inner thigh. "My team in all ways is what I mean."

Tony realized that at least one part of his body hadn't been damaged by the attack. Despite his anger, it was obvious that fighting Striker's apology wasn't a smart move in any way. "Accept what's about to happen," Phelps's words echoed in his head, "and know it could get worse." Tony had no other choice. He closed his eyes, released the morphine drip, and watched the future governor of Texas lower the sheets and go down on him. The woman was cold and duplicitous—Tony knew that—but he also understood her better than anyone. And for at least a few brief moments, the pain and anger disappeared.

———— ★ ————

Blake's palms sweated as he and Rags waited for Taylor Brooks to arrive at headquarters. Whatever news Brooks was bringing back from Nashville, it had the campaign manager plenty motivated, though Blake had his doubts. Rags had been similarly enthusiastic about the information potentially coming from Tony León, but that big revelation had never materialized. Even while excited, Rags had been careful to tamp down expectations about Brooks's investigation, especially once he recognized that his never-say-die confidence was wearing thin on his candidate. A "potential game changer about Striker's abortion," Rags had first mentioned, but that had been followed by, "but we'll see."

"He's here," Rags shouted while springing toward the hallway. Rags whipped open his office door and Brooks hurried inside.

"Good morning," Blake greeted his investigator. The three men exchanged handshakes and sat down around Rags's small conference table.

"Luke Gresham," Brooks opened, "could change everything for us. I'm convinced he has a history with Striker—although what that entails isn't entirely clear—but we're never going to know unless we extract it from him."

"What does that mean?" Blake asked.

"That's why I'm here," Brooks explained. "These next few steps have to be very carefully planned between Rags and me. One mistake and this whole thing could backfire on us."

"I'm still listening," Blake said, his eyes darting between the two consultants, "but you're starting to worry me."

"Well, Senator," Rags interrupted. "I don't think you're going to like what we have in mind, but Taylor and I believe there's only one way to make this work."

"Dammit, guys, what is it?" Blake fired back.

Rags ran his hands up and down his face and then slowly unfurled his plan. It was a three step program and each move would have to be carefully executed in the dark without leaving any tracks. Brooks sat by Rags's side nodding at each critical juncture.

As the strategy was laid out, Blake once again realized he had to make a campaign decision that the man Blake Buchanan would never make. The whole notion of turning an innocent man's life upside down for political purposes was repugnant to him. But, what choice did he have? Unless he followed his brain trust's advice, they'd likely lose all hope and his campaign would die of apathy.

"I know it's rough," Rags conceded, "but Taylor thinks we've got something here. I agree. We need your sign-off."

Blake looked at his two operatives and sighed. "Taylor," he said, "you better be right about this. I can't believe I'm buying in, but go ahead—make it happen."

CHAPTER 49

December 6

For several days, Jackson Goodrich had sat hunched over his computer screen, secluded in his apartment, rereading and editing his draft, until he was finally ready to hit Send. His patience had paid off and he now had his juicy, controversial, news-breaking scoop, the kind that would see his name slathered across major media platforms around the country. His very own Deep Throat mystery, complete with sex, drama, and high political theater. The Striker exposé carried enormous risk as well—heavy criticism or, worse, a lawsuit—but Jackson and his editors were undeterred. Groundbreaking, high-risk stories were the kind the *Enquirer* did best. Who cared if the underdog candidate was using him? Or if the article was based in most part on hearsay from a witness he'd never met? Journalistic standards had never been the highest priority in his newsroom.

Texas Attorney General Rape Story a Sham?

A conflicting story has emerged about the rape allegations that Texas Attorney General Grace Striker dramatically revealed at her November 15 debate. Sources in the gubernatorial campaign suggest that Striker, the prohibitive favorite to become the next governor of Texas, was involved in a consensual sexual relationship at the time of the alleged rape. The same sources suggest that Striker's abortion while in college wasn't a response to a devastating attack, but a personal decision to terminate an unwanted pregnancy. This information contradicts Striker's now well-known story that she was a victim forced into a life-altering decision . . .

Striker's political machinery would savage him as soon as the piece hit the wire, but Jackson was comfortable with the information he'd received from Rags Beckham. He'd studied Luke Gresham's biography as he'd sourced the story himself and every detail lined up. The few comments Striker had offered about the alleged rape—"It was a long time ago and it's up to God now to decide if he'll punish my attacker"—allowed him daylight to take some liberties. Jackson knew that Gresham might challenge the facts attributed to him if his name was leaked as the "unnamed" source, but that was a risk worth taking. Those were decisions for his editors anyway; all he had to do was birth the scandal.

— ★ —

Rags called in his team for an all-night work session at the office to prepare for the media blitz that would ramp up the minute Jackson Goodrich's feature launched. "Rich," Rags started, directing his gaze at his communications director, "I want Blake on every news station in Texas once this story goes viral. He needs to hammer her on honesty and integrity."

"On it," Rich Franks responded. "Blake's coming down now."

"Susan," Rags said, turning to his chief fundraiser, "shake the trees when the news comes out. We might find some money we'd given up on."

Wilde nodded, as if she'd already planned to do that.

"And Kristen, stay close by. I'll need you for a hundred different things over the next couple of days."

The pretty brunette bobbed her head like a teenage cheerleader, excited to be part of the team again after working in the shadows to rebuild her credibility.

At that moment, Blake burst into the room displaying an energy Rags hadn't seen in weeks, maybe months. "We ready?" he shouted.

Everyone gave the candidate thumbs-ups and affirmative smiles. For a campaign so recently mired in frustration and disappointment, it was a monumental attitude change. The sun was coming out again and maybe, perhaps, the long downpour was over.

CHAPTER 50

Marshall Phelps's made a practice of sleeping in on Saturdays, a luxury after a long week of navigating the Striker campaign. So a man who was typically drinking coffee and planning his day an hour earlier on most mornings, found his phone blaring while he was still in bed at 6:00 a.m. on this Saturday, a most unwelcome annoyance.

"Yeah," he grunted.

"Shit's hit the fan," announced the Source.

"What?"

"There's a story about Striker's abortion on the internet."

"What the fuck?"

"Some *New York Enquirer* reporter named Goodrich," the Source said. "He claims to have a mole inside the campaign who says the rape never happened . . . that the sex was consensual."

"Fuck. Can you come in?"

"Headed there now."

"What do you think?"

"The story's probably a plant from the Buchanan folks. But we've always known Striker walks on the edge, so who knows? I'll see you soon."

Phelps slammed down his phone and jumped out of bed. Nothing in the world was capable of derailing his candidate at this point other than secrets and arrogance. The fact that Striker had both in abundance had always worried him. Phelps knew he'd need to get his tanks lined up in counterattack before the sun hit his doorstep but his first call had to be the candidate. He held the phone away from his ear as he punched in Striker's cell number.

"You're kidding, Marshall," she answered.

"This couldn't wait."

"Shit."

"Yeah, shit. There's a new take on the abortion story out, relying on an anonymous source. I'm surprised the press hasn't called you already."

"I'm getting up. I'm gonna kill that little shit Tony before I get to the office." Her phone banged silent.

Phelps hadn't even considered Tony as the prime suspect for the leak, certainly not after his "meeting" with Boots Ali. And to Phelps's knowledge, Tony didn't know the real abortion story anyway. No, the Source had it right. Someone in the Buchanan campaign was the "leaker," someone like Taylor Brooks. The investigator from Dallas was the one professional on Buchanan's staff capable of building this kind of storm.

"Motherfucker," Phelps yelled before rushing to the shower.

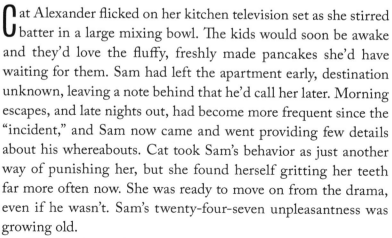

Cat Alexander flicked on her kitchen television set as she stirred batter in a large mixing bowl. The kids would soon be awake and they'd love the fluffy, freshly made pancakes she'd have waiting for them. Sam had left the apartment early, destination unknown, leaving a note behind that he'd call her later. Morning escapes, and late nights out, had become more frequent since the "incident," and Sam now came and went providing few details about his whereabouts. Cat took Sam's behavior as just another way of punishing her, but she found herself gritting her teeth far more often now. She was ready to move on from the drama, even if he wasn't. Sam's twenty-four-seven unpleasantness was growing old.

Usually the weekend news program streaming on the small

kitchen TV created background noise for Cat in the mornings, although there was always a cooking segment with some rising new chef she watched if time permitted. Otherwise, Cat rarely paid more than cursory attention to the shows. But the red scroll at the bottom of the screen screaming "Breaking News" made her take notice. While she continued stirring milk and eggs into her flour, Cat picked up the remote with her free hand and turned up the volume. At that moment, the commentator mentioned a controversy about Grace Striker's abortion just as photos of the candidate and her opponent flashed across the screen. Cat dropped her mixing spoon to the floor and clutched her chest. It was all she could do to keep from falling face first into her pancake batter.

CHAPTER 51

December 11

B lake leaned into his office speakerphone as Rags listened in. "So Taylor," he said, "what's he doing?"

The man in question was Luke Gresham. For four days, Blake had watched Marshall Phelps and his team deny Gresham's still-unattributed story and attack Jackson Goodrich and the *New York Enquirer* to the point that the air in the reporter's bombshell piece had completely deflated. Striker and her band of trained assassins had blanketed the airwaves to double down on her explanation about the rape and abortion. Meanwhile, Blake's attempts to spin the revelation into a question about her honesty took on the look of desperation. His campaign's big missile had turned into a dud.

There was one positive development, maybe. Brooks had carefully scattered around enough rumors that people from some of the more serious news outlets, including a team of Texas-based investigative reporters, had started poking around Gresham's doorstep. The Nashville man had yet to speak to anyone, but a growing horde of media now suspected him as the source of the *Enquirer* story. The pieces of his biography fit too well. Rags had said repeatedly that it was only a matter of time before Gresham would have to comment.

"Nothing so far," Brooks answered Blake's question. "But he can't duck the jackals forever."

"And you still don't think it's a good idea to reach out to him?" Blake asked.

"No!" Brooks exclaimed. "If he knows our campaign leaked the story, he'd kick us in the balls just because. Right now, he can only suspect it."

"I feel terrible about what we've done to this man." Blake shook his head.

"Senator," Rags countered, "I know how you're feeling but don't forget we're not the ones who painted the man as a rapist on national TV. Striker did that all by herself."

Blake still didn't think much of this political justification—Striker had never mentioned Gresham's name in any interview—but he'd approved the strategy and had to own it now. And no good would come from agonizing over his decision any longer. "So what's our plan?" he followed up. "What if Striker's already got to him?"

"That's possible," Brooks admitted, "but doubtful. That would be a bigger risk for them. If it came out that Striker was trying to influence Gresham's story, you can assume most would view that as an admission. My guess is they're wondering the same thing we are, except that Striker knows whatever Gresham knows."

"She seems confident he won't talk."

"Yes, sir," Brooks said. "She's certainly praying he won't."

"So we wait?"

Rags held his arm out to Blake. "Yes," he agreed. "And hope he tells the truth."

"What are the odds of that?" Blake asked.

Brooks's hesitation suggested he wasn't sure. "Senator," Brooks responded, "I don't know what to tell you, but this was the right strategy. Everything I learned about Gresham before we started down this road tells me he's a straight arrow. A solid Christian family man. He can't like what Striker's done to him and I don't think he'll lie for her. It's just a matter of how much of the truth he's willing to tell."

———— ★ ————

Phelps didn't know what, if anything, he should do about Luke Gresham. There was rarely a time when the political Svengali was uncertain of next steps but this was one. Striker had assured him that the Nashville man was a Bible-toting boy scout she'd dated only a few times in college, and that he'd never publicly discuss their relationship, but she'd felt the need to explain, "If he does, he has nothing to say." When Phelps had raised an eyebrow over that, she'd become even more adamant. "Just stick to the rape story, dammit" she'd instructed, "because he can't deny what he doesn't fricking know." But unlike his candidate, Phelps recognized that if this Tennessee family man felt vilified by Striker's lies during the debate, he might do more than just say "leave me alone" to the press.

———— ★ ————

After several days of constant observation by the media, Luke Gresham had finally cracked. He'd announced through a local lawyer, Joshua Carson, that he was going to issue a written statement to the Nashville paper, the *Tennessean*, about 4:00 p.m. that afternoon. When Rags had called with the news, Blake had hustled back to headquarters, where he now huddled with his campaign manager awaiting Taylor Brooks's call. Blake could see the sweat beads forming on Rags's face as the two men anticipated the report.

Rags scratched his chin and looked at Blake. "No one knows what it says so there's more than a few anxious folks out there," he suggested. Then the phone rang, interrupting Rags mid-sentence. Blake clicked the speakerphone on.

"I just got the release," Brooks reported. "No public comment; just a statement. I haven't looked at it yet so brace yourselves." He read:

The press has decided that I am the ex-boyfriend of Grace Striker mentioned in the New York Enquirer story. I am reluctant to comment on my relationship with the Texas attorney general that dates back almost thirty years ago, but I've been left with no choice by the media. At the outset, I want everyone to know that I have no part in the politics of my former home state and have no interest in Grace Striker's campaign for governor. I've spoken with no one other than my wife and lawyer about what I'm about to say. My life is now in Tennessee, not Texas, and I'm not doing this for any reason other than to clear my name and buy peace for my family. I doubt I'd be in this position at all but for a stranger who recently bought me a cup of coffee in Nashville. My guess is he was a reporter and I want him to understand that I find his tactics sleazy and disgusting.

Blake looked at Rags and sighed. "That's a relief," he mouthed. Brooks continued reading from Gresham's statement:

When I was a sophomore in college at Abilene Christian, I met Grace Striker. For over a year, we had an intimate, personal relationship. During the course of our time together, Grace became pregnant. I supported her when she decided to terminate the pregnancy and it was a very difficult time for both of us. Grace never mentioned a rape to me and I know nothing about that. I will have no further comment on this matter.

CHAPTER 52

December 18

The tsunami came.

Marshall Phelps watched the wave engulf Grace Striker's campaign with hurricane force, and for seven days he was powerless to stop it. "*Liar*," screamed one headline. "*Shame*," hollered another. There was no safe quarter for the attorney general after Luke Gresham's stunning announcement. The press, politicians in both parties, and most important, the voters appeared betrayed by Grace Striker's fictional tale about a rape-induced abortion. Although the candidate stood her ground, accusing Gresham now of being a spurned ex-lover who knew about the rape, few believed her. Phelps understood what the voters were feeling: Striker had lied her way to the top and one of her lies—the whopper of whoppers—had finally stopped her.

Sitting in his office, Phelps realized he was down to his last gasp. If something didn't change soon, Striker's slide would become irreversible and his candidate would drop into the wastebin of scandal-clad politicians like Gary Hart, Anthony Weiner, and Eliot Spitzer, earning the dubious distinction of becoming the first woman candidate brought down by tawdry actions of her own. Nothing less than a game changer could stop her free fall— and save Phelps's job—and for that reason he'd agreed to meet with the now mostly recovered Tony León. He would have to hold his nose while doing so, but he was out of ideas.

"Come in," Phelps said to the young man, who limped through the doorway. Phelps pointed him to a chair. "So what's this about?" he asked warily.

Tony glared at Phelps and shoved him the finger with his expression. He hesitated for a moment before speaking. "I've considered telling the police more than once about your little visit in the cemetery—you son of a bitch—but Grace talked me out of it. No reason for me to heap on that rotting corpse of yours anyway."

Phelps shook his head. "Fuck you," he replied. "What do you want?"

Tony squirmed in his chair before pulling out a news headline from his pocket. "It seems your candidate's free-falling and there's nothing between her and the ground. She's going to splat, unless you can save her."

"Yeah?" Phelps realized the young kid had come to horse-trade. He had no idea what León might be offering.

"Your boys never took Buchanan seriously in the early going and got lazy," Tony started. "No real oppo research, nothing. But I always guessed Grace would get her ass in a crack somewhere along the way."

Phelps stared at Tony, checking his emotions. He couldn't admit it, but he knew his adversary was right. It was Striker's affair with Tony that had worried him most. There'd been no need to devote precious resources to do a deep dive into Buchanan's background when they were carrying a twenty-point lead.

"Here's the deal," Tony announced. "What I have is so good that it will whack Buchanan on his heels and it will stop his surge. It may even neutralize your problem with Gresham because both candidates will then be damaged goods. I've held it back as insurance, just in case."

Phelps tried to avoid looking surprised but he was staggered. "If I was interested," Phelps hedged, "and I doubt that I am, what would you be looking for?"

"A lot more than last time," Tony replied with a fixed jaw.

"Then I'll need more than speculation before we go any further."

Tony tapped the manila folder under his arm. "I'm prepared," he said.

Phelps frowned but felt a certain respect grow for his young nemesis. If nothing else, the kid was a survivor, a good quality for an aspiring politician.

———————★———————

Blake rushed to his house after receiving Faith's impassioned call. He'd been in front of microphones almost nonstop since Luke Gresham's announcement and hadn't been home in days. His brief argument with Faith after her glass-breaking episode with Fin had pushed them even further apart.

"I need you here," she'd said without further explanation. "It's not about the girls but please come home." It was an unusually animated request for Faith and Blake's mind had wandered all over the map by the time he ran into his kitchen, where Faith waited with bloodshot eyes. She gulped down a glass of wine just as Blake entered the room.

"My God, Faith, what is it?" Blake asked.

"This couldn't wait," she replied in a somber tone. "I'm sorry to worry you." Blake could hear panic in her voice.

"I'm here. Tell me what's going on."

Faith started crying and Blake had no idea what to do next. He stood and stared with his mouth open.

"I sent the girls to dinner," Faith whimpered. "I wasn't sure when I'd see you again."

"Well, I'm here," he replied. "Please, Faith, what's going on?"

Faith walked over and took his arm. "Let's go in the den and sit down," she directed.

They walked into the adjoining room and Blake plopped down on the sofa while Faith remained standing.

"C'mon, Faith. Talk to me."

"This isn't easy," she said in a halting voice, "but I just need to . . . say it straight out. I made a mistake. It's over now—I promise—but I think the girls may know."

Blake's body twitched, but his anger, if there was any, passed in such a flash that it surprised him. *Did he even care?*

"What's his name?" Blake asked.

Faith looked away and Blake sensed she was holding back a second round of tears or manufacturing new ones. She gasped for air and shook her head, before whispering, "Her name's Meredith."

CHAPTER 53

Rags stood on the precipice of the greatest achievement of his life. Christmas was just a week away and his candidate had vaulted within range of the nomination. Striker's collapse had appeared impossible just weeks before, but it now seemed irreversible. The attorney general had fallen so far so fast that her camp had canceled the January debate, claiming a scheduling conflict. One truth even Striker understood was that voters never forgave lying. A second debate, dominated by that subject, would be devastating.

Of course, Rags appreciated that the last week had been too good to be true and that trouble lurked around every corner, so the urgent call from Blake had his heart in his throat. He arrived at Blake's house with the full expectation that some unknown problem had emerged to take their campaign down.

"Thanks for coming over," Blake said when Rags entered his home.

"Of course. What's going on?" Rags asked. He then noticed Faith standing down the hallway. He could tell she'd been crying.

"Faith," Rags acknowledged as he bowed his head. She offered a soft wave in response.

"We don't have much time before my girls get home," Blake explained. "So let's go in the study."

After they all sat down, Blake started. "Faith knows I've told you we've been having some problems."

Rags nodded but kept his lips pursed.

"And neither of us wants this to affect our girls."

"I understand." Rags felt the heaviness in the air. It was almost as if they'd gathered to mourn the passing of a family member.

"We've managed our relationship thus far," Blake continued, "but we're concerned that some of our problems could get to the public if we aren't careful." He paused to catch his breath.

Rags's spirits sank. He'd thought Blake's *thing* with Catherine Alexander was over, but apparently not. While Blake paused, Rags turned to Faith and lowered his eyes in sympathy.

Blake must have sensed Rags had the wrong idea and jumped back in. "Faith doesn't think anyone knows about *her situation* with Meredith, the tennis pro at the club, but we need you to keep it that way."

Rags pivoted toward Blake, exchanged a surprised look, and then said, "Okay, what do I need to know?"

Rags could tell that Blake was sending him all sorts of subliminal messages about his cowering wife. The most obvious—Rags saw vindication in Blake's eyes, as if his friend wanted a pass for his indiscretion because of what he was enduring at home. Why else would Blake have made Faith sit through the embarrassing confession about her affair with the *female* tennis pro, rather than just giving him the details on the phone and letting him go to work. But he also knew Blake might be underestimating the impact of his wife's disclosure. And that was the most dangerous development of all.

CHAPTER 54

December 19

Phelps tapped his foot in his office while he waited for Striker and Tony to arrive for their summit meeting. Tony's revelation that he possessed a secret tape that could undo the Buchanan campaign had changed everything. No way would Striker ever trust him again after the horrible week she'd just experienced, and now topped off by Tony's lie that Phelps had restricted the use of the damaging video earlier in the campaign—Phelps knew he was likely done. It didn't matter that he'd never known Tony possessed a tape; Striker couldn't accept that the polls had closed fifteen points and that her celebrity had been dramatically, if not permanently, damaged. A scapegoat was needed for her tragic change of fortune and Phelps understood he was the only choice. She'd have his head.

Striker arrived with Tony hitched to her side and Phelps girded himself.

"What's your advice today?" she hissed upon sitting down. Striker dug her fingernails into the cushions on the armrest. Tony positioned himself next to his candidate with a gotcha look on his face.

"Right now, we have to sit tight and continue working the media as much as we can. Remember, Gresham didn't say you *weren't* raped. We just need to keep pushing your story and have faith the tide will turn."

Striker threw her arms in the air in exasperation. "That's it? That's your *Big Idea*? You've got to be kidding me."

"I'm dead serious," Phelps continued. "We shouldn't release Tony's tape during the holidays. Let's get through Christmas and the end of the year and then hit Buchanan hard in early January. There's plenty of time. Just ask the Source—he's polled it."

"You mean you guys want me to sit back and take this crap for another two weeks?" Striker barked. "No fucking way!"

"General, that's your best option," Phelps argued. "No one pays attention to politicians during the holidays and the voters will be turned off by that kind of tape right now."

"I don't care about the Christmas season," she shot back, "and this won't be negative campaigning! It will be the truth! I want to inflict pain on that liar Buchanan. He's trying to ruin me."

Phelps was surprised by Tony's silence but he figured the kid would soon make his play. "I understand your frustration," he responded.

"You have no idea," Striker yelled. "You left me exposed to that coward, and you expect me to listen to this lame advice. Damn you, Marshall."

Phelps had anticipated the attorney general would rant but he had no good way to respond. "*You* never told us about Gresham," he said in a firm voice. "We made sure there were no records because that's what you told us about."

"Are you kidding me?" Striker hollered. "How much money am I paying you? You're supposed to handle this kind of shit. You let them *get* to Gresham . . . you should've kidnapped the bastard!"

"General, we have to talk about where we are," Phelps cautioned, trying to redirect the conversation. "What's done is done. We can't turn back the clock."

"That's rich. This is what I get for my money? Being told to sit back and wait? Cool my heels while my twenty-point lead gets flushed down the toilet."

"I didn't say quit the race. I just said wait a few weeks before deploying the video. Let's see if the polls stabilize before we get desperate. The Source is in the field every day and the data shows your numbers are beginning to creep back up. The video may be useful but we may not need it."

"This, this is nuts," Striker stammered while shaking her head. "God . . ."

At that point, Phelps had heard enough. He was about to throw up his arms and quit when Tony perked up.

"General," he said in a measured tone. "I believe there is another way."

And with that comment, Phelps knew his time as Grace Striker's campaign manager was all but over. There was a new sheriff in town.

CHAPTER 55

Cat poured herself a glass of red wine and went back to her office to take a short break from the dinner crowd. This wasn't the first time in the past few weeks she'd retreated to her private space. In these quiet moments, Cat contemplated the grim path ahead and struggled with the realization that her marriage could very well be over. As she tried to look into the new year that lay just weeks ahead, she knew that a good piece of it could be spent preparing her kids for a messy divorce. But she wasn't fully ready to accept that fate, no matter how personally unhappy she was with Sam. As a result, Cat had begun steeling herself for the holidays with a fresh resolve that Blake would have no further role in her life.

Reconciling herself to that outcome was difficult, but Cat could see no other way. What future could she possibly have with the man from Texas? Two divorces, two property settlements, four children, two states . . . it was an impossible challenge to manage their way through. How could their two separate worlds ever be truly conjoined, especially if Blake was elected governor? That thought—of the construct of her life *with* Blake—terrified her more than anything else. And what would happen to Abrazo if she moved to Texas? She realized a bitter Sam would likely force her to sell her beloved restaurant just as a leverage point in the divorce. Even if she could hold on to her business, bouncing back and forth between the two states was not a recipe for success, either personally or professionally.

With these thoughts swirling in her head, Cat returned to the dining room to visit with her patrons. That ritual always soothed her, but tonight when Cat hit the floor, she was shocked to find Sam, Mitch, and Paige waiting for her. She trembled at the sight and skipped toward the open arms of her son, Mitch.

"What a wonderful surprise," Cat said with a huge smile splashed across her face. She couldn't remember a single time, other than an occasional birthday celebration, that her family had joined her around a table at Abrazo.

"The kids wanted to surprise you," Sam replied. He pursed his lips, but she appreciated the effort.

"Mommy," Mitch hollered while squeezing his mother around the waist. Cat had to fight off tears. Her daughter, on the other hand, held back.

"You guys are going to get a special meal tonight!" Cat exclaimed. "This is such a treat." She removed her apron before sitting down and reaching over to hold Sam's hand. Her plan for a future with her husband and children crystallized for the first time in weeks, but deep in her heart, she wondered if she could pull it off.

———— ★ ————

Blake put his head down on his pillow but sleep wouldn't come. He had a million thoughts running through his mind—his wife's affair, the schedule ahead, the possibility of fulfilling an improbable dream of becoming governor—but one notion always jammed its way to the front. He'd become overwhelmed with the idea that his life's journey had led him to this place only so he could rediscover Cat Alexander. The now-real prospect of him becoming the next governor of Texas hadn't shaken that feeling at all; in some ways, it had reinforced it.

The fact that Cat was no longer responding to his messages was beginning to wear on him. Even his joyful email explaining that he was surging in the polls hadn't elicited a response.

Blake knew all the reasons Cat had gone silent, but it still tormented him how their relationship had crashed so abruptly. As the campaign was about to go dark through the New Year, Blake struggled with the emptiness of being separated from Cat during the holidays.

Blake then remembered his arrhythmia pill, swallowed it with an Ambien kicker, and prayed that morning would bring clarity to his world.

CHAPTER 56

Phelps leaned back in his office chair feeling vindicated. Christmas had come and gone, families had gathered across the state and, as the political veteran had predicted, voters had tuned out politicians. The pause had stemmed Striker's political free fall, and her standing appeared to have bottomed out, yet even then the attorney general had refused to heed Phelps's advice to stay in the shadows. That decision made it difficult to drive her numbers back up, especially when she seized every opportunity to talk about the rape, and question Luke Gresham's motivations for coming forward. Phelps had repeatedly advised his candidate to change her tactics. "Fanning this story when people aren't interested does you no good," he'd told her, but she ignored his guidance anyway.

The phone rang and Phelps reached down, expecting another angry directive from his candidate.

"Mr. Phelps," his assistant stated, "I have a Joshua Carson from Nashville on the line."

"Nashville?" he responded. Phelps wasn't sure but he thought that was the name of the lawyer who'd released Gresham's press statement. "Put him through," Phelps instructed.

"Mr. Carson?" Phelps answered.

"Thanks for taking my call. I guess you know who I am."

"I think so."

"Well, let me get right to the point. My client Luke Gresham is tired of hearing your candidate talk about him in the press. Her insults and character attacks need to stop. If they don't, he'll have no choice but to release a more specific statement."

"Sounds like a threat," Phelps responded.

"Not at all . . . and you know better than that. Luke is a private man, a family man, and he just wants this to end, but Ms. Striker won't leave it alone. Luke's previous statement was crafted to avoid damaging her campaign, but if it did, put that on me. I tried to give Attorney General Striker some leeway to explain away the rape, but not at Luke's expense. We don't care what fiction she manufactures. That's not his concern, but he doesn't want to be accused of being an angry ex-lover, complicit in her lies, or even worse, a rapist. Am I making myself clear?"

"Without a doubt," Phelps responded.

"That's all I have to say then. Luke's on vacation now with his family but I'm monitoring the press about him. Please ask your candidate to stop. I didn't call to threaten you but I assure you what I have in my possession is much worse for your candidate than what Mr. Gresham shared earlier."

"Send me what you have and that will help me with the attorney general."

Carson chuckled. "Nice try, but I guess you'll have to rely on her to decide if I'm bluffing. I think she knows I'm not."

"I'll be in touch," Phelps said.

"I hope so."

CHAPTER 57

January 6

The call had surprised Rags but not as much as the tone of Marshall Phelps's voice. Rags hadn't spoken to Striker's head man at any time during the campaign and the last thing he'd expected was a personal call after all that had gone down. Rags had scratched his head, wondering what Phelps was up to, but he'd decided there was no reason to refuse the meeting. Phelps had requested Rags come alone and insisted that he keep their breakfast between them. "A man-to-man conversation," he'd proposed.

They'd picked an out-of-the-way restaurant in suburban Houston where they would have maximum privacy. Rags was anxious but confident as he sat waiting in a corner booth at Huggy's Grill, sipping his coffee. Phelps arrived dressed in a sweater and jeans, then beelined it to the table.

"Rags," Phelps said while holding out his hand.

"Marshall . . . this was unexpected."

"Sorry about the cloak-and-dagger routine but our conversation needs to be graveyard. Too many folks watching."

"I guess so," Rags agreed. "But I do hear you like to intimidate people."

"Hate to ruin my reputation." Phelps smiled. "But that's not my intention today." The waitress came by and dropped off a cup of coffee for her new guest and topped off Rags's mug. "How were your holidays?" he asked.

"Did I miss the holidays?" Rags replied. "Damn."

Phelps laughed.

"Why are we here?" Rags asked, turning serious. He was feeling even more unsteady because of Phelps's casual attitude.

"Okay," Phelps responded evenly. "I quit Striker's campaign two days ago." He stopped, took a swig of coffee, and stared Rags in the eye. "My resignation letter will become public today."

Rags tried to maintain his composure but the comment caught him off guard. "What? You can't be serious?"

"Yes, I am. My candidate and I aren't . . . in agreement on a number of subjects, and it's no longer possible for me to do my job. She's got other voices in her ear."

Rags cocked his head. "Maybe that's true, but why this meeting? Why now?"

"I'm not getting into the details—they're confidential, as you might guess. I just wanted you to know that I'm done with Striker from here on out. I've built a reputation in this business that's important to me."

"What do you mean?" Rags wondered if Phelps was previewing a nasty move by Striker's campaign.

Phelps cocked his head. "I'll let you figure that out."

Rags didn't respond, but it appeared he'd correctly interpreted Phelps's message.

"Have you heard from Tony León?" Phelps asked.

"No," Rags lied.

"Then we should leave it at that. But it's important for me to distance myself from Striker and that kid. They're your adversaries now . . . not me. And, by the way, congratulations, you did a helluva job with that Gresham story."

"Can't take credit for that one," Rags responded, "but I have to say I was surprised she stayed after him for so long. Is that what this is about? You advised against that?"

Phelps nodded and paused for a moment. "I think she's done more to help you than Gresham did. Yeah, she did stay after him too long. Getting her to stop was my final act."

Rags couldn't believe Phelps was being so open with his comments. He figured there had to be some angle, some hidden agenda, something more than Phelps's transformation into a good guy. "What do you want, Marshall?" he asked again. "I'm not buying this resignation stuff."

"It's the truth. Believe it. Good luck, Rags. Looks like you have a great chance to win this thing now." He leaned across the table and whispered, "I hope you fucking do."

His former adversary then stood, offered his hand again, and left the restaurant, causing Rags to wonder what in the world had just happened.

———— ★ ————

Phelps left with a clean conscience and a clear path forward. He'd accomplished what he'd set out to do with Beckham, causing no harm to his former client in the process—rather, clearing the air so he could begin the next phase of his life. Phelps understood it was past time to move on. He'd played hard his entire career in politics, often pushing boundaries in support of his candidates, but this last episode with Striker had crushed his spirit. There was no way he could continue to do his job.

One silver lining prevailed. Even though he wasn't a young man any longer, Phelps had plenty of opportunities ahead. He could teach. Become a talking head. Perhaps even work with kids. He'd find a nice, clean way to tidy up his markers.

Maybe he'd finally write that book.

CHAPTER 58

Tony León's request for a conference had come the afternoon before Rags's coffee with Phelps. Rags had initially considered assembling his key political people to discuss León's invitation but had realized that might be premature. Whatever the young operative had to say, Rags wanted to downplay the meeting to avoid setting off panic within his team. Nevertheless, Rags kept Blake with him in Houston out of precaution the day of León's visit, hoping to protect his man from being blindsided by whatever León might be scheming.

Blake appeared at Rags's office door around 8:00 that morning. "Well," Blake said with mock cheerfulness, "this should be fun."

"I guess we're going to get their best shot today," Rags responded. "They've got no choice; the polls are getting away from them."

Blake paced before plopping down in the lone chair in front of Rags's desk. Rags could see the horrible scenarios racing through his friend's head.

"Phelps resigned for some reason," Rags continued, "and while he wouldn't elaborate, he left some clues. When he told me that I might be hearing from León, I acted surprised, but as you know, I'd already heard from him—back before Gresham's story broke—a million political years ago. Didn't hear another peep from him until just before Phelps warned me. I'm still wary they may be working together."

"What do we know about León?"

"Other than Phelps tried to run him off for sleeping with his candidate, not much. He's apparently very ambitious. And he has Striker's ear . . . or whatever."

Blake frowned.

"I don't know what more to tell you," Rags continued. "We need to be ready to pivot. She'll do anything to stay alive."

"I think we both know where this is going."

As Rags nodded, he wondered if there might be even more to Blake's story with Cat Alexander than they'd discussed. Phelps had suggested as much . . . that whatever León was up to went too far and he wanted no part of it. Or maybe Striker fired him because he wouldn't do what she wanted him to. In either case, he needed to brace Blake for a rough ride ahead.

"What are our folks saying about the polls?" Blake asked, still avoiding the elephant in the room.

"You're in great shape. Trends are against her in every category. Only her most ardent supporters believe her story's true. Her negatives are at sixty percent and growing and you've got endorsements coming in from all over now, even from those who think your views are the death of the conservative movement."

"So we might be able to get elected no matter what León has on me."

"True, there's a lot of damage for her to repair and not much time till March fourth. She needs something huge to turn this race around."

Blake looked down. "I get it," he said.

"You shouldn't be here when León arrives," Rags advised. "Come back at eleven and we'll figure out a response. Then we're getting you back on the road. Our next governor needs to press the flesh."

Blake hesitated and drew a deep breath. "Rags," he whispered. "I've stayed away from her . . . no contact at all."

Rags walked toward his friend and stood next to him. "This

will work out, Blake," he said with a consoling pat on the back. "You're going to make a great governor. And I hope you know I care about the man in this suit as well. Nothing about politics will ever change that."

Blake's gratitude poured from his eyes. "Thank you," he replied. "And please don't worry—no matter what he tells you—I can clean up my own mess. They're not going to extort this election from us."

━━━ ★ ━━━

Tony couldn't believe events had worked out so well for him. Not as first planned—primarily because of Phelps—but his attention to the political lessons learned at the feet of Judge Canales had paid off. Tony held the information his candidate could use to get back in the race, and he had the bare knuckles to play dirty, much dirtier than Phelps ever would. Without Tony's help, Striker was finished. The candidate had jumped on his plan the minute he'd offered it up, including his demand that she fire Phelps, and Tony now had the authority he relished. It was his game to win or lose.

Tony knew that what he had might not turn the polls around, but his plan was to use the scandalous video in a more *effective* way. Tony made his way toward Rags Beckham's office contemplating how it was all about to go down.

"Not sure we've ever met," Rags said when Tony limped into his office. Rags glanced askance at the bandage on his adversary's face.

"Tony León," he announced. "General Striker's campaign manager. I fell recently." Tony pointed at the slightly puffy area just below his left eye.

"Pretty late in the game for this kind of change," Rags stated.

"Or just in time," Tony replied with a cocksure smile.

Rags shrugged.

"Do you know why I'm here?" Tony asked.

"I have no idea."

"I'd like you to walk outside with me."

"Why?"

"I want this conversation to stay between us. No recordings."

"I'm not recording you," Rags fired back.

"If you want to hear what I have to say then you should follow me."

CHAPTER 59

Rags considered terminating the meeting with León the minute the kid barked instructions in *his* office, but he realized he had no choice but to go along with the offer. From Buchanan head-quarters, León led Rags to an awaiting car and they drove off to a mall parking lot several miles away. Very little was said during the ride.

After the driver positioned Tony's car in a secluded area, the operative motioned for Rags to follow him to a nearby patch of land. The green space was an oasis in the midst of the huge expanse of concrete, and it was next to a pair of thundering wind-turbine engines.

"Was all of this necessary?" Rags asked in an exasperated tone.

"I'm more comfortable here," Tony replied, seemingly reveling in his sudden self-importance. The young man pulled his sport coat a little tighter around his shoulders in the crisp, six-ty-degree air. "Let's not waste any more time," Tony said. "I have some damaging information in my possession, and I brought you a sample." Tony pulled out an envelope and handed it to Rags. "There's more where this came from."

"What's this?"

"I would guess you know. And just remember, the informa-tion on the flash drive in there is all mine. No one's seen it but me and my investigator. I haven't even shown it to Striker yet."

"Why bring it to me now? Why wait so long?"

"I had a few problems . . . um, structural . . . in the Striker campaign that have only recently been alleviated."

"Phelps wouldn't condone this sleaze, would he?" Rags paused as if the answer was obvious. "And you think this crap," he continued while shaking the envelope in his hand, "changes something?"

"Maybe not," Tony allowed. "I can read the polls just like you can and early voting's less than six weeks away." He paused as if to let his comment sink in. "But I'm betting your client won't be happy if this *crap* hits *You-Tube*."

"Senator Buchanan's tough enough to handle cheap political tricks."

"Wait till you see what I've given you before passing judgment." Tony smirked, a look that suggested he was secure in his position.

Rags contained his anger. He wasn't going to give an inch while pinned down by León. "Good luck with that," Rags scoffed. "If that's why you hauled me out here—to threaten Blake Buchanan—then you've wasted your time."

"Whatever," Tony replied dismissively. The young man's face was a blank canvas and his body showed no sign of nerves. "You still have some time," he continued. "I don't plan on releasing the video until after the primary. Striker probably can't beat Buchanan at this point—I'll give you that—but if he resigns after he wins the nomination, then all of this will work itself out. It really would save your man a lot of pain if he follows my instructions."

"You're a scum-bag," Rags said.

"Save your insults. And hasn't the senator always said the voters are entitled to know everything about their next governor?"

Rags stiffened but needed to verify León's proposal. "Let me get this straight. You want Blake to keep running and if he wins the primary . . . then withdraw? Since we're in fantasyland, why not just ask him to drop out now?"

"I don't have to tell you the answer to that."

That was true. Rags understood it was too late for either candidate to legally pull their name off the primary ballot. In Tony's perfect world, Blake would either lose the primary to Striker—unlikely at this point—or he'd win and then withdraw so party leaders could appoint her in his place to run against the Democrat in the general election. "Blake will never go for this," he declared, "no matter what filth you've dug up!"

Tony laughed. "Oh, really? Would you like a preview of what I've . . ."

"Screw you," Rags interrupted. "I'm getting out of here. I have a campaign to run."

"Then go run it. Just remember that every frame on that drive—I mean everything and more—will be published on social media right after the primary. You have options left until then. I have the only copies and you have one way to get them. Let me know if your man's interested."

"I'm going to turn all of this over to the Texas Rangers," Rags stated.

"Great, and what are they going to investigate? Careful what you ask for."

Rags felt enraged but knew he was losing ground fast. "You won't hear from me again," he announced. "And I'll find my own way home." Rags then stormed off toward the mall. He needed to find a place to throw up.

CHAPTER 60

Tony called Striker's cell phone the minute he got back in the car.

"What did he say?" Striker asked.

"I'm driving over," Tony replied. "He threatened me, but the old coot's clearly worried."

"Come straight to see me when you get here. I'm taking the afternoon off. The media's wearing me out."

Tony rolled his eyes. "I'll be there."

"Don't keep me waiting," she said. "Do you still think this will work?"

"It has to," Tony countered. "See you in an hour or two."

———— ★ ————

Rags had called one of his staffers to pick him up, then hurried back to his office to watch Tony León's video. Rags cleared the room, locked the door, and plugged the drive into his computer. He wasn't sure what to expect but he figured León had caught Blake and Cat in some compromising position while the candidate had been in New York. Cameras were so tiny and unobtrusive these days that a good investigator could always find a way to get one wherever it was needed.

Rags was surprised, however, when the tape opened with a panoramic shot of River Oaks Country Club in Houston. An odd start, he thought, but a new, alarming reality set in when the video quickly moved inside the gates of the private club and directly to the outdoor tennis courts. The videographer zoomed in on four women playing doubles, one of whom was Faith Buchanan. Again, this appeared to be nothing more than context because the film showed a couple of routine points, followed by smiling handshakes and hugs, and then trailed one of the players—the youngest and fittest of the bunch—as she hustled to beat her friends inside the tennis shop. There, the attractive woman stepped behind the store counter and mouthed directions to the lone staff member—who then scurried out of the building—before opening an office door and disappearing from view. Shortly thereafter, once the other two doubles players had left the shop, and the space was temporarily empty, Faith Buchanan tracked the younger woman into the back office. The videographer's vantage point then changed to inside the closed room. Rags slumped over on his desk when the images appeared. A feverish kissing scene ensued between the women, accompanied by heavy fondling that exposed one of Faith's breasts outside her thin tennis top. At this point, Rags clicked off the video.

He sucked in oxygen as fast as he could. Having fully anticipated managing Blake through some damaging, but survivable, video about his affair with Cat, Rags was stumped about what to do next. While Blake might be relieved in some ways about the subject of León's extortion, this turn of events could also send the father of two off the plank. As damaged as his marriage was, Blake would never allow his wife's infidelity, with a woman, to get in front of his beloved daughters. Exposing his own indiscretions was one thing. Doing it to the mother of his children, in graphic form, was quite another.

With Blake due in his office any minute, Rags had little time to calculate his response. If he showed Blake the video, he wasn't sure what might happen, but it was likely going to be a rash decision that an emotional Blake shouldn't make at this point. Until the last few months, Rags would never have considered withholding explosive information from Blake, but that was a different time, with a different candidate. So option one—telling Blake—was out of the question, at least for now.

The phone rang and Rags's assistant warned him that Blake was on his way toward the office.

"So?" Blake asked as he barreled through the door.

"They're desperate," Rags started. "León's threatening to go public with something on you, but he didn't give me much detail."

"What do you think it is?"

"I don't know, but I'm guessing he wants money."

"What do you mean?"

"He's holding back but I think he just wanted to gauge my interest first."

"What's the price?"

Rags studied Blake's face and could see his candidate was envisioning the worst-case scenario, but he knew Blake's thoughts were entirely focused on his own mistakes, not those of his wife. Blake's reaction confirmed, however, the campaign manager's sense that he had to withhold the scandalous video until he'd considered all the campaign's options. "He didn't give me a number," Rags finally answered. "But my instincts tell me he can be bought off."

"So how did you leave things?"

"He wanted me to talk to you. See how receptive you were to a deal."

Blake looked at the ceiling and sighed. "Jesus," he lamented. "I wouldn't pay that extortionist a dime but we don't have a choice, do we?"

Rags gave him a long look. He only wished it were that simple.

———— ★ ————

Blake realized he had to tell Rags the whole story. Every single detail. He couldn't allow his campaign manager to walk into battles half prepared any longer. Because he'd lived most of his life without a whiff of impropriety before Cat Alexander, Blake found it hard to confess his sins. Doing so might undermine all the trust he'd built up with Rags over their many years together, and that troubled him. But he knew coming clean was long past due. He eased into Rags's guest chair and motioned his friend to sit down behind his desk.

"The time you saw us in New York we didn't sleep together," Blake explained, "but that changed later."

Rags nodded.

"It was just one time. You know the weekend. I'm sorry. I should have told you before, but I couldn't."

"I'm not surprised. Anything else?"

"We haven't seen each other since and stopped communicating altogether before Christmas."

"You used dummy accounts when you did text and email?" Rags asked.

"Of course. So did she. But you should know some of the old ones got a little descriptive at times. If León had access to those and could trace them back to me, it would be embarrassing, but not the end of the world." He paused. "Do you think that's it?"

"Not sure," Rags answered. "Maybe."

Blake thought he'd heard indecision in Rags's voice, as if his campaign manager was holding something back.

"Where do the two of you stand now?" Rags followed up.

"Like I said, it's been at least three weeks since we spoke. No communications."

"You've been lucky so far," Rags suggested. "The *Enquirer* reporter got his rocks off chasing that Striker story but there are plenty of vultures hovering around for a fresh scandal about the governor-in-waiting."

Blake lowered his eyes and shook his head.

"I'll figure out what to do with León," Rags said confidently, which calmed Blake. "Trust me, he's just a two-bit hustler seizing on an opportunity. I'll get with Taylor and we'll go to work." Rags paused as if sorting through a number of thoughts. "I should have asked earlier, but how are you and Faith?"

Blake wondered about the change of subject. "What do you mean?" he asked.

"Blake, I know Faith's disclosure was tough to handle. I'm just checking on you . . . as a friend."

"Thanks, buddy." Blake reached out and gripped his campaign manager on the shoulder. "You're a better friend than I could ever possibly deserve." Blake paused and took a deep breath. "Truth is, we're a mess. Faith put an end to her relationship with Meredith—or so she says—but I really don't know what's going on in her brain. The last thing I ever expected was that she'd be having a lesbian affair." Blake shook his head in disbelief. "Faith claims that Meredith came out of nowhere and that their relationship just got out of control, but I'm guessing her drinking's what led to all of this. The good thing is Faith's seeking help now. That's a start."

"Well," Rags offered in a soft voice, "baby steps."

"Yep, I just don't know what it means for the two of us. But I'm really more concerned about the girls than anything else. It's tough on them seeing their mother this distraught . . . and me being gone all the time obviously doesn't help. As strange as it may sound, I'm actually feeling sorry for Faith. I know I'm responsible for some of what's happened and I'm just praying we can avoid doing the girls any harm while we sort through this."

"I understand," Rags replied. "But that's all the more reason to give me leeway in dealing with León. Can you do that?"

"You've got it," Blake said while standing up and rubbing his hands across his face. "And thank you, Rags. I'm lucky to have you . . . very lucky."

CHAPTER 61

Was it really him?

Cat looked to the table near the front of Abrazo, and the unmistakable bald head and angular body of the man she'd seen following her weeks earlier came into view. Cat watched her waitress Margie visit with him for several minutes and then deliver a glass of red wine to his table. For those around him, the bald man was an innocent, solitary diner about to enjoy a quiet meal, but Cat knew differently. The horrible, sick sense of fear she'd been trying to purge from her system during the holidays returned.

A little later, after spying on the bald man again, a worried Cat decided to break radio silence and punched out an email message to Blake:

Can you talk tomorrow between 9 and 10 EST? It's important.

Blake had responded with a simple *"Of course, call my cell"* but nothing more.

Given they hadn't spoken in what seemed like an eternity, Cat wondered how she'd react when she heard Blake's voice. The comforting answer came when he said hello.

"How are you, Cat?" he asked. Cat trembled upon feeling the confident aura Blake transferred through the phone.

"It's been tough," she replied, "but there's been some improvement . . . inch by inch. The kids are okay, though."

"Glad to hear it," Blake said in a hushed voice.

"Thank you, but that's not why I called."

"I suspected that."

"I think I'm being followed," she explained. "I can't be sure of it, but I'm worried someone knows about us."

"You think it's Striker's campaign?"

"I assume so. At first, I thought it might be my own paranoia, but I've seen the same man too many times. He's even coming into my restaurant now as if he doesn't care that I recognize him."

"I'll take care of it," Blake responded. "Don't worry about it another second."

"That's comforting. It's been worrying me a lot, but I didn't want to be a nuisance, especially now that things are looking so good for you."

"Nuisance, don't be silly." Blake hesitated. "I've been lucky," he went on. "The campaign's really taken off. But, forget all that. How are you, Cat—I mean, you—how are you?"

She sighed. "I'm adjusting. The rift between Sam and me will take time to heal, but we'll survive this. I don't think he wants to lose me."

"I'm really sorry about what you're going through. I really am."

Cat wished they could linger—it was so easy for her to lose herself in Blake—but she fought the temptation. "I have to hang up now," she said.

"Cat . . ."

"Take care of yourself, Blake. Thank you for checking on this." And with that, she let him go.

CHAPTER 62

Tony León made his way to Grace Striker's Dallas hotel room free of worry that one of Phelps's henchmen was watching him. Tony was a star in Striker's world again, both in and out of bed, and he didn't answer to anyone. Yet, even as he delighted in his raised status, Tony recognized that his time as a campaign chief could be very short-lived. The press had turned on Striker, her events had become angry demonstrations, and the campaign team had scattered like roaches exposed to sunlight. The one attribute his candidate had left going for her was the one indispensable element for any successful politician—a lack of conscience. Striker held steadfast to her belief that everything was going to work out if she kept her head down and relentlessly pressed on. That's what she'd done.

Dressed in a pressed gray suit, Tony pushed open the cracked door to Striker's suite at The Adolphus, then double-locked it. He strolled over to the attorney general's bed, where she'd positioned herself on her stomach in a sheer nightgown. He undressed, slid in next to her and stroked his fingers through her hair and around her neck.

"We don't have much time," Striker told him, as she reached for Tony's thigh. "Have a speech at ten to a downtown business group, and I can assure you I'm not going to answer any more questions about that asshole Gresham."

"That's right," Tony replied, his attention diverted by Striker's wandering fingers. "You're done with him. It's time to move on and start the great comeback."

Striker rose to her feet and walked toward the bathroom.

"When is our deal going to be done with Beckham?" she asked, pulling the door ajar. "He's still campaigning like nothing's changed."

"That's the way it's going to stay for a while." Tony waited until he heard the toilet flush before continuing. "I'm sure Beckham's told Buchanan by now, but they both know they have a month to figure this out. We just have to be patient and give them time to come around."

Striker emerged from the bathroom, naked but for a thick terry-cloth robe. "And you think Buchanan will buy in?"

"Doesn't matter either way. If he plays it tough, we'll release the video and go with the write-in strategy. You just need to hang in there this next month and keep working. Remember, redemption always sells in politics. Now that you've backed off Gresham, you can show contrition and allow the voters to come back to you. Humility and forgiveness are powerful tools."

"Not ones I do well," she countered. "You know most pols would've dropped that video on the internet the minute it became available . . . or at least forced his hand."

"And you would've lost for sure," Tony responded. He recognized he had to stay committed to his strategy or she might turn on him again. "There's no advantage in pushing him now that the ballot names are locked in. But if we hold tough to our threat to release the video *after* the primary, we keep the pressure on him to quit, and retain the option to pin the dirty trick on the Dems if he doesn't. Your comeback story stays pure either way."

"You better be right," she answered. "Or we'll both be done in politics. No write-in candidate's ever won shit in this state."

Tony didn't respond because he knew she was right. "Don't forget," he said, clutching at his ace in the hole, "I still might be able to trade the video to Buchanan for his support in that Senate seat that's about to open up."

"Hell no. I'm not going to Washington, at least not until I become president. Don't forget I'm a chief executive, not some one-in-fifty senator." Striker moved over to him and offered a less-than-reassuring dog pat. "And Buchanan's support will mean nothing when we're through with him anyway."

Tony sighed and looked up at her. "Just let me play this out with Dudley Do-Right, okay? I don't think he'll ever let that video of his wife hit the streets. And even if he does, he might still change his mind about the race after he sees the damage it does to his family. In the meantime, you need to be clean when the shit hits the fan."

Striker nodded, then tilted her head at Tony. "I like that confidence," she cooed while reaching down to her waist. "It's hard to resist." And with a pull of her belt, her thick robe hit the floor.

CHAPTER 63

January 16

Rags and Taylor Brooks hadn't devised a workable plan for defanging Tony León. Rags wasn't sure there was a way out of the mess at all, and the longer he kept the video from Blake, the more risk he ran that his candidate might react irrationally when finally confronted with it. The smug León was not to be trusted, that much Rags knew, but Rags needed the video at all costs and was willing to pay any price for it.

He drove back to the mall parking lot where he'd asked Tony to meet him again. Striker's operative waited for him in the same spot.

"You wouldn't try to tape this conversation?" Tony asked as Rags approached.

"Why do you think I came here?" Rags snorted. "I wouldn't waste my time if I wanted to turn you in."

Tony nodded. "I thought you understood my proposal last time," he stated.

"Blake's not quitting. We need to find another way."

"That's too bad."

"What do you want?" Rags asked. "Money? A seat in the House? A major appointment? The new governor can do a lot to help. He can help you both."

"It's not about me." Tony stared directly in his eyes. "If your guy wins and doesn't withdraw, then we'll follow through and

General Striker will become a write-in candidate for governor. In eight months, we think we can beat a weak Democrat and a disgraced former state senator with his family in tatters."

Rags almost burst into flames but he somehow maintained his composure. "The party will never go along with a slimy plan like yours," he fired back.

"Don't be so sure. Nightlinger likes the Dems even less than us slimy Republicans." Tony puffed out his chest as if to taunt his adversary.

Rags wasn't taping León but he could tell the kid wasn't going to incriminate himself. "What about Striker?" he asked. "Blake can support her for U.S. Senate when the seat opens up. He can unite the party behind her."

"She wants to be governor," Tony responded. "Now."

"You'd risk all of this for that woman?"

Tony shuffled his feet.

"Then your girlfriend's going to have to take her chances. I have nothing more to offer."

"The one video isn't all I have," Tony asserted as Rags turned his back. "That wasn't the only time Mrs. Buchanan's friend made nice with her. I bet your boy would really have a hard time handling the two of them diddling each other in his own home."

"That's bullshit." Rags took a step forward, close to losing his control. "You're bluffing."

"That's a huge gamble on your part. Just remember, I have nothing to lose. Neither does the attorney general."

"Go to hell."

Tony shrugged and stepped back. "Maybe I'll see you there."

CHAPTER 64

B lake leaned back in his office chair, took a deep breath, and started to dial Cat's private office number. They'd exchanged brief emails the night before to confirm the time of their call but nothing more.

"How are you?" Cat asked when she answered.

"Depends on your perspective," he replied. "The politician's doing pretty good; Blake, not so much."

"I'm sorry about that," Cat consoled. "I guess that makes two of us. Boy, we've made a mess of things."

Blake smiled but he could feel the tension in the line. Even if Cat wanted to reach out, he knew she couldn't. "My investigator found the guys who's been following you," Blake reported.

"So I do have a stalker?" she probed with a strange relief in her voice. "I'm glad I'm not crazy. Who is he?"

"A PI working for your husband." Blake could hear Cat catch her breath. "Sam hired him through a lawyer in New York. From what we can tell, there's no connection to the Striker campaign."

"Wow. Well, maybe I'm naïve, but I sure didn't expect that. I guess Sam still doesn't trust me. I guess it's even possible he's trying to set me up, but I feel strangely safer now anyway. Thank you for checking. At least I know what I'm dealing with, and, it won't worry me as much."

"I'm sorry, Cat."

"And I'm sorry, too," she responded. "But we should stop

there. I can't wait to hear that you've been elected governor. Texas is going to get a great man."

"Thank you," Blake said softly. "Take care of yourself. Remember, I'm out here if you need me."

Blake sat for a while holding his phone after they disconnected the line. It struck him that Cat's marriage was in as bad a state as his, yet their lives were as far apart now as they'd ever been. The threat of losing her children—or even worse, their respect—had pushed Cat farther and farther away from him and committed her even more doggedly to Sam. And he couldn't, or wouldn't, try to change her mind on that, no matter how much he missed her. Cat's priorities had become Blake's as well. His daughters were the innocents in his drama with Faith and they deserved better than to find out their father, and mother, were adulterers who'd acted without consideration for their children's welfare. He also realized that if he and Faith were going to work out their differences in a civil way—the D word hovered around but had yet to be spoken—they had to focus all their attention on what was best for Shana and Fin. If that meant they stayed married until their youngest daughter reached college, then Blake had to consider that as an option. After all, Faith could remain in Houston; she didn't have to move to Austin and live in the governor's mansion.

The hard truth was that Blake and Faith's conversation about the future of their family had taken a back-seat to his concern over Tony León's extortion attempt. Blake felt unstable and confused about that dilemma, and he'd grown weary of facing the same renewed threat every morning. Blake hadn't been sleeping well due to the troubling scenarios playing out in his head, and his tossing and turning had left him in a perpetual state of exhaustion.

Blake shook himself to emerge from his stupor and punched in Rags's number on his cell phone. He'd wondered for some time whether Rags was holding back information from him about León, and he could no longer look away from that possibility.

———— ★ ————

Rags had evaluated the problem every which way and had decided he couldn't hide the video any longer. He had to tell Blake everything, show him the evidence, and hope the man he knew so well would make the right decision.

"I talked to Cat," Blake announced as he hurried into Rags's office and took a seat. "It was a very brief conversation. Thanks for acting so quickly on that."

"Of course," Rags responded. He'd been mildly surprised, and relieved, that León wasn't the source of the stalker chasing Cat Alexander around New York.

"So what did León say at your meeting? What's he threatening us with?"

Rags dropped his head as he positioned himself behind his desk. "I've got a video to show you," he whispered. "I'm sorry, Blake, I really am."

"I knew it," Blake exclaimed. He sat stone-faced as Rags loaded a disk drive, clicked his mouse several times, and turned the monitor to face him. "This isn't going to be easy for you," Rags warned.

"Turn it on."

Blake watched for about a minute with a look of incredulity before holding up his hand. "Stop it," he said emphatically. "I've seen enough."

"We're doing everything possible to get the original," Rags stated. He pulled the flash drive out of his computer and dropped it into a drawer.

Blake shook his head. "Unbelievable," he muttered. "And I've thought all along this was going to be something about me and Cat. I never considered this. Not even once." Blake rubbed his hands up and down his cheeks as if to wish it all away.

Rags waited before walking around his desk and placing a gentle hand on his friend's shoulder.

"This is bad," Blake whispered while raising his head to look at Rags. He panted as if he needed oxygen. "So what now?" he asked.

"Striker's folks don't think the video can change the election at this point," Rags said. "The polls have moved too far away from them so they're trying to use it more strategically."

"What do they want?"

Rags hesitated. "For you to resign, but only after you've won the primary . . . assuming you do. This is where León's strategy gets complicated by Texas election law. You can't take your name off the ballot this late, but if you withdraw after you win, Striker believes the party will pick her to replace you in the general. They'll trade the video for that."

Blake took a deep breath. "Are you f'ing kidding me? She thinks she can get that done?"

"The woman's delusional—but yes. And even to withdraw from the general, you'd have to prove there's a medical emergency to clear the way for them. I don't think they've thought it through very well, and as I've considered your options—and I hope you know, I had to do that first—I'm not even sure whether your arrhythmia qualifies."

Blake held his hand against his chest. "And I walk into the sunset, medical emergency and video in hand?"

"Yes, that's their offer."

Blake nervously ran his fingers through his hair. "Have you talked to anyone about this?" he asked.

"No, just the lawyers . . . hypothetically."

"And?"

"They agree it's technically within the rules."

"But the party still has to go along?"

"And they never will," Rags replied firmly. "They want nothing to do with Striker now."

"What a train wreck." Blake sighed. "And that little asshole's still got someone following Faith around looking for more dirt."

"It's likely," Rags agreed. "He's told me he's got more."

Blake slammed his hand on top of Rags's desk. "Goddam it," he shouted. "Goddam it! This is unbelievable."

CHAPTER 65

Rags had pulled Blake's morning appearance on one of the Houston talk shows so he could meet with him and Taylor Brooks to discuss the Tony León problem. Blake had decided not to talk to his wife or to anyone else about the video, at least until his brain trust had come up with a plan of action. Taylor arrived first.

"Morning, Rags," the investigator said while entering the small conference room, which was covered with campaign flyers, signs and push cards. "I brought us some Starbucks. That shit you brew nearly killed me last time." He smiled.

"I'm wishing it had killed me," Rags joked, but he didn't laugh. "Blake will be here in a minute," he continued, "so let's make sure we're on the same page."

"I've got nothing," Brooks explained. "We're not getting that tape out of their hands without making a deal."

"What in the hell can we tell him then? We can't let him just quit the race."

"Look, you know as well as I do, its fifty-fifty that video ever goes public. But if it does, Blake will simply have to make a statement that he loves his wife, that the story is old news, and that he won't stand for dirty political tricks. That's what Senator Cruz did when that rumor was leaked about his wife and the story died pretty quickly. Plus, we can assure Blake that we'll be able to trace the video back to León and Striker and bury them with it."

"That's not much of a plan," Rags said. "And it won't do

anything to help with our biggest problem—his concern for his daughters."

"I understand that but this is the only way to realistically prepare him to move past the scandal, should that time come. We don't have anything left to offer them for the tape. There will be collateral damage."

"What about a preemptive press conference?" Rags suggested. "Cut them off at the knees."

"I'm all for it if you can convince him to do it."

Rags shook his head. "Stupid idea," he muttered. "Blake's not wired that way. He'd still worry the video would hit *You Tube*."

The office phone rang, interrupting their conversation.

"He's here," Rags said.

Blake entered the conference room with a grim, determined look on his face. He sat at the head of the table while Rags and Brooks flanked him. "So what's the plan?" he asked.

Rags glanced at Brooks and then turned to Blake. "You just keep campaigning and we'll stay on León. The main thing we need you to do is to discuss the video with Faith and make sure she knows you'll stand by her side if it ever goes public."

Blake held up his hand. "Whoa there," he protested. "This meeting isn't about me managing my family. We're supposed to be talking about how we're going to get that damn video away from those assholes."

"Yeah," Rags replied, "we know that."

"So I'm to assume we don't think that's possible?"

Brooks cleared his throat and faced the candidate. "Senator," he started, "I will use every means available to me to get that video but the reality is we have no idea how many versions he has hidden or where he's locked them away."

"I know that, Taylor," Blake replied, his frustration palpable. "I'm not an idiot. But I thought we were going to find another way to make a deal with these bastards. I want that damn video. Period. I don't care what it takes. Your job is to make it happen, and fast." Blake caught his breath before starting back up. "And no one, I mean no one, is to breathe a word of this to my wife. She's already coming apart over this affair, our marriage, this goddamned election, and I'm not going to push her over the edge."

Rags and Taylor nodded.

"Now I'm going back on the road and winning this nomination. I don't want to discuss this issue again until you have a deal worked out with León."

———— ★ ————

Blake hadn't ventured into his wife's bedroom since well before the night she'd confessed her affair with the tennis pro, but León's blackmail scheme had changed his attitude. He felt only sympathy toward his wife's situation now—the humiliating exposure facing her could easily be his own. Moreover, he felt an uncomfortable guilt over the turn of events, because the truth was Faith had never wanted to be a political wife in the first place. Making her suffer the ignominy of that video in full view of the world was cruel and unusual.

Blake walked into his house around 6:00 p.m. on a rare off night from campaigning, headed upstairs, and found Fin sitting in a chair across from her mother who was lying on top of the bed. The family's faithful dog, Red, was curled up by Faith's side. Several popular magazines lay scattered around them. Blake was unsure just how Faith was spending her days, beyond her treatment and her therapist visits, but he was pleased to see some color in her cheeks and a look of genuine happiness spread across her face.

"Hey guys," Blake said while entering the room.

"Dad," Fin yelled, beaming a big smile. She jumped up and hugged her father.

"Great to see you honey," Blake responded, squeezing his daughter. "How's school?"

"Oh, you know, with mid-terms over, my last semester's going to be a breeze. I was just talking about it with Mom."

Blake grinned and patted his daughter on the back. "Why aren't you at practice?" he asked.

"They canceled it. Tonight's the opening of the school musical and a bunch of the players are in the cast. I'm going over to Maggie's later on and we may go see it." She paused. "Then again," she cracked, "we may not. Either way, I'll check on you guys later." Fin pecked her dad on the cheek and hustled out of the room.

"We got lucky with her," Blake said while sitting in the chair his daughter had vacated.

"Yes," Faith agreed in a mild voice. "And with Shana."

"Where is she, by the way?"

"Already at the musical. It's a bigger deal to the underclassmen." She smiled warmly, and Blake realized he hadn't seen that in some time.

Blake smiled back. "No thespians in our crowd, I guess."

"Blake," Faith started while scooching up on her bed, "Thanks for checking on me. I really appreciate it. I asked Fin to leave when you got home because there's something I've really been wanting to say to you." She took a deep breath. "Please don't interrupt me; I need to get this out all at once." She grabbed a tissue off her bedside table as if to prepare herself. "I'm incredibly sad and sorry for what's happened to us . . . what I've done to us." She cast her eyes away for a moment. "Whatever that was . . . with Meredith, the truth is I'd been lost for some time before it happened. I told you this before but it's even clearer to me now. Meredith just appeared at a time when I was depressed and lonely—only now I'm just embarrassed and ashamed. I really am very, very sorry." Tears formed in her eyes as she slumped forward.

The images of his wife and her girlfriend stomach-punched Blake but he remained calm. "It was a shock to me, that's for sure," Blake replied, "but I'm not blind to my role in what's happened to our marriage." He reached over and cupped his wife's hand.

Faith whimpered but didn't otherwise respond to his gesture, dabbing her eyes with the tissue she clutched in her free hand. "I told my therapist today that I'm ready to put this whole episode behind me. And I want you to know I haven't had a drink—not one—since I started my treatment. Fin and Shana saw too much of that and I know I scared them. I'm committed to improving myself and being a better mother . . . and wife." Faith hesitated as if finding it difficult to come up with the right words. "And, Blake, I know it's a late offer, but I want to do anything I can to help you over this last month with the primary . . . that is, if you'll let me."

An odd mix of emotions churned through Blake's body. When he'd walked in the door, he'd contemplated telling Faith about the tape and letting her reaction to that disclosure dictate his next move, but he was now certain that was a terrible idea. And it wasn't even close to the right time to deal with the heavier subjects like divorce or their future.

"Faith," Blake said in a soothing tone, "I appreciate the offer, and you know you're welcome anytime you want to help in the campaign. I know I wouldn't be in this position if it wasn't for all that you've done for me over the years." He squeezed her hand a little tighter. "We have a lot of things to figure out in our relationship; we've both made more than our share of mistakes. Although I can't make any promises, let's see where the next month takes us. That's the best I can do."

Faith raised up out of bed and leaned over and wrapped her arms around her husband's shoulders. "Shhh," she whispered in his ear. "I don't want, or deserve, any promises right now. I know that. All I ask is that we care for our girls . . . and get you elected governor. There'll be plenty of time to sort out the rest later on. I still love you, Blake."

CHAPTER 66

February 18

Blake flicked on his office computer, plugged in the flash drive, and turned up the volume. Rags had given him a copy of Grace Striker's latest political ad with the warning that he should prepare himself to gag. Although it was the day before early voting started, and Blake had a comfortable six-point lead in the polls, Striker was still trying to rehabilitate her image.

The spot opened with a solemn attorney general dressed in black, her once shoulder-length hair shorn in an act of penance, staring at a crucifix in a rustic church. From that opening the camera panned back to take in the entire sanctuary as scripture scrolled across the bottom of the screen:

In him we have redemption through his blood, the forgiveness of our trespasses, according to the riches of his grace—Ephesians 1:7

Blake creased a wry smile as the video faded to black. Even though he'd come to expect anything from Striker, her audacity still amazed him. The new Grace Striker had been on display for over a month now, and in that time, she'd stopped defending her decision to get an abortion (now calling it an "emotional act of a desperate young woman"), embraced Gresham as a man of honor and conscience, and asked the voters to forgive her sins. Striker's transformation had captured a certain compassion among a growing segment of voters and, surprisingly, had even won a few newspaper endorsements as well. In a strange way, even Blake had started imagining the college-age Striker's dilemma and how anguished she might have been by her decision to end her pregnancy.

But the conniving Tony León, and his tape, always brought Blake back home.

Blake had campaigned like a madman over the past month. He hadn't wanted Striker or her henchman to sense he was at all worried about their threat to go public with the scandalous video. Even as he played it down the middle and pulled back on some of his more progressive positions, Blake was a man on a mission, a twenty-four-seven guided campaign missile. There was no doubt anywhere in Texas—other than in Striker's brain—that he would be Texas's next governor.

Despite all the optimism, Blake hadn't rested easy one night. The stress over his wife and daughters' plight had tormented his irregular heartbeat and sudden arrhythmias had disrupted him several times on the road. Thankfully, his relationship with Faith had steadied some, but even then their previous pattern of superficial communications had returned, and this lack of intimacy, whether at home or during their recent joint appearances, reminded him just how much they'd lost as a couple. Added into this mix of emotions was Cat, who'd been radio silent since their brief conversation about her stalker, which left Blake strangely isolated amidst all the euphoria about his campaign.

The candidate shook his head to clear his thoughts and prepare for the day ahead. He needed to do the mind trick he'd learned to perform so well over his many years in politics—push the noise out of his brain and just focus on what was directly in front of him. Nothing past that. In an hour he'd be meeting with Jim Bob Tate and later with the Booze Brothers, both to discuss large additional contributions to fuel his television spots through election day. Every new commercial, appearance, and handshake was more insurance in securing his victory. Yet even with the prize so tantalizingly close, Blake remained troubled by what lay ahead. Rags and Taylor had yet to pry the video from León's clutches and Blake's team was running out of time.

———————— ★ ————————

Rags turned to Taylor Brooks and slammed his hand down on his rickety wooden desk. "We're nowhere with León," Rags yelled.

"I think our only play here is to go to Nightlinger," Brooks replied as he stepped over one of the stacks of paper on Rags's office floor. "I've exhausted all other avenues. The kid's got the video locked up tight and there's no other option."

"A damn extortionist who won't take a bribe," Rags bristled. "Can you believe that?"

Brooks shook his head.

"Nightlinger can't help us," Rags continued. "Anything he says will have no force or weight and may even embolden León, the punk. Striker knows she isn't going to win but she's positioned herself for a write-in candidacy or to become the fill-in nominee. It's a smart strategy, however disgusting."

"Is Blake ready for that?"

"I'm not sure. He's stayed out of it and hasn't said much, but I know the guy too well. He couldn't live with himself if that video comes out. He loves those girls too much and he'll protect Faith even if it's just to protect them. I can tell it's on his mind every day. The irony is he's campaigned better the last month than I've ever seen him. This whole damn mess seems to be fueling him."

Brooks's face hardened. "Blake's going to be the governor," he said, "and a fricking good one. We just have to convince him to ride this thing out. I hate to say it, Rags, but this one's on you."

Rags looked to the sky, then stared at his investigator. "I know that and I'm doing everything I can to keep him focused on the prize. In his heart, I think Blake still believes Striker will crack at some point, but I'm losing confidence in that every day."

CHAPTER 67

March 3

Cat maneuvered her day around so she could be in her office at the restaurant to take Blake's call. "I need to talk to you," Blake had said in an email earlier that morning, and Cat hadn't stopped worrying since. She prayed he just wanted to report on his race now that he'd made it to election eve.

The phone rang at the precise time Blake told her he'd call, which made her smile. Always punctual, her Blake.

"You're almost there," Cat said when answering.

"Maybe," he replied. "Too late to turn back now." He hesitated as if he'd chosen the wrong words.

"Is there a problem?"

She heard Blake sigh. Cat girded herself for bad news. "What's going on?" she asked.

"I'm being blackmailed by my opponent."

Cat fumbled her phone. "Oh my God. How bad is it?"

"Sorry," Blake replied. "It's not about us."

Cat held her chest and looked to the heavens. For a moment, she'd thought her heart might explode. "What is it then?"

"It's a long story, but it's about Faith."

"Oh no, Blake. I'm so sorry." Cat tried to evoke empathy but she couldn't hide the palpable relief in her voice.

"Striker's desperate and is trying to use my wife and family to extort the election."

"How? I don't understand."

"I can't get into the details but I just needed to talk it out with you. I apologize. This was probably a bad idea."

"No, don't say that. I'm glad you called. You've been on my mind every day."

"You know," Blake whispered. "This should be the crowning achievement of my career. Why do I feel so bad?"

Cat wished in the worst way that she could console him. Hearing the sadness in his voice crippled her. "I know you can't discuss the details," she told him, "but I know you. All I can say is trust your instincts. They'll point you in the right direction."

"Thanks, Cat. I appreciate that more than you know. Maybe I just needed to hear that reassurance from you."

"You'll be the presumptive governor by tomorrow," Cat reminded him. "Don't forget all the good you can do once you take that office. That has to count for a lot."

"I wish it was that simple. Thanks for making time for my call. You'll be on my mind tomorrow, just like every other day."

"Good luck," she closed. "My heart's with you."

———— ★ ————

Blake dropped his head onto his desk once he said goodbye. Cat's encouragement had comforted him and given strength, even if it had offered no insight into the crisis confronting him.

Blake's cell phone buzzed and he looked down to see it was the call he'd been waiting on. At that moment, his life crystallized in front of him. He was about to realize the dream of his lifetime—becoming governor of the State of Texas.

CHAPTER 68

As he waited for León to make contact, Rags closed his office blinds and shut his eyes to think. He'd known for a long time Blake's marriage was unhappy—which certainly didn't disqualify him for a life in public service—and he'd always appreciated that despite it all Faith had stood by her husband in most public settings, shoulder to shoulder, hand in hand. Admittedly, sometimes the standing came with a frown, or a less than sunny disposition, but Faith had never caused any problems for Blake in the many years Rags had known them as a political couple. The contributions from her father and his rich network of friends had also eased the Faustian bargain of their relationship. Why then had Faith chosen, of all times, the biggest race of her husband's life to dive off the deep end? Rags continued reminding himself of the one truth all good strategists understood: he was a consultant, not a family counselor, and like all good campaign managers, his job was to win. Sometimes a little pain, maybe even a lot of pain, was necessary to achieve the end-game.

With the election a day away, Rags had run out of ideas for securing the León video. He now had to keep Blake focused on closing the deal and chasing votes throughout the night. Blake would be enraged when he found out that León had rejected Rags's final overtures, but Rags believed the soon-to-be governor would accept the bigger picture. Becoming governor of the greatest state in the nation was a prize worth the heartache the release of that video might bring.

And maybe, if they were lucky, Striker and León would see the light and back off. Maybe.

———★———

Striker headquarters was empty except for a couple of phone operators. The attorney general and her entire team were barnstorming on the road until election day, except for the solitary Tony León. He'd decided to stay in Houston to monitor the tenuous situation with the Buchanan campaign. Tony had pushed all his chips into the center of the table and the next forty-eight hours would tell the tale. Striker was going to lose the election—he was prepared for that—even if his candidate was still actively campaigning as though the race was a dead heat. Tony needed Blake Buchanan to blink. His life and career depended on it.

CHAPTER 69

March 4

Blake scanned the two large, flat-screen televisions sitting on pedestals in the front of the makeshift reception area of the busy downtown Hyatt Regency suite, watching for early voting results. The festive atmosphere in the room was accentuated by a huge Texas flag draped across one wall and the helium-filled red, white, and blue balloons that bobbed around the corners of the ceiling like june bugs near light. Blake waved at a couple of friends seated on one of the three large sofas positioned in front of the televisions in a U-shaped pattern, while he grabbed a finger sandwich off a nearby food tray. The energy and excitement presaged a big victory ahead.

The door to the suite opened and Faith, Finley, and Shana walked in. The beautiful trio entered the cozy, rectangular room smartly outfitted in short-sleeved, color coordinated dresses, with accent jewelry around their necks and sweaters over their arms. Blake smiled with pride at how cleverly they were attired—Faith wore white, Fin blue, and Shana red. All three ladies' hair and make-up were camera ready, too. As Blake had come to expect, Faith had her girls primed for their spotlight moment.

"You look beautiful," Blake said to each of his daughters as he hugged them. "And especially you, Mom." Blake kissed his wife on the cheek and then leaned toward her ear. "Thank you," he whispered. "Perfect picture, straight out of a movie."

"We're proud of you," Faith replied. "We . . . I want to share in this moment tonight."

A swarm of people quickly surrounded the Buchanans and started greeting the family members. Blake did a double take when he saw Faith's parents, the Cantrells, walk in just behind her. He greeted them with warm, although awkward, hugs. The candidate then stole his three girls away to meet his key contributors who'd been invited to join him for the evening—Chance Mitchell, Jim Bob Tate, and the Booze Brother, who were milling around the back of the room with the campaign team.

After these short introductions, Blake guided his family to the middle sofa at the front of the suite to join Faith's now-seated parents so they could watch the returns together. Then Blake made his way over to Rags, who was working three phones, chasing down updates from political operatives across the state, and talking a mile a minute. Taylor Brooks stood by Rags's side.

"The early returns look very strong," Rags exulted.

"How much longer till they call it do you think?" Brooks wondered.

"My guess is it should be within the half hour," Rags replied.

"Can I have all of your attention?" Blake announced as he stepped away from his advisers. "I want to say a couple of quick things before the night gets away from us." The still-noisy room had yet to quiet and Blake waited a moment. "I want to first thank all of you," he yelled over the cacophony. "Without your help, none of this would be possible."

Taylor Brooks whistled and the chatter stopped.

"Thank you, Taylor," Blake said with a chuckle. "All of you've done so much for me and my family," Blake continued. "Whether it's volunteering your time, hosting events, or helping finance this very expensive operation, you've been essential to our effort." He paused. "And you guys," he said, pointing at his team. "Rich, Taylor, Kristen, Susan, you're the best." Blake clapped at them and the crowd followed his lead. "I'm so fortunate to have you on my side."

"Most of you know," Blake went on, "that it's a huge sacrifice for any family to go through a long campaign . . . and mine's no different. I want to thank Faith, Finley, and Shana, my anchors, my support system, and my heroes." Blake's heart stuck in his throat as the last words left his mouth.

Faith, Fin and Shana stood up, smiled, and waved as several cell phones captured their images.

"Hold on," Rags shouted. "Houston came in early. The *Tribune*'s just called the election. Blake's the Republican nominee for governor!"

A cheer broke out and Blake slumped forward with his hands held to his chest before straightening his body to take in the moment. His family ran to his side and they all gathered together in a group hug as the applause continued. "I love you guys so much," he said quietly inside their huddle. "Thank you."

After several seconds, Blake eased away from his women, inhaled, and raised his arms to suspend the praise. "Incredible news," he yelled. "Thank you, thank you, thank you." The room slowly returned to order.

"Let me finish what I started before Rags's interruption," he said with a broad smile. "Most of you know I was a long shot at best to win this nomination. I was once told Jim Bowie and Davey Crockett had better chances at the Alamo than I did with Grace Striker. But here we are. This win, this celebration, and my political life are due to one man. I want to thank my great friend and campaign manager, Rags Beckham. I would never be here without him."

An even bigger roar followed for Rags. He stepped forward and bowed but then melted back into the scenery.

"I've got to study my remarks before we greet our supporters downstairs," Blake added, "but I want you to know I'm humbled—and very grateful. Thank you again. I can never repay what you've done for me and my family." Blake's emotions gripped him as he looked at the smiling faces—the images of his deceased mother and father flashed before him—and his voice broke as the reality of what was about to happen overcame him. "We're truly blessed." He fought to steady himself before he turned and walked to Faith and his daughters, kissed them on the cheeks, and then saluted the assembled group one last time. Blake signaled to Rags, who nodded and stepped to his friend's side. From there, the two men walked amidst a smattering of applause to the bedroom portion of the suite. Blake needed to visit with his campaign manager one last time before making the biggest speech of his life.

———— ★ ————

Tony paced around his twelfth-floor suite at the Driskill Hotel in Austin desperate for the clock to move faster. It had been a long, tough evening listening to Grace Striker and the Source complain, just the three of them now remaining to suffer in the wake of the crushing election returns. The Source had told them that Striker's redemption story had stabilized the polls, but once the early returns came in he'd admitted that it hadn't done enough to change Buchanan's trajectory. But Striker continued to hold out hope, still in disbelief that the *Tribune* had called the race so early. The margin was currently eight points and widening as the larger urban centers reported, and Tony realized these results now jeopardized the possibility of the party turning to Striker for anything. This demoralizing reality was highlighted by the fact that the once-committed group of Striker supporters, previously reveling in the now-cavernous banquet hall ten floors below them, had flooded away to drown their sorrows on Sixth Street.

After sending Blake a one-word email: "Congratulations," Striker had made her concession speech short and to the point. "I'm disappointed," she'd started, "with the results, but I believe that Republicans must come together to assure victory in November. I'm ready to do my part." No mention of Blake, and no trace of the humility she'd campaigned with over the past month.

And now she, Tony, and the Source stood in front of the television to watch Buchanan accept the party's nomination. Despite Tony's efforts to shoo the press away, a gang of reporters—eager to pounce on Striker's now-dead political body—waited outside the suite like predators stalking a kill.

"Prick is dragging this out, isn't he?" Striker observed.

"I suspect he still isn't sure what to say," Tony offered.

Striker frowned and rolled her eyes.

"He's coming on," the Source interrupted.

Tony grabbed the remote and turned up the volume. His hands trembled. The three viewers settled into their chairs and watched as the newscaster introduced Blake Buchanan.

Blake eased in behind the podium surrounded by Faith, Fin, and Shana, and the camera soaked in the familiar scene. Balloons filled the background as well as a red-white-and-blue sign that read *Buchanan for Texas*. Supporters shouted cheers and words of praise from the floor, most waving Blake's trademark placards in expectation of getting noticed by the television crews. Tony watched morosely as Buchanan's team did its victory lap but was struck by the fact Blake looked less than exuberant when he leaned into the microphone. Tony's body tensed as the candidate-elect began to speak.

"Tonight," Blake thundered as the crowd went wild with applause that forced him to back away for a moment. "Tonight, we celebrate a great victory . . . not only for those who worked tirelessly on this campaign . . . but for all Texans ready for a fresh start. Those wanting to move out from behind the cloud of cynicism and backroom dealings of modern-day politics into the world of transparency and government by, for, and through the people."

The audience cheered but Blake held up his arms to stem its enthusiasm.

"But we have much work to do. The Democrats will not rest till they turn this state blue so I ask all of you to redouble your efforts to ensure our party maintains the governor's mansion."

The room erupted again.

"My candidacy," he continued, "was never about me or any special qualities I brought to the race, but about you, and bringing our party back to a place where all Republicans—all *Texans*—can live together under one tent. About giving you, the *people*, a government you could be proud of and trust would listen to your concerns. I'm here to tell you the age of extremism and intolerance is over. Our party is now one, our divide is healed, our future assured." More clapping and yelling.

Tony looked over at Striker and she appeared ready to explode. But Tony sensed something was off in Blake's speech. The man he'd watched on the stump so many times before always joked or offered a lighthearted comment to open his remarks. Whether it was the gravity of the moment or a reflection of how far he'd come, Blake seemed off, preternaturally earnest, almost grim.

"I'm proud," Blake continued, "of what we've accomplished . . . together. And I'm so very lucky to have worked with the finest group of people any campaign's ever known. I want to thank each and every one of them now, especially my wonderful family."

Striker turned to Tony with a look intended to vaporize him, as if every phrase spoken by Buchanan twisted a knife deeper into her back.

"Texans deserve a lot from their next governor," Blake said while staring into the camera. "I want the next four years to be a vigorous time of transformation in Austin. I don't want a single voter ever to question that he or she put the right Republican, the right person, in office. You—every one of you—deserve that and a whole lot more."

Tony's heart jumped as Blake stopped for a moment and appeared to choke up. Blake then looked into the crowd, paused, and continued.

"Tonight, as we savor this magnificent victory, I need to tell you why that person can't be me."

———— ★ ————

Cat had gone to her restaurant office to watch Blake's acceptance speech online. She felt elated as her former lover assumed the podium, then an odd displacement when Faith Buchanan cozied up next to him with her daughters. Cat listened to the speech attentively, proud of Blake's accomplishment, then grew sad and wistful for what might have been.

Throughout his remarks, Cat had sensed something was slightly off in Blake's delivery, but even she wasn't prepared for what came next.

CHAPTER 70

"Texas Surrender!" screamed the headline in the political section of the *New York Enquirer*. Jackson Goodrich hadn't participated in the story, feigning a deadline on another matter, and so his colleagues weren't aware of his suspicions about the reasons behind Blake Buchanan's bombshell withdrawal. Blake's heart condition may have been the public story—the paper did speculate about why he'd waited so long to announce it—but Jackson figured that delay more accurately reflected Blake's agonizing indecision about giving up the governorship for Catherine Alexander. Jackson had wondered if it made sense to re-trade the deal he'd made long before with Rags Beckham, in which he'd exchanged writing about Blake's improprieties for a groundbreaking exposé on Striker, but he remained satisfied with, and committed to, the deal. He'd benefited handsomely as a result of his exclusive on Striker's secret abortion and his status had grown exponentially at the *Enquirer* as a result. The phone rang as Jackson pondered the situation.

"Jackson Goodrich," he answered.

"This is Rags Beckham."

"Funny, but I was just thinking of you."

"Good timing then . . . figured I'd better check in."

"I haven't written a word, if that's why you're calling."

"I know that. I just wanted to thank you for honoring our deal."

"Not sure I've made my final decision on that."

Rags's silence signaled his response. "Blake's done . . . finished. And his decision to withdraw has nothing to do with Cat Alexander. I wanted you to know that."

"I find that hard to believe. Everyone suspects something more even if his health issue is real. Tell me—off the record—is the heart condition bullshit?"

"Are we good? None of this will be printed?"

"Yeah, yeah, this is all off the record."

"He's had arrhythmia for some time, and it's flared up quite a bit during the campaign, but this was ultimately a personal decision based on his family. That's all I can tell you."

"You think the heart condition qualifies as a *serious* medical condition under Texas election law?"

"The Democrats will argue otherwise but yes, I do."

"Striker had something on him, didn't she?" Jackson speculated. "So damaging your man gave up the governorship." He paused. "And you guarantee you're not spinning me on Alexander? It's really not about her?"

"No spin; it's not her," Rags repeated. "Blake's a good man, Jackson. I can't tell you any more than that but it looks like he's going to need a pacemaker inserted to control his arrhythmia, so there's really no reason to doubt his story." The campaign manager paused as if he had more on his mind.

"When did all of this come down?" Jackson asked.

"I wasn't in favor of it, if that's what you're asking."

"He didn't tell you, did he?"

The silence answered Jackson's question even before Rags spoke. "Not until last night," Rags explained, "right before he gave that speech. He hadn't decided until then."

"Wow."

"You can imagine it wasn't what I wanted, but I've grown to admire the man even more overnight."

Jackson shook his head in amazement. He could write a

novel about this one day. "Do you think the Republicans will put Striker on the ballot now?"

"It's possible," Rags conceded, "but her terrible showing yesterday makes me doubt they will. I'll sure encourage them to look elsewhere."

The comment triggered Jackson's reporter instincts. "Does that mean you have another reason for calling?"

"You're figuring this out, aren't you?"

Jackson chuckled. "You owe me. So what've you got?"

"I didn't want Blake's sacrifice to be for nothing, so I brought a bit more to trade . . . if you're listening."

"And you know I don't care much for Striker. I'm listening."

"Well, it also has to do with your friend Tony León."

"Then I'm all ears," Jackson said.

"Get your pen out."

CHAPTER 71

Blake drove off to headquarters to meet Rags and thought through the previous night's events. He was devastated over the price he'd been forced to pay to protect his family but knew in his heart that he'd made the right decision.

His agreement with Tony León ensured that all copies of the video were now locked up. They'd been placed in the possession of a mutually trusted lawyer who also held damaging admissions signed by León and Striker as a counterbalance, neither to be released unless one side double-crossed the other. Blake had fulfilled his part of their contract by withdrawing from the race; Striker's would be satisfied once the video was destroyed.

Blake still couldn't believe he'd managed to finalize the side deal without Rags's knowledge. And it wasn't until those final moments before his acceptance speech—when Blake admitted to Rags that he'd misled him and had his lawyer deal directly with León about the video—that he'd arrived at his final decision.

"Dammit, Blake," Rags had yelled at him while slamming his fist into the wall. "You can't do this. Goddammit, get your head on straight. The kid's bluffing. You're not going to throw the whole election away over this. I won't let you!"

"I've made up my mind," Blake had responded calmly. He'd been prepared to ride out Rags's storm, knowing his campaign manager would be crushed. "I won't ruin my girls' lives," Blake had continued. "Faith's humiliation, the jokes, and the internet posts would stalk her forever. And the girls. Their relationship with their mother would be ruptured, and they'd never escape that disgusting video. How in the world could I focus on governing if my family was imploding the minute I got into office? Rags, I'm sick about it but there's no other way. I'm sure of it." Blake had gasped to fight back his emotions. "God, I'm sorry Rags," he'd said. "I'm so very, very sorry."

"Fuck," Rags had hollered, loud enough for the guests in the suite to hear him, and then he'd slumped into a chair, defeated.

The episode the previous night had reinforced what Blake already knew—he had a true friend in Rags Beckham. Although their dreams had died in that moment on election night, the campaign manager had embraced Blake like a true brother and hadn't looked back once the speech was delivered, quickly accepting his role as crisis manager for the fallout after Blake's stunning announcement. Blake would never forget Rags's gestures of support. Few men—much less politicians—had friends like Rags Beckham.

Rags was waiting for Blake when he arrived in his campaign headquarters' office. "Don't tell me you've been working," Blake said with a halfhearted smile. They sat down next to each other at Blake's small conference table.

"Wanted to confirm Jackson Goodrich wasn't going to make all this for naught," Rags explained.

"And?"

"He isn't going to speculate about you and Ms. Alexander, but he does have a new story that kinda interested him."

"I suspect that has something to do with the attorney general and her campaign manager."

"He seemed to like it."

Blake grinned. "I don't know what to say."

"What did you tell Faith and the girls?"

"Nothing at all about this sordid business with Striker. And given all we've been through, Faith didn't push too much. I'm not sure if I'll ever tell her more beyond the heart story but in some ways, I think she knows this was about her. The girls seemed very concerned about my health issues, although they're very disappointed. They know how hard this process has been on me."

"Probably best you don't say any more than that," Rags counseled. "But let's be real for a minute. Your decision obviously has national implications. Republicans in the rest of the state, and country, are now deathly afraid that Texas could go blue over this. Your money boys want to string you up. Yet no one—and I mean no one—wants that toxic woman back on the ballot."

"Other than keeping this from you," Blake replied, "that worried me more than anything else. But you know as well as I do they could put Vladimir Putin on the ticket and still beat the Democrat. As much as it sickens me, even after her showing last night, Striker's base still loves her, and if they pick her, she'll win."

"Are you kidding me?" Rags boomed. "You're willing to accept that?"

"I don't have a choice."

"Well, I do. And I'm not done with her yet."

"What do you mean?"

"Do you think I'm going to let you just walk away and let her win? That bitch is going to get what she deserves. And don't worry. Nothing I do will undermine your deal."

"I know you're too smart for that but please be careful. I withdrew—once and for all—and I've fulfilled my side of the deal. Striker has no outs, unless we give them to her." Blake paused. "Okay," he said as if redirecting them. "Time for you to get out of here. I've got a long, ugly day of telephone conversations ahead."

Rags nodded. "You're right; that's what you need to be doing. And it's going to be rough. The Booze Brothers looked like they'd taken a couple of cyanide capsules last night." Rags leaned over and patted his friend on the knee. "Blake, you've always been too good for this cesspool. But just don't give up yet. There's always another way."

Blake turned his head as if confused. "No, that's not possible. There's no wiggle room in my deal."

Rags chuckled. "For a smart guy, you can be a dumb son of a bitch. There's always wiggle room." Rags stood up and paced around the floor for a minute. "I've been thinking about your options for some time. I guess I always kept a backup plan, just in case. I called Nightlinger last week. Sit back for a minute and listen."

CHAPTER 72

Cat's mind wandered as she stirred the eggs in her frying pan, waiting for her kids to wake up for breakfast. Her emotions remained on edge after her words with Sam the night before. Maybe her decision to raise *the Blake issue* was a mistake, but she'd worried about leaving his big announcement hanging out there unaddressed with her husband, especially when every network had been running coverage about it for twenty-four straight hours. Cat had understood that a messy conversation with Sam might imperil all the small gains she'd scratched out with him since the *discovery*, but she'd gone ahead anyway.

"Can you turn that off for a minute?" Cat had asked when Sam had flicked on the TV in their room as they prepared for bed.

"What for?" Sam had responded. "Something bothering you?"

"Please, Sam, just turn it off."

Cat hadn't been sure what the right words were, but after pacing for a few seconds, she'd decided dancing around the subject wasn't the answer either.

"Did you see the news about Blake?" she'd asked.

"Why in the hell are you bringing him up?" Sam had shot back. "How could I miss *the news*? It's been running on every station constantly since last night." He'd stopped what he was doing and had frozen in place, staring at her.

"Sam, I've done everything I can to put that bad decision

behind me, and the last thing I want is this story to create new problems for us."

"I don't know what you want me to say," Sam had replied. "But I can tell you one damn thing—hearing you say his name in our house doesn't make things better."

"I know that but having you mad, and our not talking about it, is worse. I have no idea why he's pulling out of his race and I don't care. You need to know that."

Sam had shaken his head. "Cat," he'd growled, "I frankly hope the guy really is sick. In fact, I wouldn't lose a minute's sleep if he drops dead of a heart attack tomorrow." Sam's face had reddened. "Look, I don't want to talk about him anymore. I never want to hear or talk about the man again. Period."

That was not the way she'd wanted the conversation to go. Cat had hoped for forgiveness, resignation, maybe even reconciliation, but Sam had offered nothing more than vitriol. Maybe it had been too soon. Maybe she'd been wrong to anticipate anything more of her husband, but she'd been reminded again there was still a very long journey ahead with him.

After that, a jittery silence had prevailed. Sam had avoided her as they'd brushed their teeth and swished mouthwash, but eventually he'd been unable to deal with the tense atmosphere. He'd grabbed his pillow and left the room.

As Paige and Mitch spilled into the kitchen from the hallway this morning, and looked at their mother with expectant eyes, Cat remembered. Her kids still needed her, and that's all that mattered.

———★———

As he'd watched the press reaction the past few days, Tony began wondering if his strategy might actually work. Deep down, he'd never truly believed his plan had a chance to succeed, but now that Buchanan had done his part, Tony was feverishly attempting to push Striker over the goal line. His problem was that he'd failed to fully consider how her poor performance in the primary election might push the A.G. down the list of Republican prospects for the nomination. But that was counter-balanced by Striker's gutty finish to the campaign, which had impressed some of the big cigars in the party. And while the scandal had constricted her loyal base, Striker still seemed the safest choice to lead the GOP to victory in November. Equally important, Tony's team had stoked the rumor that denying the A.G. the nomination would infuriate her supporters and might even keep these most reliable Republican voters home on election day. That was a risk the party really couldn't afford. At least Tony hoped so. He'd always known the write-in route wasn't a practical option.

"Nothing's assured yet," he'd told Striker in their earlier call. "We'll know more tomorrow. Nightlinger's coming to town and asked you to meet at four at his lawyer's office with reps from the State Republican Executive Committee. He wouldn't come right out and tell me anything but he hinted the SREC's going to offer you the nomination."

"Mmmmm," Striker had cooed. "Amazing. Pick me up then and let's not be late. And Tony, honey, either we're celebrating tomorrow night or you'll have a lot of explaining to do."

CHAPTER 73

Blake and Rags drove off to the meeting at Chairman Nightlinger's office in downtown Houston with very different expectations. Blake understood Rags's plan and agreed to go along with it out of respect for his campaign manager, but he had no belief the party chair could spin any magic into his relationship with Grace Striker. His deal with the woman was ironclad, and he couldn't risk undoing it by trying to lawyer around the agreement. Moreover, Blake had spent the last few days reconciling himself to a future of rebuilding his private life, far from the public eye. He was almost excited about his liberating new course.

A bear of a man at six foot five and over two-hundred-fifty pounds, Chairman Nightlinger welcomed Blake and Rags to the meeting standing alongside two associates. "Thank you both for coming," Nightlinger said as he walked toward the duo with his thick arm outstretched. They shook hands before the party chair wheeled around to introduce his colleagues. "I think you both know Sheila Blackwell and Roger Honeycutt. Sheila's our SREC chair and Roger's my general counsel. The full State Republican Executive Committee will meet tomorrow to select the new nominee."

After several minutes of welcoming one another, the assembled politicos seated themselves around the table. "I want all of you to know," Blake started, "how sorry I am for putting you through this."

Nightlinger held up his hand, displaying shiny, gold cuff links and a pressed French-cuff shirt. "Senator, we all understand you made your decision based on the best interest of your health—and by extension that of our state. None of us doubt your integrity. And while we don't relish this responsibility, we're prepared to take it on. What we need to do today is verify your illness. You can imagine that once the Dems sue us to keep the party from putting another name on the ballot, we'll need to be covered. And if we lose that suit, we're all screwed."

Blake grasped that a lawsuit investigating his *critical illness*— the legal standard to permit the party to seat a replacement—was a probability, but he was confident his situation qualified. "I'm sure," he stated, "that my arrhythmia is a critical illness. My cardiologist tells me I'm at risk for a sudden-death heart attack or stroke given the severity of my condition. Even once I insert a pacemaker, I'm still going to need some downtime to recover. My doctor has signed a sworn statement to this effect and I'm confident his opinion will hold up in court."

"That's one issue we called you about," Honeycutt interjected, "but not the only one."

Blake glanced at Rags and could tell he was going to force Blake to handle this discussion alone. *Was that a smirk on his face?* "What are the others?" Blake asked.

"The real reason you withdrew," the lawyer replied.

"I don't follow," Blake countered.

"Senator, what happens between us is privileged business," Honeycutt continued. "I'm acting as legal counsel for the party and all of us are covered by the privilege, except Rags. He'll have to leave now for us to speak freely. You understand we don't want a record created that the Democrats can get their hands on."

"I'll be back." Rags nodded with a smile and hustled out of the room.

Rags hadn't been entirely candid with him but Blake wasn't upset. This was the discussion he'd expected although he had to be very careful, given his deal with Striker. "So you believe our conversation is now privileged?" he asked.

"Yes," Honeycutt confirmed. "We have precedent to support confidentiality in this setting. So be frank with us, please."

"And you should know Rags didn't violate your confidence," Nightlinger added. "We heard from Marshall Phelps yesterday and he gave us the full story. Rags chose not to correct me when I told him what I'd heard . . . that's it. But we know your illness doesn't cover the whole story."

Blake paused for several seconds to examine the hungry eyes before him. "I'm not sure where you're going," he said.

"Let's be blunt," Nightlinger stated. "We understand this medical procedure won't keep you down very long and we want you back on the ballot. It's the safest bet for the party and we believe it's best for the state. Hell, you're even growing on the SREC and they disagree with you on most of the issues. Blake, we're willing to help manage your other problem."

Blackwell nodded her agreement.

"I'm not following," Blake said, shaking his head. "How do you plan to do that?"

"Senator," Nightlinger responded, "in a few minutes Grace Striker's going to walk through that door and we're going to demand she release you from whatever she's holding over your head. We have no idea how that's going to play out but we have to try."

Blake wasn't sure what Nightlinger's endgame was, but he couldn't allow the chairman to unravel the deal he'd cut with the A.G. "She's coming in here?" Blake asked. "Right now?"

"I just got a text," Honeycutt interrupted. "She just walked in the building with Tony León. Hold on a minute and I'll go get her."

Blake threw up his arms and prepared himself for the circus. "I can't say a word once she gets here," he stressed, "and I won't violate our deal. Do you understand?"

Nightlinger nodded.

Thirty seconds later, the storm hit.

"What's he doing here?" Striker challenged when she burst through the door in front of Honeycutt looking like a woman ready to take control of the nomination. The attorney general swayed her head side-to-side to express her dissatisfaction. León was not with them.

Blake stared at Striker in stoic silence. God, how he detested the woman.

"Senator Buchanan's here at my invitation," Nightlinger responded tersely. "He didn't know you were coming either."

"So he's here to bless my nomination?" Striker offered, straightening the bottom of her crisp blue suit.

"Please sit down, General," Nightlinger instructed, "and we'll get started." Striker plopped down in the chair at the head of the table.

"Oliver," Striker said with a charming smile. "I'm ready to go. What more do we need to discuss?"

Nightlinger stood up, surveyed each person at the table, and fixed his gaze on Striker. "General, you're not getting the nomination," he announced. "You must understand that. But you can have a future in our party if you will help us convince Senator Buchanan to put his name back on the ballot. We need him or the party could lose this race."

Striker shook her head in defiance. "No, no, no," she exclaimed. "I'm going to be the nominee. It's me. Do you understand? It's me!"

For the first time, Sheila Blackwell perked up. "Grace, that isn't going to happen. The SREC wants Senator Buchanan or it will look in another direction. We need your help for the sake of our party."

Striker's face flashed red and Blake began wondering if she was about to start a tantrum. The attorney general's desperate eyes scanned the room, searching for a lifeline, before she exhaled and slammed her hands on the table. "That man," she said, pointing her trembling finger at Blake, "ruined my life. He'll be governor over my dead body. There's nothing to discuss. Nothing at all. I'll file as a write-in if he goes on the ballot."

"That's unfortunate," Nightlinger cut in. "Do you want some time to think about it?"

"I don't need another minute. You name him and I'll guarantee you the Democrats will win." Blake could see that Striker wanted to mention their deal but caught herself. "You don't have a choice," she went on, "but to give me the nomination. I'll win and you'll all look like heroes."

"We do have other options," Blackwell interjected.

"No, you don't," Striker responded. "Not if you want to win."

"Is there any way we can change your mind?" Nightlinger asked.

"Nominate me!" Striker demanded.

"This meeting's over then," Honeycutt stated. "Thank you, General. I'll show you out."

After a touchy moment facing down the room, Striker whipped her head to the left and stared at Nightlinger. "Mr. Chairman," she said in a calmer tone, "I'll be waiting to hear about next steps." Striker then turned to Blackwell. "C'mon, Sheila," she pleaded, "the SREC knows me. It knows we're aligned on every issue the members care about. Let's go win this together."

"Thanks for coming, General," Blackwell said. "But it's too late to change the SREC's mind."

Striker sprang up as if she'd been electrocuted, surveyed the table one last time, and glared at Blake before calming herself. "You all know it has to be me," she roared. "I've earned it!" She locked her hands in a vise grip and stood in a defiant posture, as if waiting for her friends to come to their senses.

"Let it go, General," Honeycutt said. "It's over."

Still indignant, Striker stared at Blake with menacing eyes before turning to Honeycutt and following him out of the room.

Blake had enjoyed watching Striker make a fool of herself. She'd buried her future with the Republican Party—at least it appeared that way—but her hostility toward him assured once and for all that his run for governor was probably done.

"We have a lot to consider," Blackwell said. "Blake, we'll call you tomorrow. We're sorry it's come to this."

"Thank you," Blake replied. "There's no need to apologize. I'll support the nominee, whomever you choose."

Rags had waited in the hallway to see Blake when he walked out of the meeting.

"Listen," Rags said with a smile, cocking his head.

From somewhere at the far end of the floor, Blake heard an earsplitting wail: "T—O—N—Y."

CHAPTER 74

Blake had little hope the State Republican Executive Committee might cut a deal with Striker to put him back on the ballot, and he forced himself not to think about it. Having grown even more comfortable with his decision to withdraw over the past few days, Blake had disregarded the encouragement Nightlinger had given him at their meeting. The fact was, Striker would never let him out of their agreement.

As he leaned back in his favorite chair in his study, Blake contemplated a life ahead without politics. That reality started with Faith. She'd gone to such lengths over the past month to support him, and his campaign, that Blake had begun having second thoughts about their prospects as a couple. Yet, in his heart, he still didn't believe his relationship with his wife was salvageable. It wasn't just his feelings for Cat or Faith's lesbian affair that led him to that conclusion; it was the sense that Faith's efforts over the past month had been more stagecraft than real. Even as the tension between them had eased, the emptiness Blake felt every time he was alone with his wife hadn't changed. The fact that Faith hadn't asked a single probing question about why he'd stepped away from the nomination troubled him. While his disappointment was profound and palpable, she seemed thoroughly comfortable, maybe even happy, with his decision.

But no matter what problems existed in his marriage, Blake knew his priority remained the welfare of Fin and Shana. And given the girls needed their mother more than ever at the critical stages of their lives, his future with Faith was clouded with uncertainty.

The doorbell rang and Blake knew the time had come. He walked to the front of the house and found Rags pacing nervously on his porch.

"Come in," Blake said. "And wipe that look off your face. Whatever it is can't be all that bad."

Rags walked past his friend and then swung around to face him. "They picked Governor Johnson. The old goat said he'd serve another term if it was best for the party."

"I expected as much," Blake reflected. "He was the logical, and safest, choice."

"Striker's already put out a press release saying she supports the governor and will do everything in her power to defeat the Democrats."

"How noble. What a team player."

"Yeah, I think she plans on succeeding him. There's already speculation that he'll only serve a couple of years and step down. The feeding frenzy's underway."

"She's a resourceful one. A survivor, no doubt."

Rags placed his hand on Blake's arm. "That feeding frenzy has a place for you. Just cut me loose so I can get to work on it. That contract with Striker won't keep you out of the next battle."

"Slow down, Rags. I'm not sure about any of this now. Maybe I need to rejoin the real world first and get my life in order. I can't bring myself to start plotting again."

Rags muttered to himself before he fixed his jaw. "What am I going to do with you?" he asked. "I need to break you out of this funk!" He paused for a moment before firing back up. "Blake, you were born to lead—and the state needs you. I may seem angry over how all of this went down, but I respect the hell out of what you did for your family. Now it's time to lock all that away and move forward. When Nightlinger told me they were going with

Johnson, I realized he was just a place-holder. Your time will come, and I'm going to make sure of it."

Blake was moved by Rags's heartfelt appeal, but even as he wanted to leap at Rags's encouragement, a voice in his head said *slow down*. His life might need a jump start, but he wondered if politics was the right fix. It had taken a while to figure out, but Blake realized that his push into the public arena had always come from external sources, whether his father or now Rags did the shoving. That could no longer be the case. "I made a great decision when I hired you, Rags Beckham," Blake observed. "But I'm not even sure where I'll be . . . by the time the next campaign fires up."

Rags held out his hand to clasp Blake's outstretched one. "This isn't over," Rags said. "Not by a long shot."

"Get some rest," Blake responded as he nudged Rags toward the door. "We'll have plenty of time to sort this out."

Blake watched Rags drive away and then returned to his favorite chair. He had so much to mull over. He stared at the cell phone lying on his desk and wondered if he dare call Cat. He wanted to know what she was thinking, how she'd interpreted his speech, and whether she felt his decision had opened any doors for them. He shook his head, then moved his eyes around the room, glancing at the political pictures and memorabilia that had come to define his career. He sighed while reaching out and picking up his favorite picture of a beaming Walter Buchanan, hugging his son after his first political victory, and mumbled, "Some mess you got me in."

In his search for answers, Blake now realized that the overriding voice that guided him was no longer that of his commanding father, or even that of Rags Beckham, but instead the encouraging one in his own head. The one that reminded him about priorities, about his love for his daughters, and the importance of finding contentment in *his* life, with or without public office. Until that evening when Cat had reappeared in Houston, too many years had passed where politics was all he'd known . . . or valued.

Blake exhaled and took a deep breath. He picked up his phone, stared at it for a moment, then punched in Cat's number.

AUTHOR'S NOTE AND ACKNOWLEDGEMENT

This is the second novel I've published, and it's a significant departure in style from my first work, *Come and Take It—Search for the Treasure of the Alamo*. From historical fiction to a politically fueled romance. What gives? The question reflects the great journey of a writer. The only limitation on a novelist's work is his or her imagination. I didn't set out to create a love story in *The Election*, but Cat and Blake became irresistible forces. In fact, when I wrote "The End" in my manuscript, what I realized most is that these two characters are nowhere close to the conclusion of their story. I hope you will be intrigued enough to find out what lays ahead in their lives in *The Next Election*.

There are a few people I want to thank for helping me bring this novel to publication. I've been blessed with angels in my life, and this writing venture wouldn't be possible without any of them. My wife, my daughters, my sister, and my mother all provide me encouragement, occasional harassment, and daily doses of humility. I'm very lucky that all three are delivered with equal shares of love and affection. I also want to thank the numerous readers, editors, special friends, and professionals who helped me deliver this final story to the page. These people are too numerous to mention individually, but I'm grateful to each one of them for caring enough to provide honest and valuable feedback. Four persons who deserve special mention are Susan Leon, Camille DeSalme, Sheila Cowley and Trudy Catterfeld. They all performed critical roles for me on this book and each is a true professional who makes my writing life work. I'm not sure how I found my way to each one you, but I'm deeply indebted.

One final thought. As with my first novel, many readers have asked if I modeled any of my characters after real persons I've met in my life. Once again, I refuse to answer that question under fear of reprisal, and choose to leave that answer to the readers' imaginations; however, I will admit that I did have someone in mind when I named the Buchanan's dog Red. Enough said.

Made in the USA
Columbia, SC
03 March 2024